LEMON CURD KILLER

Titles by Laura Childs

Tea Shop Mysteries

DEATH BY DARJEELING
GUNPOWDER GREEN
SHADES OF EARL GREY
THE ENGLISH BREAKFAST MURDER
THE JASMINE MOON MURDER
CHAMOMILE MOURNING
BLOOD ORANGE BREWING
DRAGONWELL DEAD
THE SILVER NEEDLE MURDER
OOLONG DEAD
THE TEABERRY STRANGLER
SCONES & BONES
AGONY OF THE LEAVES

SWEET TEA REVENGE
STEEPED IN EVIL
MING TEA MURDER
DEVONSHIRE SCREAM
PEKOE MOST POISON
PLUM TEA CRAZY
BROKEN BONE CHINA
LAVENDER BLUE MURDER
HAUNTED HIBISCUS
TWISTED TEA CHRISTMAS
A DARK AND STORMY TEA
LEMON CURD KILLER

Scrapbooking Mysteries

KEEPSAKE CRIMES
PHOTO FINISHED
BOUND FOR MURDER
MOTIF FOR MURDER
FRILL KILL
DEATH SWATCH
TRAGIC MAGIC
FIBER & BRIMSTONE

SKELETON LETTERS
POSTCARDS FROM THE DEAD
GILT TRIP
GOSSAMER GHOST
PARCHMENT AND OLD LACE
CREPE FACTOR
GLITTER BOMB
MUMBO GUMBO MURDER

Cackleberry Club Mysteries

EGGS IN PURGATORY
EGGS BENEDICT ARNOLD
BEDEVILED EGGS
STAKE & EGGS
EGGS IN A CASKET

SCORCHED EGGS
EGG DROP DEAD
EGGS ON ICE
EGG SHOOTERS

Anthologies

DEATH BY DESIGN
TEA FOR THREE

Afton Tangler Thrillers
writing as Gerry Schmitt

LITTLE GIRL GONE
SHADOW GIRL

LEMON CURD KILLER

Tea Shop Mystery #25

LAURA CHILDS

BERKLEY PRIME CRIME
New York

BERKLEY PRIME CRIME
Published by Berkley
An imprint of Penguin Random House LLC
penguinrandomhouse.com

Copyright © 2023 by Gerry Schmitt & Associates, Inc.
Excerpt from *Honey Drop Dead* by Laura Childs
copyright © 2023 by Gerry Schmitt & Associates, Inc.

Library of Congress Cataloging-in-Publication Data

Names: Childs, Laura, author.
Title: Lemon curd killer / Laura Childs.
Description: New York: Berkley Prime Crime, [2023] | Series: Tea shop mystery; 25
Identifiers: LCCN 2022041577 (print) | LCCN 2022041578 (ebook) |
ISBN 9780593200926 (hardcover) | ISBN 9780593200933 (ebook)
Subjects: LCGFT: Novels. Classification: LCC PS3603.H56 L46 2023 (print) |
LCC PS3603.H56 (ebook)| DDC 813/.6—dc23/eng/20220831
LC record available at https://lccn.loc.gov/2022041577
LC ebook record available at https://lccn.loc.gov/2022041578

Printed in the United States of America
1st Printing

LEMON CURD KILLER

1

✤

When life hands you lemons, you're supposed to make lemonade. Theodosia Browning had adopted a slightly more creative approach. She was smack-dab in the middle of hosting a fanciful Limón Tea Party.

Picture this if you will: Five dozen Southern ladies dressed in gauzy florals and wearing hats and gloves. All seated at elegant tea tables in the fairy-tale setting of an actual lemon grove strung with hundreds of white twinkle lights. Postcard perfect, yes? Now add in a delicate waft of lemon-scented tea, large glass bowls amply heaped with fresh-picked lemons, and lemon scones served as the first course. For the pièce de résistance, a fashion show was about to begin and a camera crew was on hand to capture all the highlights of the runway. Naturally, the usual gaggle of high-strung designers, stylists, and business partners paced about nervously in the background.

A lot to contend with. Almost too much for Theodosia. It was one thing to serve morning and afternoon tea at her charming

Indigo Tea Shop on Charleston's famed Church Street, another to juggle a major event such as this Limón Tea Party.

"Grab another pitcher of lemonade, will you?" Theodosia said to Haley, her young chef and baker. "And that silver ice bucket as well."

Theodosia blew a wisp of curly auburn hair off her face as she stood in the kitchen of the Orchard House Inn, home to South Carolina's only lemon orchard. All the food and beverages were being staged here with the help of Drayton, her tea sommelier, Haley, her chef, and two additional waitstaff. And each course was (thankfully!) going out on time. Seemed to be, anyway.

"That woman is driving me batty," Drayton said as he measured out scoops of lemon verbena tea. A natural orator, each of his syllables was rounded and carefully cadenced.

"You're talking about Delaine?" Theodosia asked. She gazed at him with crystalline blue eyes that were complemented by a peaches and cream complexion and an abundant halo of auburn hair. With her slender, athletic build, Theodosia always gave the impression that she was infused with energy and about to come uncoiled.

"Delaine *always* drives me crazy," Drayton said. "That's nothing new. No, I'm talking about her overbearing sister, Nadine. The woman is positively outrageous. Not only is she bullying the poor models, she's been braying out orders to the film crew. And seriously ragging that dilettante of a film director whose name escapes me at the moment. My fear is that our lovely guests might pick up on the dissonance and frenzy wafting through the air."

Haley looked up from where she was stacking lobster salad tea sandwiches on three-tiered trays. "You mean bad vibes?" Haley was sylphlike and blond, cute as a button, and in her early twenties—still easily impressionable.

"Precisely," Drayton said.

Theodosia glanced out the window over the sink and saw Nadine rushing around, waving her arms, looking as if she were jacked up on an entire bottle of Ritalin.

"Tell you what. You and Haley make one more round with scones, tea, and lemonade, then carry out the tea sandwiches. I'll go see if I can wrangle Nadine."

Theodosia, ever the peacemaker, didn't want trouble. She also didn't want Drayton to lose his cool. He was her steadfast, sixty-something tea sommelier and right-hand man who rarely got ruffled. But today he was edging toward it. Not that you could tell. In his cream-colored silk jacket and pale pink bow tie he was the picture of a Southern gent dressed for a lovely spring afternoon. Not a wrinkle in sight, nary a hair out of place.

Walking across the grass, Theodosia tilted her face up slightly to catch the warm sun. This was such a fun idea to host a tea party in an actual lemon grove on Johns Island, just a few miles outside Charleston's city limits. The Orchard House Inn was the perfect spot, a lovely plantation-style B and B with a chef's kitchen and plenty of parking. And to think that the inn's owners had actually imported all these trees, planted them, and then carefully nurtured them so that they were all producing edible fruit. Quite amazing.

Theodosia walked past the fluttering white tent that served as a temporary dressing room and where a dozen underfed models were squeezing their slim bodies into leggings and halter tops. She passed a small shed where a maintenance man in green overalls was stowing a rake and noticed the film director fidgeting with a camera on a tripod. Even though the day was warm, the director—she remembered his name was somebody Fox—wore a dark green Burberry blazer with a linen scarf looped lazily around his neck.

Theodosia smiled to herself. Like he was at the Cannes Film Festival ready to pick up an award instead of filming an afternoon tea and fashion show.

Finally, a few steps into the lemon orchard, she found the two sisters, Delaine and Nadine, locked in a heated argument. Delaine Dish was sputtering like a manic gopher, her face turning pink as she lectured her younger sister, Nadine.

"You *always* send the sportiest looks down the runway first," Delaine shouted. "Then work your way up to the more fashion-conscious outfits." Delaine was the high-maintenance owner of Cotton Duck, one of Charleston's premier clothing boutiques. She was also a semi-socialite, confirmed gossip, and veteran of countless fashion shows. Today Delaine wore a flouncy rose-colored skirt with a matching, tight-fitting peplum jacket.

Nadine, grim faced and posturing awkwardly in her yellow dress, barely acknowledged her own sister.

"Ladies," Theodosia said, breaking into their conversation. "Please don't tell me we have a problem."

Delaine spun to face her. "A problem? There's *always* a problem when Nadine's involved."

Nadine's expression turned even more sour. "You're always accusing me of being stupid," she sneered at Delaine. "Well, Lemon Squeeze Couture is *my* project and *I'm* creative director. So I'd appreciate it if you'd kindly back off!"

While Delaine was size zero skinny with flowing dark hair and a heart-shaped face, Nadine was her polar opposite. Light blond close-cropped hair, zaftig figure, and a temperament more mercurial than Delaine's. If that was even possible.

"Please," Theodosia said. "Let's all take a deep breath here." Yes, it may have been Theodosia's tea party, but these two ladies had the potential to turn it into WrestleMania if they continued to go at it tooth and nail.

"B-b-but the timing," Delaine began. "With so many moving parts . . . you want everything to be perfect. The food, the fashion . . ."

"Relax," Theodosia said in what she hoped was a soothing

tone. "For one thing, the tea party is nothing to worry about. Drayton and I have done this a million times. As far as the fashion show goes, it looks as if all the models are dressed, glammed up, and eager to strut their stuff." She forced a smile. "Why don't you both take a deep breath, sit down, and enjoy the show. I have a feeling it's going to be terrific."

Nadine's waxed brows shot up as she fought to pull her pink-glossed, over-injected lips into an unhappy line. "So you say, but this is an *enormous* challenge for me. It's not just the kickoff event for Charleston Fashion Week, it's the very first time my partners and I have staged an actual Lemon Squeeze Couture Fashion Show!"

Theodosia sighed. Lemon Squeeze Couture was a new line of workout clothing, or as Nadine preferred to call it—athleisure wear—that was debuting today at the Limón Tea Party.

And just to throw a monkey wrench into things, adding a film crew had been a last-minute decision cooked up by Nadine's two business partners, Harv and Marv. They suddenly had their hearts set on a fun, bouncy fashion video that could be set to music and played on the Lemon Squeeze Couture website. Not a bad idea entirely, just a little late in the game.

Theodosia consulted her watch and waved a hand as a bumblebee buzzed lazily past her head. "Tell you what," she said. "We have ten minutes before the fashion show is scheduled to start. Delaine, why don't you check on the models. And, Nadine, perhaps you could take a quick break. I know you have people from the press here, so before you speak to them maybe you could grab a glass of lemonade and . . ."

"Chill out," Delaine snapped.

Nadine, her nose out of joint because of the confrontation with her sister, walked to the back door of the Orchard House Inn.

Still steaming with anger, she hesitated for a moment, then pulled open the screen door and stepped into the empty kitchen. It was large with lots of metal shelves stocked with stewpots, stacks of fry pans, and sheet cake pans. Acres of counter space held what remained of today's tea party bounty—extra three-tiered trays and pans mounded with lemon cream scones covered in plastic wrap. Six blue coolers that had recently held a myriad of tea sandwiches stood empty. There was also a scatter of tea tins, teapots, and tea accoutrements.

Nadine didn't give a fig about tea or tea sandwiches. What she really wanted right now was a cigarette to help settle her nerves—and who cared if this was a no-smoking zone? Who was going to know? All the tea people were running around like crazy chickens serving the guests while her silly, domineering sister was trying to take over the show and ingratiate herself with her business partners. Hah. Delaine always had been the pushy one.

Dipping into her skirt pocket, Nadine grabbed a half-empty pack of Marlboro Lights, shook one out, and lit up. She inhaled greedily, then exhaled slowly. Tried to calm her jangled nerves as well as her intense worry over the fashion show. And just as her shoulders started to unkink, just as she was beginning to relax, she heard, on the other side of the door that separated the kitchen from a rather large parlor, two people arguing.

Curious now (Nadine was *always* curious), she wondered if it might be her erstwhile business partners, Harv and Marv, sniping at each other yet again. She tiptoed over, put an ear to the door, and heard . . .

More arguing. Insistent and growing increasingly heated with every passing moment. Still, the voices were pitched so low it was virtually impossible to make out actual words.

Could they be talking about me? Nadine wondered as her paranoia kicked in big-time.

She hadn't been getting along all that well with Harv and

Marv. They'd finally tumbled to her utter lack of knowledge concerning fashion and their new product launch. Once that had happened, once she'd been unmasked, it seemed as if they were *constantly* shouting and ranting at her about one thing or another. And it was upsetting to Nadine. Could she help it if she was a neophyte when it came to design and sales and marketing? Sure, she'd embroidered some of her résumé (okay, most of it), but for goodness' sake, she was *trying* to contribute. Could she help it if she lacked actual know-how about manufacturing and distribution? What about all the sweat equity she'd poured in? Surely, that must count for something!

Listening harder, trying to discern exact words, Nadine leaned closer. And as she did, she bumped her forehead against the swinging door, causing it to emit a loud *creak*. At that exact same moment, Nadine lost her balance and—doggone high heels!—teetered hard against the door.

The door swung open, causing her to practically fall into the parlor.

Embarrassed, cartwheeling her arms to try and regain her balance, Nadine stared at the two people and recognized them instantly. "Oh jeez," she sputtered. "I'm so sorry. I was just . . ." Before she got halfway through her apology, her eyes fell on a large black duffel bag stuffed with . . .

Oh no.

Realizing she was suddenly in serious trouble, Nadine spun about frantically, hoping to beat a hasty retreat.

Too late.

As she lurched back into the kitchen, legs churning, veins coursing hot with adrenaline, something sharp struck the back of her head. It was an exquisitely well-defined pain, almost like the sting of a hornet. The sudden assault made her cry out. Then, a millisecond later, the pain was excruciating, as if the entire back of her head were on fire. Nadine wondered what strange thing had just happened as a million jumbled thoughts spun crazily through her brain and she crashed to the floor.

And the very last thing Nadine was cognizant of before she winked out for good, for all eternity, was being dragged . . . dragged into a place that was cold and dark and sticky.

2

"Is it my imagination or do some of these fine Charleston ladies have appetites that rival a burly truck driver?" Drayton asked Theodosia. "I just made the rounds again and almost everyone requested a second lemon scone. One woman wanted a *third*!"

"That's because our scones are so ridiculously delicious," Theodosia said. "Don't spill the beans, but I think Haley uses a special cake flour to get them so light and fluffy."

"That's lovely, of course. But now we're in need of additional lemon curd."

"I'll run and grab a few more bowls," Theodosia said. She spun on her heels and headed for the back door of the Orchard House Inn. Put a little urgency into her step because she knew the fashion show would be starting anytime now and she didn't want to miss a second of it. After all, it wasn't every day she got to host a tea party that served as the kickoff for Charleston Fashion Week.

Grab the lemon curd, scoop it into those little glass slipper bowls, Theodosia thought to herself. *I hope Haley packed a few extra.*

One glance in the wicker basket on the counter told her that Haley had. How perfect.

This tea is going to go off as planned come hell or high water.

Theodosia set a half dozen of the small glass slipper bowls on the counter, crossed to the walk-in cooler, and pulled open the door.

That's when hell or high water showed up.

Or at least a dead body. On the floor of the cooler. Facedown, arms and limbs akimbo, the head practically submerged in a bowl of lemon curd. *Her* lemon curd.

Whose dead body? was the first thought that streaked like lightning through Theodosia's brain. Then she bonked into hyperdrive and thought, *Oh, dear Lord, I recognize that bright yellow dress. It's Nadine!*

Theodosia drew a sharp breath even as she put a hand to her mouth. She blinked, swallowed hard, then pulled it together. Let the shock subside a little.

What just happened here? Well, she was no forensic expert, but as she stared at Nadine with a mixture of horror and curiosity, she saw what looked like a small black hole, jagged and ringed with blood, at the back of the poor woman's head. Really more at the base of her skull. And even though Theodosia knew in her heart there wasn't much hope, that Nadine had pretty much left the building, she bent down anyway and, with a shaking hand, gently touched two fingers to one side of Nadine's neck.

Nothing. No throb of pulse. No hint of warmth in the carotid artery. No chance of resuscitation.

Theodosia backed away from Nadine's body but left the cooler door wide open. And wondered what to do next.

Well, she knew what should be done. She had to alert the authorities. And then try to put the entire luncheon and fashion show on hold.

Not gonna be easy.

But she had to do it anyway.

Yes, go, Theodosia told herself. *Do it now!*

Flying out the back door, phone in hand, she had the bad luck of running smack-dab into Delaine. Actually crashed into her, her left shoulder jamming hard against Delaine's shoulder, giving them both a hard shaking up.

"Ouch," a grumpy Delaine cried. "What's your problem?"

"Don't go in there!" Theodosia warned.

Delaine gazed at her with suspicion. "Why not?"

"Because there's a . . . a problem." Theodosia was already tip-tapping 911 into her cell phone.

Delaine wiggled her nose and frowned. "What's that you're doing there? Three digits? Did you just punch in an emergency number?"

Theodosia didn't have time to answer because the dispatcher was suddenly on the line saying, "911, what's your emergency?"

"There's been a death," Theodosia said. Then her words tumbled out in one long stream. "At the Orchard House Inn on Bohicket Road. We need help, law enforcement, and whoever else you can send. Immediately."

"A death?" Delaine said. "What are you talking about? Who died?"

Theodosia paid her no mind as she listened carefully to the dispatcher's words, fought to comprehend them.

"You'll radio Sheriff Burney? . . . Yes, thank you, we'll watch for him," Theodosia said. "And could you maybe send the county coroner as well?" She was breathless and jumpy as she tried to focus on the dispatcher's questions, then said, "No, I don't know the *exact* cause, but it looks like a gunshot. . . . Yes, that does seem fairly suspicious. So it could have been . . . murder?"

"Murder!" Delaine screamed.

Theodosia listened to the calm voice of the dispatcher for an-other half minute, then said, "I don't know," and "We'll try." And then, "Got it, nobody's to leave the premises."

Delaine reached a hand out and gripped Theodosia's arm as she hung up.

"What's going on?" Delaine demanded. "You said death—maybe a murder. Who's been murdered?"

"Delaine," Theodosia said, "you need to take a deep breath and hang on. Try to stay strong."

Delaine looked suddenly petulant. "You're not making any sense at all. What are you *blathering* about?"

"The murder victim? I'm afraid it's your sister, Nadine."

Delaine's face blanched white, overriding multiple layers of bronzer and blusher. Her forehead puckered, she made a soft mew-ling sound, and she said, "You're joking, right? Theo, please tell me you're joking!"

"I wish I were."

"No, it can't be. That would . . . uh . . ." Delaine suddenly stopped mid-sentence, as if she'd been flash frozen or her internal engine had seized. Then her eyes rolled back in her head and she crumpled to the ground.

So. Theodosia made the dreaded announcement that the fashion show was on hold. Delaine was eventually revived. And Bettina, Nadine's daughter, was informed, as gently as possible, about the death of her mother.

A few minutes later, Sheriff Clay Burney, his two deputies, and an ambulance with two EMTs came screaming onto the scene.

Tall and lean with short silvered hair and a craggy face, Sher-iff Burney had been county sheriff for more than twenty-seven years and had seen his share of accidents, killings, and death.

"Did you move her?" were his first words to Theodosia.

"No," she said as the EMTs went crashing past them. They immediately fell to their knees and futilely checked Nadine's airway, breathing, and pulse.

"When you found her, did you know she was dead?" Sheriff Burney asked.

"Pretty much," Theodosia said.

"Okay then," Sheriff Burney said as he glanced at his two deputies. "Seth, Roscoe, you boys stay here and secure the scene while I go out and talk to this group of people."

"Got it, Sheriff," Seth said. Seth was languid with shaggy blond hair like a surfer dude. Roscoe had a crew cut and looked as if he'd just escaped from the marines.

If Theodosia's somewhat cryptic announcement of the fashion show's cancellation had been met with disappointment, Sheriff Burney's words were met with outright hostility from the crowd.

"A situation? What kind of situation?" one woman demanded.

"Why are we all being detained?" another shouted.

This from one of the partners: "Tell us what *happened*!"

Once Sheriff Burney elaborated on the circumstances as delicately as possible, the guests fell silent. His announcement of Nadine's murder cast a terrible pall over the group. Many of them dabbed at their eyes; some glanced about fearfully as if some kind of rogue militia might be planning to storm the place.

Delaine sat at a table and sniffled, while Harv and Marv, the two managing partners, skulked about and whispered to each other, and the models lazed around and smoked.

Theodosia spent her time trying to soothe Bettina's tears over her mother's death and explaining the bizarre turn of events to Andrea Wilts, the owner of the Orchard House Inn.

Ten minutes later a shiny black Crime Scene van showed up with two men who immediately donned white Tyvek suits. One of the men shook hands with Sheriff Burney and said, "Once we finish here, we'll transport the victim to the Charleston Medical

Examiner's office. Per our contractual arrangement with them."
Then they all three disappeared inside the inn.

Drayton sidled up to Theodosia. "I have to tell you something."

"What's that?"

"Earlier today, I overheard Nadine having a knock-down, drag-out fight with that film director, Eddie Fox."

"What are you saying?"

"Just that . . ."

Theodosia lifted an eyebrow. "Do you think Fox might have killed her?"

Drayton shrugged. "Maybe, maybe not. It's just a thought. On the other hand, it seems as if everyone associated with this Lemon Squeeze Couture project harbored a secret desire to wring Nadine's neck. All day I kept hearing whispers of how she was caustic and overbearing, treated everyone so badly."

Theodosia looked out at the crowd and wondered who could have killed Nadine. Correction, who could have *shot* Nadine. Someone here must be carrying a concealed weapon, right? Or maybe they'd already ditched it somewhere in the woods. Or nearby Bohicket Creek.

And how long had Nadine been dead?

Theodosia racked her brain. From the time she'd separated Delaine and Nadine until the time she'd discovered Nadine's body in the cooler had to be nine or ten minutes. A lot could happen in that time. A lot *had* happened.

Was the killer still on the premises? Was it someone in this crowd that she'd rubbed shoulders with? Or someone who'd snuck in from the outside? It would have been a piece of cake to waltz in here, given the frantic activity of the tea service and film crew. To say nothing of all the guests, models, stylists, and makeup artists. Really, it would have been a snap.

Theodosia gave a reflexive shudder. She let her thoughts wander for a few moments, reached for her phone, then changed her mind. Rethought her idea and then made her call anyway.

"Howdy there." Pete Riley's voice was warm and engaging. Clearly, he'd checked his caller ID and knew that it was Theodosia, his girlfriend, sailing buddy, and fellow foodie, on the line.

"You'll never guess what happened," Theodosia said.

"Did it rain on your fancy-schmancy tea?"

"Look out your window. Do you see dark clouds?"

"Nope, I'm looking out over Charleston Harbor and the sun does seem to be shining." A pause. "So what happened? What's wrong? Your voice sounds funny."

"You remember Nadine, Delaine's sister?"

"Met her once. That was enough," Riley said. "The lady was too high-strung for my sensibilities."

"Not anymore. Nadine was just murdered."

"What!" he cried.

3

Pete Riley was a D-2, a detective with the Charleston Police Department's Robbery and Homicide Division. Theodosia knew the scent of a good murder would make him sit up and take notice.

Theodosia cleared her throat. "I said Nadine . . ."

"No, no, I heard that part just fine. But . . . what? Who?"

"Who," Theodosia said, slowly drawing out the word. "It could have been someone attending our Limón Tea Party. Or, possibly, one of the folks from the fashion shoot. Or maybe some maniac just wandered in and didn't like her looks."

"Unlikely," Riley said. "Tell me, how was Nadine killed?"

"Don't quote me on this, but it looks like a small caliber weapon to the back of the head."

"Huh," Riley said. "Maybe that's why they call it a fashion shoot."

Theodosia wanted to laugh but didn't. Longed to dispel the horrible ball of anxiety that was slowly building inside her. A ruined tea, a murdered woman, a grieving sister and daughter.

"You're not helping," she said.

Riley was suddenly serious. "But I *could* help. That's why you called, isn't it? Do you want me to drive out there and lend a hand?"

Theodosia thought for a few quick moments. Riley didn't have jurisdiction, but he was clever enough not to step on anybody's toes. Plus, he was a trained investigator and a darn good shoulder to lean on. Or cry on if necessary.

"That would be great," Theodosia said finally.

Pete Riley was, as always, an oasis of calm. Even in a maelstrom of shock and uncertainty. He arrived some twenty minutes later and swept Theodosia into his arms.

"Thank you for coming," Theodosia said. She could feel his newly acquired Glock 22 press up against her as she hugged him tight. It made her feel . . . safe.

Pete Riley nodded and kissed the top of her head. He was used to dealing with tragedy, used to investigating homicides and serious crimes. At age thirty-seven, he was one of the up-and-coming detectives on Charleston's police force, a tall, intense man with an aristocratic nose, high cheekbones, and cobalt blue eyes. Theodosia tended to call him Riley instead of Pete, and he called her Theo. It was what worked for them. And had for a couple of years now.

When Theodosia knocked on the kitchen door, Sheriff Burney cracked it open and peered out. The sheriff might have been surprised when Theodosia introduced him to a CPD detective, but he had the good grace not to show it. Even seemed to welcome Riley's presence.

"Tell me again how you found her?" Sheriff Burney said to Theodosia. They were all crowded into the kitchen now. The sheriff, Pete Riley, Theodosia, the deputies, EMTs, and two Crime Scene investigators. Even Drayton seemed to have acquired a hall pass to get inside. The Crime Scene guys had set up lights on stanchions, marked a few things with red tape, made a video of the area, taken still photos, and checked the scene for possible fibers, hair, and trace evidence.

But they still hadn't moved the body. Poor Nadine still lay facedown in the lemon curd, her arms and legs splayed out like a rag doll.

"I opened the walk-in cooler and there she was—boom! Facedown in the lemon curd," Theodosia said. She glanced at the blobs and spatters of yellow that were all around Nadine and thought, *She must have landed hard.*

"Do you think she went in there to get something?" Riley asked.

"I don't think so," Theodosia said. "Basically, it looked as if she'd been shot and then kind of dragged across the kitchen floor. You see over there? Where that red tab marks her shoe? Obviously one of her high heels flew off. So there must have been some kind of struggle during which . . ." Theodosia took a quick swipe at her eyes. "During which Nadine was overpowered and shot. Then she was tossed into the cooler all haphazard like."

"Why was Nadine in the kitchen?" Sheriff Burney asked.

"There was a cigarette on the floor," one of the Crime Scene techs said. "Burned down some but not extinguished. I think she came in here to sneak a smoke."

"In the kitchen. With all your food around," Riley said.

Theodosia sighed. "Nobody ever said Nadine was considerate."

Drayton still couldn't wrap his head around the murder. "If Nadine fell into the lemon curd like that, is it possible she was unconscious and drowned?"

Sheriff Burney shook his head. "She was probably dead by the time she hit the floor. Or I should say that bowl of . . . what did you folks call it? Lemon herb?"

"Lemon curd," Drayton said in a glum tone.

Sheriff Burney shook his head. "Huh. Never heard of that before."

"And none of us heard the fatal gunshot," Theodosia said.

"Not surprising," Sheriff Burney said. "Whoever did this probably used a suppressor."

"Is that common?" Theodosia asked.

"It's not uncommon," Sheriff Burney said.

One of the Crime Scene techs sidestepped into the cooler and, with gloved hands, gently probed the back of Nadine's skull. "Stippling," he said. "So she was shot at close range."

"Ghastly," Drayton said and turned away.

Theodosia was repulsed as well. By the crime and the seeming cold-bloodedness of it all. But deep down inside her DNA, where her curiosity gene resided, she was more than a little intrigued.

"Can you test for gunpowder residue?" she asked.

"Paraffin test," said Seth the deputy.

"We could if we had a viable suspect," Sheriff Burney said. "But to test everyone here, all those folks outside, that would be seventy or more people . . . well, we can't just do that willy-nilly. Not without probable cause."

"Or a court order," Theodosia said. "Yes, that does present a problem."

"Theodosia," Riley said in a cautionary tone, "don't get ahead of yourself. In fact, best not to get involved at all."

"I don't intend to. I'm just . . . curious," Theodosia said. "I mean, why Nadine? What did she do to provoke this kind of deadly response?"

"That," Riley said, "is what investigations are all about."

Drayton turned back for another look, grimaced, and said, "Is the bullet still in her?"

"Probably," Sheriff Burney said. "But we'll let the ME deal with that."

"Pretty clean shot though; must have caught her by surprise," one of the techs said.

"No," Theodosia said. "I don't think so. Nadine knew she was in trouble and was struggling to get away."

"You're surmising all that because she lost her shoe?" Drayton asked.

"That and a feeling I have." Theodosia had a very *bad* feeling deep down in her gut, but for now she decided to keep it to herself.

With names and addresses all jotted down and more than a few people interviewed, there wasn't much left to do but call it a day. Guests streamed to their cars looking nervous and upset while the film crew packed up their equipment and the models piled into a beat-up station wagon.

Theodosia tried to talk to Bettina, Nadine's daughter, to offer some words of comfort, but Delaine wanted to hustle her back to Charleston as soon as possible. She also spoke with Harvey Bateman and Marvin Chauvet, Nadine's two partners, but they seemed shell-shocked by it all and anxious to make their escape.

Once most everyone had left, the coroner arrived in a black van. He and his assistant went into the kitchen, carefully placed Nadine's body in a black plastic body bag, and loaded it into their vehicle.

As Riley talked to Sheriff Burney, Theodosia made her way back into the kitchen for a final look-see.

One of the Crime Scene techs had just picked up the bowl of lemon curd.

"You're taking the lemon curd, too?" Theodosia asked him.

He nodded as he slipped it into a large plastic bag. "Evidence." He gazed around. "You can pack up your stuff now. We're going to poke around one last time in the room next door."

* * *

It was late by the time Theodosia, Drayton, and Haley packed up all their dishes, serving trays, and leftover food. Theodosia and Drayton worked steadily while Haley kept stealing glances at one of the coolers.

Finally, she said, "We're not going to keep those leftover scones, are we?"

"Heaven forbid," Drayton shuddered. "They're part of a murder scene."

"Then I'll toss them out for the birds when we get back," Haley said.

"I saw you talking to Delaine and Bettina," Drayton said to Theodosia. "How are they handling Nadine's death?"

"Not well," Theodosia said. "Delaine has a huge case of the guilts because she was so nasty to Nadine. And Bettina is just plain heartsick about her mom."

"Poor Bettina," Haley said as she picked up two coolers and muscled them out the door. "I feel so sad for her."

"Me, too," Drayton said. He covered six teapots in Bubble Wrap, then placed them in a large cardboard box. "I'll be back for the rest," he said as he picked up the box and headed out as well.

Theodosia stood there looking around. The cooler door was still open, and the lid for the lemon curd was lying on the floor. She was about to pick it up when she decided, *No, let it go. It's not important.*

"Hey, are you okay?"

Theodosia spun around to find Riley gazing at her.

"As good as can be expected," she said. Then, "Thanks for coming."

"You want me to follow you home? If you're feeling down I could hang around." He smiled at her. "You know, for recreational purposes."

"No, I'm okay."

"All right, then, you take care." He gave her a quick kiss and was gone.

Theodosia took one more look around the kitchen. Then, with a heavy heart, she stepped outside into the dying light.

4

"Can you believe our rotten luck yesterday?" It was Monday morning at the Indigo Tea Shop, and Drayton had a death grip on his teacup as he spoke across the table to Theodosia and Haley.

"Actually, it was Nadine's rotten luck," Haley said.

"Haley's right," Theodosia said.

Drayton sighed. "I suppose. Though it's awful to think that our tea party was completely ruined. All that planning turned out to be for naught. And now our poor guests probably think the worst of us."

"Or maybe not," Theodosia said. "The ones that didn't want a full refund all got make-goods. I gave them tickets for next Saturday's Tea Trolley Tour."

"And they were okay with that?" Haley asked.

Theodosia smiled. "The ones who accepted tickets were especially pleased when I told them the Tea Trolley Tour would ferry them around to three different venues in the Historic District for three different tea courses."

Haley cocked a finger at her. "That's some smart thinking, boss lady."

"It was the least I could do, given the circumstances," Theodosia said.

Drayton blew out a breath. "Circumstances. Which begs the question of possible suspects. I wonder who . . . ?"

"No idea," Theodosia said. "That's for Sheriff Burney to figure out."

"But thank goodness Riley showed up when he did," Haley said. "He asked some good questions and turned out to be a calming influence."

"It was good of him to come, yes, but of course it's not his turf," Theodosia said. "So he can't properly investigate the murder."

"Pity for that," Drayton said. "His skills would certainly come in handy." He glanced at his watch, an antique Patek Philippe that ran a perpetual five minutes slow, and said, "Oops, almost nine, dear people. Our guests will be arriving any moment."

Theodosia took a last sip of Darjeeling and stood up. "I'll hang out our sign." She grabbed a small hand-lettered, curlicued sign that said OPEN FOR TEA AND LIGHT LUNCHES and stepped out the front door. And just as she hung her sign on the brass hook to the left of the door, she heard a shuffle of footsteps directly behind her. Followed by a muffled sob. Turning, curious now, Theodosia was shocked to find Delaine standing there.

"Delaine, this is . . . unexpected." Theodosia gazed at Delaine who stood like a statue, looking grim, a white linen hankie pressed to her nose. She wore a sharply tailored black skirt suit with a pink blouse and matching bag, and tottered unsteadily on black stiletto heels. Diamond studs glittered from her earlobes.

"Theo," Delaine blurted out, "you're the *only one* I can turn to at a time like this. The *only one* I can trust."

Theodosia put an arm around Delaine's shoulders and pulled her close. "I'm so sorry about your sister."

Delaine let loose another little sob, then nodded and wiped at her eyes.

"I know, Theo, and I do appreciate your concern. You of all people know that Nadine and I didn't always see eye to eye. Well, actually, we never did. But for my poor sister to be murdered like that—gunned down in cold blood—at her own fashion show. It's almost too much to bear."

"Come inside," Theodosia urged. "Have a nice cup of tea." She pushed open the door and called, "Drayton? Something strong in the tea department, please?"

Drayton caught sight of Delaine, nodded, and immediately went to work.

Theodosia got Delaine situated at one of their small tables, then sat down across from her. Reached over and squeezed her hand. "You'll get through this, honey."

"I suppose," Delaine said without much conviction.

"How's Bettina doing?" Theodosia knew Delaine hadn't been all that close to her sister, often made snide remarks about her. But Bettina was a whole different case. She was young, early twenties, and obviously distressed that her mother had been wantonly murdered.

"Bettina is . . . handling it," Delaine said. "In her own way."

Theodosia took this to mean that poor Bettina was beside herself with grief.

"Bettina seemed terribly upset yesterday," Theodosia said as Drayton carried a Chinese blue-and-white teapot to their table along with two matching cups.

"A Nepalese oolong," he said. "Nice and strong with notes of honey. Warming, too."

"Thank you," Theodosia murmured as Drayton retreated to the front counter where he began lining up his various teapots.

Theodosia poured out a cup of tea and pushed it across the table to Delaine. "Drink it. You'll feel better."

Delaine clasped both hands around the ceramic cup, inhaled the rich aroma, and said, "At this point I'm not sure *anything* will make me feel better."

"That's because you're still in a mild state of shock. But that will eventually wear off, maybe even faster than you think. Go ahead, this tea is one of Drayton's favorites. Very soothing to the psyche."

Delaine took a delicate sip. "Mmn. It is good."

"You have to allow yourself time to get past your sister's death. Practice a bit of self-care."

"A little financial self-care is more like it," Delaine said.

"Excuse me?"

"You don't know this, Theo, but *I'm* the one who gave Nadine the money to invest in Lemon Squeeze Couture."

"I had no idea." Theodosia had secretly wondered how the perpetually broke Nadine had come up with enough cash to buy into a business. Now she knew.

"That was *my* hard-earned money," Delaine said. "You know as well as I do that Nadine was poor as a church mouse. Always has been. Now I don't know how I'll ever recoup my investment!" She flicked her wrist, sending the floating diamonds in her Chopard watch spinning.

"Can't you just ask the partners?" Theodosia offered.

Delaine wrinkled her nose. "I already tried that. Spoke to Harv and Marv about it late yesterday. It felt as though they were basically stonewalling me. Then, first thing this morning, I called the bank that put up the guarantee money. And that horrible banker, Frank Wetzel, wouldn't even *talk* to me."

Delaine snuffled again as giant tears rolled down her cheeks.

"I'm sure something can be worked out," Theodosia said. "Perhaps the right attorney . . ."

Delaine just shook her head.

Theodosia decided to switch the subject away from finances.

"How did Nadine get involved with these fashion people in the first place?" she asked.

Delaine made a comical grimace. "Silly me, that was *my* fault I hooked them up. When Nadine came for a visit a few months ago, she moped around like she always does, then began taking an interest in the orders I was putting in for Cotton Duck. One thing led to another, and she started making connections of her own."

"In the fashion industry," Theodosia said.

"Right," Delaine snorted. "How was I to know it would all go sour? I should have never supported her, never lent her all that money." She started to reach for her teacup, then jumped as her mobile phone shrilled inside her pink Chanel bag. "Goodness!" she cried, touching a hand to her heart. Then she pulled out her phone, glanced at the caller ID, and frowned.

"Problem?" Theodosia said.

"Could be." Delaine lifted the phone to her ear. "Hello?" she said in a clipped voice. "I really can't imagine we have much to discuss at this point so . . . hmm?" Delaine pursed her lips, suddenly stopped talking, and listened. Then, "What did you say? Could you please repeat that?" Her eyes darted back and forth and she began to look a little less flustered. "Oh, you think so? . . . Really . . . No, I hadn't considered that aspect at all . . . Well, I *suppose* I could. If it means I wouldn't lose my *entire* investment." Delaine's tears had magically dried up, and her demeanor seemed to be improving by leaps and bounds. "Yes, at the Fashion Dazzle Show tonight? I'm sure I could handle that. Happy to, in fact. Okay, see you shortly. Yes, you, too."

Delaine hung up. She stared at her phone for a few moments, then dropped it in her bag.

Theodosia gazed at Delaine. "I take it that was good news?"

"Stunning news," Delaine said with a slightly crooked smile. "That was Marvin Chauvet. You know, the partner who also owns Chauvet's Smartwear over on Broad Street."

Theodosia remembered Marvin Chauvet from yesterday. A tall, silver-haired gentleman who'd been pacing about restlessly. Even before everything had gone ka-pow crazy. Before Nadine had been murdered.

"You'll never in a million years guess what Mr. Chauvet just asked me," Delaine said.

Theodosia knew something was up because there'd been a tectonic shift in Delaine's attitude. Yes, she was famously mercurial, but this transformation seemed far too abrupt. She'd gone from speaking in dour tones to the breathy little girl voice she was using now. And her scowl had been replaced by a curious cat-who-swallowed-the-canary smile.

"Tell me. What did Mr. Chauvet want?"

"It's terribly interesting, really. He asked if I'd step in and take over the job of brand ambassador." Delaine's false eyelashes suddenly fluttered like newly hatched butterflies. "Can you *imagine*?"

From behind the front counter, Drayton said, "What on *earth* is a brand ambassador?"

Delaine turned toward him, a smile suddenly lighting her face. "It's the hottest new thing ever, particularly in the case of high-profile luxury goods. A brand ambassador is a well-spoken, well-respected individual who represents—who embodies—a company's brand."

"That brand being Lemon Squeeze Couture?" Theodosia said.

"And that's going to be *you*?" Drayton sounded just this side of amazed.

"It is now," Delaine said. "What an honor." She lifted her chin, pushed her shoulders back. "I have to say, this invitation couldn't come at a more opportune moment."

Theodosia couldn't believe what she was hearing. Yes, Delaine was known to have her ditzy flashes, but this was world-class.

"You're accepting this . . . this *position* the day after your sister was murdered?" Theodosia said. "When basically everyone involved with Lemon Squeeze Couture is a suspect?"

"That's not what I meant at all," Delaine hastened to say. "Of course the investigation will go on, but this position as brand ambassador means I'll be able to recoup a good portion of my investment." Now her eyes shone clear and bright. "I know it sounds cray-cray, but possibly, as an essential member of the team, I'd stand to make even *more* money."

"There's only one word for Delaine," Drayton said once Delaine had finished her tea and scurried off.

"Cray-cray?" Theodosia said. "Wait, that's two words."

"I was thinking more like greedy."

"It was her money that helped launch the company."

"Yes, but who can negotiate such an about-face? Delaine went from anguish to ecstasy in five seconds flat."

Theodosia made a face somewhere between a grin and a grimace. "You know Delaine; she majored in theatrics."

"And graduated with honors," Drayton said.

"Still, if she was about to lose a small fortune . . ." Before Theodosia could get the rest of her words out, the front door flew open and guests began to pour in.

"Guests," Drayton exclaimed, happy to shift his type A, task-oriented persona into high gear.

Within minutes Theodosia had seated three tables of guests who'd been recommended by Angie at the Featherbed House B and B, and four more tables of tourists. There was also the usual assortment of Church Street shopkeepers who dropped in for their morning scone and cuppa.

From her post in the kitchen, Haley helped fulfill everyone's baked goods fantasies with butterscotch scones, cranberry-walnut scones, and lemon tea bread.

Drayton, as resident tea alchemist, brewed pots of Assam, Russian Caravan, and Chinese black congou tea. All selected to please and tantalize discerning palates.

Theodosia was also caught up in the morning whirlwind. She continued to welcome guests, serve tea, and take orders, delighting in the fact that, once again, her cute little tea shop hummed with activity.

And what a tea shop it was.

Situated directly on Church Street, a block from historic St. Philip's Church, the Indigo Tea Shop was a veritable jewel box of a shop. A little bit country French, a smattering of Olde England, Theodosia's tea shop had wavy leaded windows hung with blue toile curtains, pegged pine floors, faded Oriental carpets, and a small stone fireplace. A French chandelier imparted a warm glow—Drayton always referred to it as Rembrandt lighting—while antique highboys were bursting with popular retail items such as tea towels, tea cozies, tins of tea, jars of honey, and a selection of Theodosia's proprietary T-Bath products. Brick walls were hung with grapevine wreaths decorated with teacups and threaded with pink and green ribbons.

To make all this happen, Theodosia had put together a bit of inheritance, her savings, and some 401(k) money from a previous marketing job. Then she'd bit the bullet and bought the shop outright, never once regretting her decision. Drayton as tea sommelier had been her first hire—now he was practically a full partner. Haley, her chef and chief bottle washer, had casually answered a want ad and suddenly found that her kitchen creativity and prodigious baking skills were very much desired. Together Theodosia and Drayton vowed they'd never let her go.

The rest of the decor and tea accoutrements had come about

organically, with Theodosia hunting through antique shops, flea markets, and tag sales to find the perfect vintage teacups, teapots, goblets, and silverware.

After a half dozen years together, Theodosia, Drayton, and Haley had become a confident, well-oiled team that never failed to delight visitors and neighbors with their baked-from-scratch scones and muffins, dazzling array of fine teas, extraordinary catering, and ever-popular special event teas.

Theodosia had just finished folding white linen napkins into a showy bishop's hat arrangement when Haley came wandering out, bringing with her a drift of wonderful aromas.

"Smells good in your kitchen," Theodosia said.

Haley grinned. "Getting everything ready for a tasty lunch today. Even though . . . you know."

"Even though we're all still on edge," Theodosia said. "And I take it you're all set menu-wise for tomorrow's Sterling Silver Tea?"

"Yup, pretty much. Except for . . ." Haley stopped midsentence and held up a finger. "Give me a couple seconds and let me *parlez-vous* with one more supplier before I give you the final-final, okay?"

"Works for me. Oh, and you do plan on cluing us in on today's luncheon? Hopefully sometime soon?"

"Oops. Better run and grab my menu card."

5

Haley's luncheon menu turned out to be a delicious lineup that included shrimp bisque and Caesar salad for starters and entrées of Chicken à la King on baking powder biscuits and cheddar cheese quiche with a side salad. Her tea sandwiches consisted of roast beef with English mustard on sourdough bread, smoked salmon with cream cheese on dark bread, and roasted red pepper hummus on pita bread.

By twelve fifteen the tea shop was literally packed with customers and Theodosia was spinning and hopping from table to table. She took orders, ran them to the kitchen, zipped back out and grabbed pots of tea that Drayton had brewed, and chatted with customers.

Yes, they were crazy busy, but what was the alternative? Not being busy at all? No, thank you. Theodosia loved the Indigo Tea Shop with all her heart and always sought to give her guests a truly unique experience. In today's 24-7, hurly-burly world, she regarded her tea shop as an oasis of calm. Where the relaxed atmosphere could be savored just as much as the food and tea.

At one o'clock Theodosia got her second surprise of the day when the front door whooshed open and Nadine's two business partners walked in.

Theodosia recognized Marvin Chauvet first. His silver-gray hair was swept back in a lush tidal wave that ended an inch below his collar. His posture was ramrod straight, and he wore a pink button-down shirt tucked into powder blue slacks. As if his peacock wardrobe wasn't enough, Chauvet looked perpetually suntanned, as if he played golf all year round, from Hilton Head on down to Miami and over to the Caribbean.

Interestingly enough, his business partner, Harvey Bateman, wasn't even close to being a fashion plate. He was short and stocky, with close-cropped dark hair and a perpetual five-o'clock shadow. Unlike the sartorial splendor of Chauvet, Bateman wore a rumpled green polo shirt with a pair of awful brown-and-yellow plaid slacks. He came across as fidgety, brash, and pushy, like the kind of guy who'd be selling time-shares in Cabo.

Delaine had told Theodosia that Chauvet had serious retail experience by way of his upscale clothing shop, while Bateman was a whiz at buying distressed and overstock clothing, then turning it around and selling it to discount retailers. And making a tidy profit in doing so.

"Gentlemen," Theodosia said, hurrying to greet them at the door. "How may I help you?"

She assumed they'd come to talk about yesterday's fashion show fiasco. They had, but they also wanted to have lunch.

Okay, no problem. Theodosia seated them at a table by the front window, took their orders, then brought them the pot of Nilgiri tea they'd debated over and finally ordered.

"Do you have a minute to talk?" Chauvet asked.

Theodosia glanced around. Most of her guests were either finishing their lunches or savoring second cups of tea, so yes, she had some time. And she was curious.

"What's up?" Theodosia said, slipping into a chair at their table.

"You know we're going full speed ahead with our fashion launch," Bateman said.

Theodosia nodded. "I assumed you would. In fact, Delaine was in here this morning and mentioned that you asked her to sub in as brand ambassador."

"She's got a lot more retail experience than that sister of hers," Chauvet said.

"And better connections," Bateman said.

"I'm sure she does," Theodosia said.

She studied them carefully, wondering if either of them could have had a hand in Nadine's murder. Then decided to follow Riley's advice and leave it alone. But there *was* something . . .

"I have to ask," Theodosia said. "Does Bettina know about Delaine's new arrangement with you?" She figured that Delaine stepping in to fill her dead sister's shoes might go over like a lead balloon with Nadine's daughter.

"As far as I know, she's unaware of the change in circumstances," Chauvet said. He glanced across the table at Bateman.

"It's not really any of the daughter's concern," Bateman said in measured tones. "Bettina's never had any involvement or financial stake in Lemon Squeeze Couture."

"I suppose you're right," Theodosia said. "But you'll no doubt be looking for another creative director. That was Nadine's role, right?"

"That was her *title*," Chauvet said. He was casually studying his manicure as if his life depended on it.

"But we didn't come here to talk about yesterday's murder, or any fallout caused by it," Bateman said.

"But it happened," Theodosia said. Finding Nadine's dead body was still fresh in her mind, and she wasn't willing to drop the subject quite yet. "And I was part of it. So, naturally, I'm wondering if either of you have any ideas on who might have wanted Nadine dead?" There, she'd set it on the table like the big steaming mess it was. Surely, they'd have some suspicions, right?

Turns out they didn't.

"We're clueless," Chauvet said. He wrinkled his brow, trying hard to look concerned.

Theodosia turned her gaze to Bateman.

"We're as stunned as everyone else," Bateman said, not looking particularly stunned at all. "We've huddled with Sheriff Burney, talked at length with his investigators, and told them everything we know."

"Which isn't all that much," Chauvet hastened to add.

"I see," Theodosia said. "No rifts in your relationship with Nadine?"

Both men shook their heads.

"Outside issues or jealousies, then? Problems with creative people or vendors?"

"Nothing we can think of," Bateman said. "And, believe me, we've tried. Racked our brains, turned everything upside down and over sideways, but couldn't find a doggone thing. No reason at all to murder that poor woman in cold blood."

"It's a complete mystery," Chauvet said.

No kidding, Theodosia thought as she started to get up from her chair. "In that case . . ."

"Hang on a minute, will you?" Chauvet lifted a hand. "We want to ask you something."

Theodosia sat back down. "Yes?"

"You've heard of the Concours d'Carolina?" Chauvet said.

"Sure," Theodosia said. The Concours d'Carolina was a major car show that took place annually, usually at a local country club. It featured classic and high-end cars, attendance was limited, and tickets generally cost upward of a hundred dollars each.

"It's happening this Friday at the Juniper Bay Country Club, and we were wondering if you and your staff could cater our portion of the event?" Bateman said.

"We'll have a hospitality tent and do informal modeling. You know, a few girls wearing Lemon Squeeze Couture," Chauvet said.

Theodosia thought fast. She didn't have a tea party scheduled for Friday, so an afternoon catering gig would definitely help fluff the week's receipts. And she wanted to stay close to these two men because she still wasn't sure of their complete and total innocence.

"We could probably accommodate you," Theodosia said. "What sort of menu did you have in mind?"

"Kind of like what you did yesterday," Chauvet said. "Only we'll be serving gin fizzes and salty dogs, so we'll need something that pairs well with cocktails."

Theodosia glanced toward the counter and curled a finger at Drayton. He came over to the table and stood there while she explained the event to him.

"Any recommendations?" Chauvet asked him.

"What about crab salad tea sandwiches for starters?" Drayton said.

"Not bad," Bateman said. "But we were thinking of something more in the heartier appetizer realm. There'll be lots of men at the show."

"In that case," Drayton said, "how about duck pâté on crostini, steak bites, and shrimp tartlets? And maybe a nice charcuterie board of meats and cheeses?"

Chauvet nodded. "I like it. Very upscale. So you can *do* all that for us?"

"I don't see why not," Theodosia said. "As long as it's in your budget."

"The budget's not a problem," Bateman said. He stood up, dug in his wallet, and handed Theodosia a business card. "Here.

If you have any questions, call our office and talk to Julie Eiden, our intern."

Bateman hurried out of the tea shop while Chauvet stayed and dawdled.

"Tea, huh?" Chauvet said. He looked around the shop. "You make any money at this?"

"We do okay," Theodosia said.

"I'll say one thing, it's a cute place. A little flouncy for my taste, but I'm sure your customers love it."

"Our customers are all very loyal," Drayton said.

Chauvet took a final sip of tea, looked at his watch, and stood up slowly. "Well, time to bounce. I've got a session with my personal trainer." He patted his stomach. "You two work out?" He looked from Drayton to Theodosia.

"Heavens no," Drayton said.

"Run a bit," Theodosia said.

Chauvet smiled. "Good for you."

"They're strange ducks, aren't they?" Drayton said from behind the counter. The lunch rush was over, only a few guests lingered, and he was getting ready to taste test some new teas.

Theodosia walked over to the counter and leaned on it with her elbows, stretching the kinks out of her neck. "You're referring to Chauvet and Bateman? Yeah, I got a weird vibe from them, too."

Drayton measured tea into a teapot as he talked. "I hope you don't mean a murder vibe."

"Not sure. But there is something a little off about their attitude."

"Are you referring to their utter lack of empathy concerning Nadine's murder?" Drayton said. "Or the way they hastily dimed her out in favor of her sister?"

"I hear what you're saying. On the other hand, it *is* fashion week, and they're business people with a lot on the line. This is when they need to connect with clothing buyers."

"Meaning the partners gotta do what they gotta do?"

"Something like that," Theodosia said.

"Here." Drayton poured tea into a small dark green ceramic cup, then slid it across the counter. "I'd like you to try this."

Theodosia raised the cup and took a sip. She tasted green tea with fruit. "It's delicious."

"This is mango-apricot green tea from Plum Deluxe. Light with a lovely fragrance." He poured her another cup of tea. "And this is their sugar plum cardamom tea."

"They're both wonderful. I think we should feature them on our tea menu."

"And here's a dessert tea to top things off," Drayton said as he poured her a third cup. "Harney and Sons chocolate mint."

"I taste peppermint and chocolate, kind of like a yummy cookie."

"Exactly," Drayton said, pleased. Then the front door yawned open and Drayton suddenly looked unhappy. "Oh my, look who's come to call," he said under his breath.

Theodosia looked. It was Bill Glass, the publisher of *Shooting Star*, a weekly tabloid that was filled with glitzy photos, gossip, and ads for local clubs and watering holes. Today Glass wasn't wearing his usual photojournalist vest and scarf. Today he was dressed like a refugee from a California commune, circa 1968. He wore faded jeans, a patchwork shirt, and leather huaraches on his feet. Two Nikons were slung around his neck.

"I ran into that Chauvet guy on the street," Glass said as he slouched toward the counter. "Was he just in here?"

"Could have been," Theodosia said. She harbored no love for Bill Glass. He was nosy, pushy, and arrogant. Plus, he was always on the prowl for a juicy story.

"Doing business?"

"If he was, that's none of your business," Theodosia said. She noticed that Drayton had turned away from them and was busily measuring out tea.

Glass peered at her. "I bet he was at the death tea yesterday, am I right?"

Theodosia just gazed at him. Better not to engage. Be polite, but never negotiate with a terrorist.

"Sure. 'Course he was," Glass said. "Chauvet's one of the partners in that Banana Peel line."

"Lemon Squeeze Couture," Theodosia said.

"Whatever."

"Do you think he could have murdered that chick?"

"Honestly," Theodosia said, "at this point *anybody* could have."

"Want me to sniff around? See if I can scrape up any dirt on him?" Glass asked.

It was tempting, but Theodosia decided no. Instead, she dropped two butterscotch scones into an indigo blue bag and shoved it at Glass, anxious to be rid of him. "Here you go. Two for the road."

Glass touched a hand to his heart. "You're kicking me out?"

"Apologies. But we're awfully busy."

At three o'clock Haley came out of the kitchen, brandishing a notebook and pen, a serious look on her face.

"We need to talk," she said.

Looking worried, Drayton put a hand to his bow tie and said, "About . . . ?"

"Bridal shower teas," Haley said.

"Ah," Drayton said, relaxing.

Haley shook back a curtain of blond hair and tapped her pen. "As you know, we've got six or seven bridal showers coming up in the very near future, and I'm fairly sure we don't want to keep doing the same old thing."

"I prefer to view each tea we cater as something unique and lovely," Drayton said.

"Well . . . yeah," Haley said. "But . . ."

"But it couldn't hurt to brainstorm, right?" Theodosia said as she joined them at the counter.

"It sure would help," Haley said. "When we have a few different themes we can present to prospective brides, it helps me develop the menus to go along."

"So it's a business decision," Drayton said. "In that case why don't we consider doing a Spa Tea?"

"Explain, please," Haley said.

"I've been dying to serve some of our wonderful herbal teas," Drayton said. "And we've already got Theodosia's T-Bath products to use as favors."

"We could even bring in someone to do shoulder massages," Theodosia said. "And I know we could probably get a couple of makeup artists as well."

"Does that give you menu ideas?" Drayton asked Haley.

"Yup. I'm already thinking quinoa salads, tomato and goat cheese tea sandwiches, avocado toast, and grilled cauliflower steak."

"Okay, here are a couple more ideas," Theodosia said. "We could do a Paris Tea, a *Great Gatsby*–themed tea, or even a Shabby Chic Tea."

"Why not bring in a string quartet?" Drayton said. "Do a Music Tea."

"Slow down," Haley cautioned. "I'm writing as fast as I can."

"For something really outside the box we could give our guests basic calligraphy lessons," Drayton said.

"And there's always a Pretty in Pink Party or a champagne brunch," Theodosia said.

"I'm loving this!" Haley cried. "But it's almost too much. You guys are way over-the-top creative."

Drayton smiled as he took a step back. "Does all this seem strange to you?"

"What do you mean?" Theodosia said.

"Nadine was murdered yesterday, and today we're brainstorming ideas for bridal shower teas?"

"I guess . . ." Haley stopped mid-sentence.

"You guess what?" Drayton said.

Haley closed her notebook and said, "I guess life goes on."

As if to underscore Haley's words, the front door flew open with a loud bang. Looking over to see what the ruckus was, they saw Bettina standing there, a look of anguish on her young face.

"Or maybe I spoke too soon," Haley murmured under her breath.

6

"Bettina!" Theodosia cried. "What are you . . . ?"

Bettina stumbled toward Theodosia on shaky legs and said, "Please, I need to talk to you."

"You poor thing," Theodosia said. She met Bettina halfway, put an arm around the girl's shoulders, and led her to the nearest table. Haley was there to pull out a chair while Drayton hovered nearby.

Once Bettina sat down she looked up at the three of them and said, "You are all so kind, but I'm okay. Really."

"Let me grab you something to eat," Haley said.

"I'll fix you a nice cup of tea," Drayton said.

Theodosia sat down across from Bettina and said, "What's going on? How can I help?"

Bettina tried for a smile but failed miserably. "I need to talk to you about . . . you know."

"About your mom," Theodosia said.

"About her murder." Bettina seemed to cringe inwardly, then said, "There, I've said it. Her murder."

"Okay," Theodosia said gently. "What about it?"

"Mainly the circumstances surrounding it. Because the thing is . . . it feels like Sheriff Burney is giving me the runaround. I'm sure he thinks I need to be protected from the awful truth, even though I was right there and pretty much know all the grisly details."

"Uh-huh," Theodosia said. She decided to simply let Bettina talk. Let the poor girl get it all out. Do a kind of emotional purge.

"But the circumstances are all so *mysterious*. There doesn't seem to be a logical explanation for Mom's murder and there still aren't any suspects."

Theodosia patted her hand. "I know."

"And even though your boyfriend, Detective Riley, was super helpful yesterday, even made a few suggestions, I know it's not his jurisdiction."

"It's not mine, either."

Bettina sat up straight in her chair and gazed at Theodosia. "That's not what I've heard."

Drayton walked over, placed two cups and a steaming pot of tippy Yunnan tea on the table, and peered at Bettina. "What have you heard?"

Bettina drew a deep breath and said, "A lot of people think Theodosia is Charleston's very own Miss Marple. That she's smart and dogged and has even solved a couple of murders."

"More like been involved in," Theodosia hastened to say.

Bettina had come loaded for bear. "Oh no, you're being far too modest. I remember when that poor girl got killed last Halloween at the haunted house. And then that nice older lady at her fancy Christmas party." Her brows bunched together as she stared intently at Theodosia. "I know you were instrumental in figuring out who the killers were in both cases."

"That was then," Theodosia said.

Bettina reached across the table and gently touched a finger to Theodosia's arm. "The thing is, I desperately need your help. Delaine needs your help, too, even though it would kill her to admit it."

Drayton cleared his throat. "Um."

Bettina turned her attention to him. "Yes, I already know. About Aunt Delaine taking over the brand ambassador position."

"And you're okay with that?" Theodosia asked.

"Lord, no," Bettina said. "It's totally wack. I mean . . . one of those Lemon Squeeze people could have easily *killed* my mother. Why would I ever trust them in a million years?"

"It could have been someone else," Theodosia said. "From outside the group."

Bettina bobbed her head. "I suppose that's a possibility. But who? One of the makeup and hair people? Certainly not those skinny models. I bet the only thing on their minds was their next bite of food."

"I meant the partners, the banker, or someone from the film crew," Theodosia said. "Your mother could have seriously ruffled some feathers."

"She does that . . . *did* that," Bettina said. She wiped another tear away and said, "Here I am, talking about Mom in the past tense already. How awful."

"I know," Theodosia said. "And I'm so sorry."

Bettina drew a deep breath and said, "I get that Mom's personality was hard to swallow sometimes. But do you really believe someone would murder her for being obnoxious?" She sat back in her chair. "No, there has to be another reason. Something bigger. Maybe something financial, don't you think?"

"It would be a place to start," Drayton said.

Bettina looked hopeful. "So you'll agree to help? Both of you?"

Theodosia tried one last excuse. "I hate to involve Drayton in something as dangerous as this."

"I'm already involved," Drayton said.

Theodosia knew she'd already emotionally capitulated but still tried to temper her answer.

"I don't know how far I'd get," she said.

"That's okay," Bettina said. "Just knowing you guys are poking around would make me feel a whole lot better. Like I had a couple of guardian angels."

"Such a lovely analogy," Drayton said.

But Theodosia continued to hedge. "I'm not sure how deep I'd be able to dig."

Bettina tapped a finger on the table. "Is that a yes?"

"It's an agreement to look into things and have conversations with a few people," Theodosia said. "Though I'm not exactly sure where to start."

"I might have an idea," Bettina said.

"You have a suspect in mind?" Drayton asked.

"No, but here's the thing," Bettina said. "Mom had been extremely upset lately. I mean more so than her usual funk and fury."

"Do you think she was worried about her situation in the partnership?" Theodosia asked.

Bettina nodded. "Absolutely. Mom was terrified because she'd jumped in feetfirst with no fashion experience whatsoever."

"Wait a minute," Theodosia said. "How could she have gotten so deeply involved in a brand launch if she didn't know what she was doing?"

"Because she lied. Mom did a complete puffery job on those two guys, Harv and Marv. She concocted a fake résumé that completely embellished her experience in the fashion industry—in other words, she gave them her usual line of bull."

"And the partners went for it?" Theodosia said.

"Hook, line, and sinker. They never questioned her, never checked her veracity, never bothered to call a reference," Bettina said.

"Wait a minute, I thought Nadine was *in* the fashion business,"

Drayton said. "I thought that's why she'd been living in New York."

Bettina made a face. "Mom sold overpriced shoes at a boutique in Soho. She maybe helped style a few window displays, but that's a far cry from doing an actual fashion launch."

"Oh my," Drayton said. "It would be worlds apart."

"Except Mom gave her business partners the impression that she understood the fashion business from the ground up. That she knew how to write a business plan, sketch and come up with workable designs that would appeal to their target audience, and that she understood marketing and distribution channels." Bettina looked glum. "She was good at giving impressions, not so good at implementing things. Unfortunately, she was creative director for Lemon Squeeze Couture in name only."

"She didn't come up with the preliminary sketches?" Theodosia asked.

"Not a one," Bettina said. "They had to bring in an outside designer. A guy named Mark Devlin."

"Nadine had no design ability at all?" Drayton said.

"Mom didn't know the business end of a Magic Marker," Bettina said.

"So the partners might have discovered her complete lack of experience and wanted to get rid of her," Theodosia said.

"Might have, but don't you think murdering someone because they lied about their experience is, like, totally radical?" Bettina asked. "I mean, they could have just fired her or hired a lawyer or, I don't know, just yelled at her and kicked her out the door." She stopped and gulped a breath. "But *kill* her? At a fashion show? That seems awfully far-fetched."

"Good point," Drayton said.

"So the question is . . . what really *did* happen yesterday?" Bettina said.

"That's exactly the question I put to your mom's two part-ners," Theodosia said.

Bettina looked confused. "You spoke to them yesterday?"

"No, today—a couple of hours ago," Theodosia said. "The two of them dropped by for lunch."

"That's weird," Bettina said.

"Actually, they asked us to cater their event at the Concours d'Carolina," Theodosia said.

"Unless that was a ruse," Drayton said.

Theodosia and Bettina both gave him a questioning look.

"You know, maybe the partners were trying to determine how much *we* know about the murder," Drayton said.

"Or maybe they genuinely needed a caterer," Theodosia said. "And we were top of mind."

"I suppose that's possible," Drayton said.

Theodosia thought for a few moments. "Okay, maybe it does look a little fishy."

"So what do we do now?" Drayton asked. "Where do we start if we're going to help Bettina?"

"Right here," Bettina said. She reached in her purse and pulled out two tickets. She handed one to Theodosia and one to Drayton. "These are for the Fashion Dazzle Show tonight at the Winder Arts Center." A hopeful note crept into her voice. "A lot of the major players will be hanging out there—so it might be a good opportunity to snoop around and ask a few questions?"

"I like that idea." Theodosia ticked the corner of a ticket with her thumb. "I like it a lot."

"What does one wear to a fashion show?" Drayton asked, once Bettina had left the tea shop.

Theodosia studied him. Today, Drayton wore a linden green

Harris Tweed jacket, dove gray slacks, white shirt, and gold tie with white polka dots.

"I'd say you're fine as is," she said.

Haley came out of the kitchen, carrying a plastic tub of just-washed teacups.

"Or you could switch it out to something a little more hipster," she said.

Drayton's brows crinkled. "Pray tell what that would be?"

"We could style you in ripped jeans, leather jacket, and maybe a knit cap," Haley said. She was bent over, laughing silently, barely able to keep a straight face.

"You know the problem in talking to me about current fashion?" Drayton asked.

"What's that?" Haley said.

He grinned. "It's in one ear and out the other."

Drayton might have been wearing his standard tweedy look tonight, but Theodosia had gone home, walked her dog, Earl Grey, and changed clothes. Now she was juiced up in shiny black leggings, a fluttery pink and yellow silk top, and stiletto sandals.

"You look like a fanciful floral bouquet in that outfit," Drayton remarked as they strolled through the lobby of the Winder Arts Center. It was a large space with redbrick walls, gray industrial carpet, and a bustling crowd of eager fashionistas. Colorful posters for upcoming art exhibits, theater productions, poetry slams, and dance events hung on the walls.

"Is looking like a bunch of flowers good or bad?" Theodosia asked.

"I didn't mean it as a value judgment. I meant that you fit right in."

Theodosia glanced around at what was definitely a fashion-forward crowd. Lots of logos and labels, tailored jackets paired with flowing skirts, skinny T-shirts with the occasional ripped jeans, and a few corsets, sharp-shouldered leather jackets, and, oh my, was that a grunge redux? This crowd was definitely not the ladies who lunch bunch. Or, if it was, they'd all undergone a radical fashion metamorphosis.

A waiflike girl dressed head to toe in black handed Theodosia and Drayton programs as they walked into the auditorium. Bill Glass was waiting inside, snapping photos like mad. Luckily, they managed to avoid him.

"Looks like the fashions will be mostly fun and casual tonight," Theodosia said, studying her program. "Pieces from four different lines are being showcased—Ruff 'n Ready, Lemon Squeeze Couture, Paragon Sport, and Echo Grace."

"If Lemon Squeeze Couture is represented, then the two partners should be here as well," Drayton said. He'd already rolled up his program and stuck it in his jacket pocket.

"Probably." Theodosia lifted herself up on her tiptoes to survey the crowd. "In fact, I already see Marvin Chauvet. We should probably go say hello to him, try to slip in a few probing questions."

"Lead the way."

But before Theodosia and Drayton were able to take a single step, they were accosted by Delaine Dish. Gushing and giddy, wearing an electric blue Lemon Squeeze Couture jacket and matching leggings, she glad-handed them as if she were the duly appointed hostess for the entire show.

"You came to our *show*!" Delaine exclaimed. Tonight she was doing her thing where she talked mostly in italics and exclamation points. "The *both* of you. How *fabulous*!"

"Bettina was kind enough to give us tickets," Drayton said.

Delaine clutched his arm. "Oh, she *did*? She's such a *thoughtful* girl, isn't she? Carrying on in spite of her mother's *death*!"

Theodosia decided Delaine had to be completely tone-deaf. Nadine wasn't just Bettina's mom, she was Delaine's sister. Thus, the death should have affected her, too. Right? Well, maybe not. Apparently not.

"Yes, well, Bettina is hoping we'll turn an investigative eye on a few people tonight," Theodosia said. Might as well be up front and let Delaine know the real reason they were there. She'd figure it out eventually.

Delaine's shoulders hunched forward as she gave a worried, quizzical look. "Do you think that's *wise?*"

"I can't see what it would hurt," Theodosia said. "After all, we are talking murder."

Delaine reached out and clutched Theodosia's arm nervously. "Please don't rock the boat, dear, if you know what I mean."

"Heaven forbid we do that," Drayton said in a weary tone.

"Oh." Delaine fluttered her hands as she gazed at the buzz of people that continued to pour in. "I'd better keep moving. There's so many people to talk to." And off she galloped looking like a bright blue social butterfly.

"What ridiculous behavior," Drayton snorted. "Delaine is acting as if the murder of her sister is a mere inconvenience."

Theodosia shrugged. "Maybe it is. They weren't close, that's for sure." *Or maybe Delaine is masking her sorrow with overblown theatrics. Could go either way.*

Drayton pointed at a camera that was positioned right at the end of the raised runway. "Looks like the show is being filmed tonight."

Theodosia followed his gaze past a DJ twiddling at his soundboard and saw two men hovering near the camera. Probably discussing lighting or angles or production values. Then, with a start, she recognized one of the men.

"Drayton, that's the guy who was supposed to film the Lemon Squeeze Couture show yesterday."

Drayton narrowed his eyes. "The one who dresses like a French film director."

"I thought it was Italian. Fellini."

"Whatever his ilk, he strikes me as a bit pretentious."

"Let's go talk to him anyway," Theodosia said.

But as they pushed their way through the crowd, they ran smack-dab into Marvin Chauvet. Tonight his silver hair was slicked back and he wore a pale green cashmere sweater, cream-colored linen slacks, and Tod's loafers. Very country club–ish.

"Hello again," Chauvet said to Theodosia and Drayton, a broad smile lighting his face. "I didn't expect to see you folks here."

"Last-minute tickets," Drayton said. "Lucky us."

"We're looking forward to finally seeing Lemon Squeeze Couture on the runway," Theodosia told him.

"I'm afraid you won't see our complete line tonight. It's more like six or seven pieces since we're sharing the runway with three other designers," Chauvet said.

"But it seems as though you've generated a good deal of excitement," Drayton said. "It looks like a packed house tonight."

Chauvet swept both arms open wide. "What can I say? Charlestonians are famous for their sartorial sense of style."

"After you and your partner dropped by for lunch today, Nadine's daughter came in," Theodosia said.

Chauvet's broad forehead crinkled. "Oh?"

"Bettina was hoping that Drayton and I could poke around and ask a few questions. She's convinced her mother must have made an enemy somewhere along the line." As she spoke, Theodosia studied Chauvet for any possible reaction.

"Like I told you before, nobody I can think of," Chauvet said quickly.

"How big is your fashion team?" Drayton asked.

"Um, six of us in all," Chauvet said. "Well, five. Not counting outside reps."

"Everyone at Lemon Squeeze Couture gets along just fine?" Theodosia asked.

"Like gangbusters," Chauvet said.

Theodosia was pretty sure that wasn't true, so she decided to switch up her approach.

"If you can think of anything that might have impacted Nadine's personal life, it would be of great help," she said.

"I don't know what that would be," Chauvet began, then stopped and said, "Well . . . I suppose there might be one thing."

"What's that?" Theodosia asked.

"It has to do with Eddie Fox over there," Chauvet said. He hooked a thumb in the direction of the camera setup.

"The director?" Theodosia said.

"Fellini," said Drayton.

"He heads Foxfire Productions," Chauvet said, "which is a fairly well-known outfit. I think they won a gold medal from the South Carolina Arts Board for some documentary they produced about great blue herons. Or maybe it was for great horned owls . . ."

"Okay," Theodosia said to keep him rolling.

Chauvet rocked back on his heels, pursed his lips, and said, "Anyway, a few days after we hired Fox to shoot our show—the one that was supposed to happen yesterday—I heard a rumor that Nadine might have had an affair with him."

"Nadine and the director?" Theodosia was surprised but recovered immediately.

"An affair?" Drayton said in a disapproving tone.

"Wait," Theodosia said. "You said you *heard* they were having an affair. But you don't know that for a fact."

"It's just a rumor, can't even remember who passed it on. Or maybe Nadine herself dropped his name in conversation, I don't know." Chauvet let loose a snort. "You think maybe there's a reason they call him Fast Eddie? Anyway, if the two of them *were* cozy, it would have been right under the nose of Nadine's boyfriend."

New facts were coming to light so fast and furiously that

Theodosia struggled to take them all in. "Nadine had a boyfriend?"

"Seriously?" Drayton said. He'd been caught off guard as well.

"*Had* one anyway," Chauvet said. "I think she mentioned that it was a guy named Nardwell. Yeah, that's it, Simon Nardwell. He's from right here in Charleston and has something to do with antiques."

"Don't know him," Theodosia said as Drayton made a sound in the back of his throat.

"If you want the whole story—and it seems like you do—then maybe you should talk to Nardwell." Chauvet gave Theodosia a nod and a sideways glance, then hurried off as the theater lights dimmed and rock music began to blare.

"Theo, let's go." Drayton touched Theodosia's shoulder. "The show's about to start." They hurried to find their seats as Drayton glanced at their tickets. "We're in row two, seats eight and nine. Over this way."

The two of them murmured, "Excuse me," as they squeezed past guests who were already seated, then made themselves as comfortable as possible on hard folding chairs. The music continued to build as the DJ worked his soundboard. Adele's cool tones switched over to Mick complaining that he "can't get no satisfaction." Then the footlights blazed brightly as overhead rotating spotlights cast circles of red, yellow, and blue on the elevated runway.

"Do you know anything about this Nardwell guy?" Theodosia asked Drayton just as the first leggy model set foot onstage.

"I don't know him personally, but I've heard of him."

"And he's in the antiques business?" she whispered.

"He specializes," Drayton said, as lights flashed brilliantly and the second model hit the runway, "in antique firearms."

7

❧

Drayton's words practically electrified Theodosia, made her sit bolt upright in her chair.

Nardwell specializes in antique firearms? And Nadine had been shot? What were the chances?

Now Theodosia watched the fashion show with only a modicum of interest as she pondered the idea of a jilted boyfriend who owned a gun collection. Really, an entire gun shop.

Was that just too strange, too convenient, too . . . something?

Of course it was. But what could she do about it? Well, nothing right now. But tomorrow morning . . . yes, tomorrow she would definitely get in touch with this Nardwell guy.

Theodosia forced herself to try and switch off her overtaxed brain and focus on the remainder of the fashion show. Let herself be seduced by the music, models, and bright-colored clothes, which were actually quite exciting.

A few deep breaths and she was finally able to semi-relax and enjoy the rest of the show.

The music switched from high-energy to kind of a world beat

as the Lemon Squeeze Couture line came on. And, amazingly, the clothes turned out to be punchy and cute. Lots of yoga pieces accented with fun graphics, a few pieces done in scuba material, some in cozy fleece. One pair of joggers looked like it would be perfect for her nightly runs—it featured a small, lined zip pocket that could carry Earl Grey's dog treats!

Next up was a line by local designer Echo Grace. These clothes were romantic to the max with plenty of pastels, ruffles, feathers, and fluttery sleeves. But instead of looking fusty and old-fashioned, they were amazingly contemporary. Like something with a cool factor that you'd wear to Coachella.

"You like this Echo Grace clothing line, don't you?" Drayton whispered.

"I do," Theodosia said as she applauded. "The designer has a real point of view."

As the show ended, all the models came back out for one last jaunt down the runway, and the music rose to a crescendo. Theodosia was suddenly jolted back to reality—and thinking about the murder.

"Do you suppose Nadine was killed with an antique gun?" she asked Drayton.

He turned to her and lifted a single eyebrow. "If you're thinking that Simon Nardwell was the killer, I can't imagine he'd use an antique gun. Wouldn't that be simplistically traceable?"

"It would be if that were a real term."

"You know what I mean," Drayton said.

"I do. But now we know for sure that Nardwell, Nadine's possibly jilted boyfriend, is someone who can readily lay his hands on a firearm. Probably any kind of firearm, right?"

"I would assume he's a licensed gun dealer, so yes."

They stood up as the audience around them rose to their feet and continued to applaud.

"What do you want to do now?" Drayton asked.

Theodosia gazed across the crowded theater to the end of the stage where Eddie Fox, who'd just finished shooting footage of the show, was fiddling with his camera and talking to one of his lighting guys.

"I want to talk to Mr. Fox."

Eddie Fox saw Theodosia coming and broke into a wide grin, "Hey, I remember you. You're the tea lady from yesterday." He pointed at her and snapped his fingers. "Theodosia something, right?"

"Theodosia Browning," she said. "I was also the one who discovered Nadine's body in the cooler."

"Oof." Fox slapped a hand against his chest. "What a shock, huh? Such a crazy thing to happen!"

"I'd say a brutal murder is beyond crazy," Theodosia said. "It's downright terrifying." She was surprised that Fox was taking Nadine's murder so lightly.

Fox shrugged. "Yeah, well . . . what can you do?"

"Solve Nadine's murder for one thing."

Fox looked suddenly interested. "*You're* going to do that?"

"Probably not, but I would like to ask you a couple of questions."

"Concerning . . . ?" As his gray eyes focused on her like lasers, Theodosia decided this man's name might be Fox, but he had the eyes and bearing of a predatory wolf.

"Concerning Nadine, of course," she said.

"What's your interest in this?" Fox asked. "Aside from the fact that you were there yesterday."

"Let's just say I'm making a few inquiries on behalf of Nadine's daughter."

"Her kid. I see."

Theodosia took a deep breath and plunged right in. "I understand you and Nadine were somewhat cozy."

"Is that a euphemism for enjoying each other's company?"

"I don't know, you tell me," Theodosia said.

"Yeah, well, we knew each other, sure. And, as they say, we were both consenting adults. Nadine was a good-looking woman, maybe a little self-centered, but what woman isn't?"

Jerk, Theodosia thought.

"We hung out a couple of times, had a few laughs. But nothing seemed to click."

"Still, you were friendly."

"Why wouldn't we be?" Fox said.

"It's funny, you don't seem particularly broken up about Nadine's murder."

"Like I said, we never really hit it off. Besides, people express their emotions in lots of different ways." Fox favored her with what felt like a forced look of sadness.

"I suppose you're right," Theodosia said. She wasn't exactly getting bad vibes from Fox, though he did seem somewhat evasive. "Do you know if Nadine was having personal problems with anyone?"

"I can tell you she wasn't enamored with Mr. Fancy Pants."

"You're referring to . . . ?"

"The big honch-o-roo, Marvin Chauvet," Fox said. "They were constantly at each other's throats. And I'm talking about down and dirty screaming matches."

"What about?"

"Money, mostly. I don't think Chauvet is as well-off as he pretends to be. Anyhoo, I'm surprised Nadine lasted there as long as she did." Fox paused. "Well, I guess she didn't."

"Because someone wanted her out of the picture," Theodosia said.

Fox shrugged. "Looks like."

"Aside from office-related conflicts, is there a chance Nadine had an enemy outside of work?"

"Having an actual *enemy* sounds very Special Forces clandestine and maybe a little too out-there." Fox stroked his chin as if deep in thought. "But I get what you're saying. Still, nobody comes to mind that I can think of . . ."

"You're sure?"

"Let me noodle this around and get back to you, okay?"

Fox gazed at her, a sudden eagerness in his facial expression and body language.

"Or maybe we could go out for a drink sometime," Fox added.

Or maybe not.

Theodosia smiled. Better not to react at all, to simply ignore his quasi-invitation.

"Okay, then," Fox said. "Where would I find you if I wanted to get together and talk?"

"At the Indigo Tea Shop over on Church Street."

Fox threw back his head and laughed, as if caught in the throes of an amusing story. "I love it. Such a quaint business for a modern woman."

"Who says I'm a modern woman?"

"Honey," Fox said, "have you looked in a mirror lately? You're a knockout."

Theodosia dropped Drayton off at his home, then drove the few blocks to her own place, relieved to be done with this day. She parked her Jeep in the back alley and walked through the gate into her small backyard where a magnolia tree swayed in the light breeze and a tiny fishpond burbled. Her key ring jangled as she let herself into her house and . . .

Earl Grey hit her like a cannonball.

Woof.

"Nice to see you, too," Theodosia said. Though practically doubled over, she reached out to grab her dog's sweet muzzle and plant a kiss. Earl Grey, not to be outdone, kissed her back, oodles of exuberant doggy kisses that left her happy and giggling. Because that was the thing about pets. You have a tough day, you come home, and they make it all better.

Theodosia let Earl Grey into the backyard where he ran around, sniffing for bunnies or any other critter that may have left its scent. For her, the sweet Charleston air served as a gentle balm. A subtle blend of magnolias, camellias, and salty sea air that soothed and relaxed.

"You know what?"

Earl Grey, a dalmatian and Labrador mix (a Dalbrador), lifted his head and gazed at her with warm brown eyes.

"We should take a spin around the block."

So they did. Down the alley, past a couple of pocket gardens, turning left at a Charleston single house at the end of the block, then back around. Not many cars out tonight, not a single jogger or dog walker. As they came back down the alley from the other end, Theodosia noted that the much larger house next door to her—the Granville Mansion—was still empty. A previous renter, a true crime writer, had vacated the place a few months ago, and she assumed the mansion's owner must still be in London on business.

Back home in her small Queen Anne–style cottage with its thatched roof and curls of ivy up the walls, Theodosia and Earl Grey retired to their upstairs suite. When Theodosia had first moved in, she'd converted the entire upstairs into a bedroom / bathroom / walk-in closet master suite (aka her sweet retreat), with the bonus of a cozy reading area tucked in the side tower room. Baroque mirrors, Laura Ashely wallpaper, Stickley lamps, and a four-poster bed gave the place a girly-glam feel. And her mother's antique vanity with its round mirror and myriad side drawers was the perfect spot for doing her hair, putting on makeup, and stashing jewelry and collectibles. Right now, the top of the vanity held a scatter of earrings and bottles of Opium by Yves Saint Laurent and Eternity by Calvin Klein. A large white bowl held a Majolica tile bracelet, a Kendra Scott bracelet, strings of pearls, gold chains, and carved wooden bangles. Two candles—one a Jo Malone and another a Tom Ford—stood ready to improve the mood even more.

They were both tucked in, all cozy like, when the phone rang. Theodosia in her queen-sized bed, Earl Grey on his overpriced dog bed, his head and shoulders snuggled up against the built-in bolster.

"Hello," Theodosia said in a drowsy tone, knowing it was Riley.

"What were you up to tonight?" he asked. "Or did you hang around home reading *InStyle* or, better yet, *Guns and Ammo*? Ever since I took you to the shooting range that time . . ."

"I'm afraid it was nothing that exciting. I went to a fashion show."

"Fashion show? Uh-oh, I thought you weren't going to get involved in all that."

"My involvement went as far as making cordial conversation with one of the Lemon Squeeze partners and sitting in the second row."

"No snooping? No asking of questions?"

"Well . . ."

"Just as I suspected," Riley said.

"So tell me," Theodosia said, anxious to change the subject, "what are *you* up to tonight?"

"Would you believe I'm slouched in the front seat of a way-too-compact car that's rendered my knees completely numb while parked a half block from a craft brewery?"

"Getting up your nerve to go in and have a beer?"

"Don't I wish. No, I'm on what a TV writer would call a stake-out."

"What do you call it?" There was amusement in Theodosia's voice.

"Tedious."

"But it must be important."

"Ah, it has to do with this drug thing we're working on. We got word from the DEA that a bunch of Florida lowlifes are supposedly bringing in drugs from South America so they can do a deal with our local criminal element."

"Sounds fascinating," Theodosia said, meaning it.

Riley just sounded bored. "Tell me about it," he yawned.

8

"I've been thinking about Simon Nardwell," Theodosia announced as she hurriedly polished a dozen silver spoons. It was Tuesday morning at the Indigo Tea Shop and morning tea was firmly underway. The aromas of fresh-baked cinnamon scones and apple tea bread perfumed the air and mingled with Drayton's steaming pots of English breakfast and Darjeeling tea.

"What about Simon Nardwell?" Drayton said. He shoved a yellow teapot across the counter and said, "This one's for table five, but it needs to steep another two minutes."

"Just the fact that Nardwell owns a gun shop is fairly strange, don't you think?"

Drayton touched a hand to a bright yellow bow tie that matched his teapot perfectly. "I'd have to say it doesn't bode well."

"I'm thinking about paying Nardwell a visit." Theodosia glanced around at the almost-full tea shop. "That's if we don't get frantically busy and Miss Dimple shows up on time."

"She *is* on time."

"Hmm?"

"Guess who just walked through the front door."

Theodosia whirled around to see Miss Dimple shrug out of her sweater coat and hang it on the brass coatrack. Because she was only a titch over five feet tall, Miss Dimple had to practically stand on tiptoes. Then, with a broad smile on her lined face, she whirled around and headed for the counter to greet them.

"Am I late?" were Miss Dimple's first words.

"Dear lady, you are punctual as ever," Drayton said.

Miss Dimple was their seventy-something crackerjack book-keeper who often helped serve at event teas. She was a grandmotherly type—the twinkle-eyed, apple-cheeked kind that also gave a nod to fashion with curly, pink-tinted hair and painted fingernails to match.

"Long time no see," Theodosia said. "How are the cats?" Miss Dimple had a pair of Siamese cats.

"The fur babies are adorable and as demanding as ever," she chuckled. "Of course, as Siamese cats it's their God-given right." She grabbed an apron, put it on, and turned to face Drayton. "What can I do to help?"

"You can deliver this pot of Keemun to table five," Drayton said. "Then run in the kitchen and grab some more scones to put in our pie saver. Honestly, our takeout customers have cleaned us out!"

Theodosia relaxed some as Miss Dimple buzzed about the tea room, pouring refills, clearing plates, and chatting with customers. And just as she'd poured herself a nice fortifying cup of Darjeeling, the front door opened and Bettina walked in. Bettina spotted Theodosia immediately and made a beeline for her.

"The visitation," Bettina said, a grim look on her face. "It's set for tonight. And the funeral's tomorrow."

"So soon," Theodosia murmured.

"It's all Aunt Delaine's doing. You know how frantic she is, always in a tizzy to hurry things along."

Theodosia glanced about the tea shop. Everyone was sipping

tea and munching scones, Miss Dimple seemed to have things covered, so . . .

"Bettina." Theodosia grabbed the girl's hand and led her over to a table in the corner. "We need to talk some more."

"Okay." Bettina slid into a chair and placed her hands flat on the table. Even though she looked tired, as if she hadn't slept for the last two nights, her eyes burned with fervent hope. "Do you want to ask me about the various players again? Possible suspects?"

"Something like that, yes. I'd hoped you'd remembered a few more things about your mom and who she hung out with. Even if you don't think something's important, it could figure into her murder."

"I guess."

"So far I've spoken with your mom's two business partners . . ."

"Harv and Marv," Bettina said. "And you went to the show last night." She seemed faintly pleased.

"Yes, and while I was there I spoke with Eddie Fox, the director."

"Fox," Bettina said. "Though not without talent, he imagines himself as a big-time Hollywood director. Wants to have his own IMDb page." She leaned forward. "But do you see any of them as suspects?"

"At this point I'm still gathering basic information. And wondering who else I should be talking to."

Bettina closed her eyes and thought for a minute. "Probably that designer I told you about who was part of the Lemon Squeeze team, Mark Devlin."

"Was he at the Limón Tea on Sunday?" Theodosia asked.

Bettina frowned. "I'm not sure."

"Okay, you said Mark Devlin was the actual designer for the line."

"Right. It's kind of a deep, dark secret, but he did all the preliminary sketches and then worked with the partners to winnow down the designs that would go into production. Then he helped supervise a lot of the fabrication and manufacturing."

"Sounds as if Mark Devlin is highly competent," Theodosia said. *More so than Nadine was*, she thought. On the other hand, Nadine was an investor. By way of her sister's money, anyway.

"Oh yeah, Devlin's got major experience designing for labels like Denim Canoe and Ladybug Cotton."

"Those are fairly hip sportswear labels," Theodosia said. "Based in New York, I'd guess?"

"I think so."

"But Devlin lives here in Charleston?"

"He's from here originally and recently moved back. Rumor has it that Devlin's extremely difficult to get along with, a complete prima donna, and that didn't fly well in New York. Mom once told me that Mr. Chauvet wanted to make a change to one of the yoga tops—add a vent or something—and Devlin freaked out."

"But Chauvet still let Devlin have major input."

Bettina shrugged. "I guess."

"Was Mark Devlin friends with your mom?"

"I don't know. Maybe." Bettina brushed a fluff of hair out of her eyes. "Gee, this is difficult. Like pointing fingers and tattling. I feel like I'm back in third grade."

"Just remember, you're doing it for a very good reason."

"I know."

"Is there anyone else you can think of? Anyone at all?"

"Mom had a sort-of boyfriend, but I think they'd broken it off a while back," Bettina said.

"Simon Nardwell."

"Oh, you already know about him?"

"Just that he owns a gun shop," Theodosia said.

"And specializes in antique weapons. Which I guess, now that I think of it, looks kind of fishy . . . seeing as how Mom was shot to death."

"Were your mom and Nardwell close? How long had they been dating?"

Bettina hunched her shoulders. "I don't know. They dated some, but Mom didn't exactly . . . share. I know Aunt Delaine didn't think much of Simon Nardwell. Thought he was kind of boring and dreary. She always referred to him as Simon Ne'er-do-well."

"Snarky."

Bettina rolled her eyes. "Well, yeah."

"Just so you know, I intend to pay Nardwell a visit. Today if possible."

"Good. Thank you."

"Okay, Bettina, I want you to think hard about this. Do you know if your mom had any enemies or if she had a recent falling out with someone?"

Bettina squeezed her eyes shut, then opened them. "I'm sorry, I'm so upset I can't remember what I told you."

Theodosia reached across the table and patted Bettina's hand. "That's okay, you're doing fine." She paused. "What about the film director, Eddie Fox?"

"I don't think Mom got along with him. Anyway, I remember her calling him a smug dilettante."

"Is he?"

"No idea. All I know is that Fox shot a documentary and won a big award for it. And then he was hired to shoot—" Bettina's voice was a strangled knot in her throat. "The fashion show that never happened."

"Do you know if your mom ever *dated* Eddie Fox?"

"No!" Bettina cried. "I mean, I don't think so." She pursed her lips. "If she did, she sure didn't tell me."

Theodosia wondered if Nadine had actually had an affair with Eddie Fox, or if they'd just had a few laughs together as Fox had mentioned. If they hadn't been romantically involved, perhaps

Marvin Chauvet was intentionally trying to misdirect her. If that was Chauvet's game, then maybe he was more than an innocent bystander.

"Who else?" Theodosia asked.

Bettina shook her head. "There isn't anyone else. Mom didn't *know* anybody else. So her killer has to be someone from work or in the fashion business."

Theodosia wasn't totally convinced. "There were a lot of people there Sunday. Guests, models, a film crew . . ."

"And the Lemon Squeeze Couture people."

"And maybe someone else," Theodosia said. She knew that Nadine's caustic personality could have rubbed somebody—anybody—the wrong way.

"You mean there could have been a surprise guest?"

"More like an uninvited guest."

Bettina stood up abruptly. "I should go. Your tea shop is getting busier by the minute, and I'm taking up valuable time."

"You needn't apologize," Theodosia said as they strolled toward the front counter. "Drayton, do we have a takeout cup for Bettina?"

Drayton reached for a pink-and-white teapot, poured a froth of tea into one of their indigo blue takeout cups, then snapped on a lid. "Peaches and ginger to go. Freshly brewed, nice and hot. Oh, and we should give you a few scones as well."

Theodosia lifted the lid on their glass pie saver and plucked out four raisin cream scones. "You can take these back to Delaine's boutique, if that's where you're headed."

"I am, and those scones look beyond yummy, but Delaine won't touch a single one because of the carbs."

"Tell her they're carb-free."

"Are they?"

Theodosia smiled. "What do you think?"

Bettina offered a sad smile. "Okay, mum's the word."

*   *   *

The morning continued to slip by, and Theodosia never did get a chance to visit Nardwell's shop. Instead, by eleven fifteen, she was cashing out tables, trying to hurry her customers along (without making them feel rushed, of course) so she could get the tea shop ready for their Sterling Silver Tea Party.

"I'm guessing you want to use the white damask tablecloths?" Miss Dimple asked.

"That's right, with the matching lace napkins," Theodosia said.

"And for dinnerware?"

"The Lenox Montclair with the silver trim. In fact, let's each grab a stack of those plates and run them into the kitchen for Haley. Except for the scones, she'll be plating the entire lunch."

"Perfect. And for flatware?" Miss Dimple seemed to be having the time of her life.

"Let's go for broke and put out the sterling silver Chantilly by Gorham. Then we'll finish off the tables with white tapers in silver candlesticks, silver bowls filled with Devonshire cream, and, naturally, our silver tea service."

"What about those gorgeous silver trays you have?"

"I'd say they're just about perfect for serving scones. We can each carry out a tray stacked with scones, then serve them using silver tongs. Oh, and Floradora delivered two buckets of white tea roses this morning, so we need to pop a few buds in silver vases."

Once the tables were set, the candles were lit, and the tea shop was practically gleaming with silver accents, Drayton walked over to survey their handiwork.

"Delightful," he proclaimed. "I believe you could bring in any number of fancy magazines and they'd kill to have a photo of our tea room to use on their cover."

Kill, Theodosia thought, wondering if one of those photographers had shown up at last Sunday's tea.

9

✿

Guests began lining up outside the Indigo Tea Shop at fifteen minutes to twelve.

"It's a noon event and people are already here!" Drayton cried as he pulled back a blue toile curtain and peered out the window onto Church Street. "Are we ready? Is everything shipshape in the tea room?" He ran back to the counter and fluttered his hands above a lineup of teapots, tea tins, spoons, and strainers. "Do I have everything I need?"

"The answer is yes," Theodosia told him as she stepped into the front hallway. She smiled at her reflection in the mirror and assured herself that it was all going to be fine. Better than fine. This tea luncheon was shaping up to be one of their premier events. Tickets had completely sold out, the menu was deliciously upscale, and the tea room looked like the kind of cozy shop you'd find if you wandered the picturesque back alleys of London's Notting Hill.

As Theodosia stood at the door and greeted her guests, a mixture of old friends and fresh faces tumbled through the doorway, everyone eager to take their seats and enjoy the tea. There was Jill, Kristen, Judi, Linda, and Jessica. Followed by Joy, Arlene, and Monica.

Leigh Carroll, her lovely African-American neighbor who owned the Cabbage Patch Gift Shop just down the street, brought her friends Kenesha and Tiara.

And one of the newer faces to show up was Cricket Sadler, the proprietor of Wildflower, a soap and perfume shop that had recently opened some two blocks away.

At the very last minute, Theodosia's dear friend, Brooke Carter Crockett, the owner of Hearts Desire Jewelers, showed up with fashion designer Echo Grace in tow. Brooke was in her fifties, bright-eyed and athletic-looking, with a cap of silver hair. Echo was petite, fine boned, and crackling with energy. Her rose-blond hair was gelled into spikes, she had inquisitive pale blue eyes, and her skin was so white you could almost trace the veins in her long neck. Dressed like a contemporary hippie-chick, she wore a suede jacket with a fringe of feathers at the bottom and three long, clanking silver necklaces laden with charms.

"OMG," Theodosia said after introductions had been made and hugs and air-kisses exchanged. "How on earth do you two know each other?"

"Echo contacted me to see if she could borrow some of my silver jewelry to help accessorize her clothing," Brooke said. "I took one look at her fabulous fashions and said absolutely yes."

"I've seen Echo's line," Theodosia said. "And I loved it."

Echo looked thrilled. "You have? You did?"

"Well, some of it," Theodosia corrected. "I attended the Fashion Dazzle Show last night."

"That was just a teensy tiny sampling," Echo said. "I think you need to see my entire line."

"I totally agree," Brooke said. "And since there's an informal showing at the Imago Gallery later this afternoon, I think Theodosia should plan on dropping by."

"Yes, why don't you?" Echo said.

"I will," Theodosia said. "I'd love to."

"It starts at five," Echo said. "A kind of cocktail show. Well, art and cocktails, anyway."

When all the guests were seated and sipping cups of tea that Drayton and Miss Dimple had poured, Theodosia stepped to the center of the room.

"Welcome to the Indigo Tea Shop," she said, doing a slow spin so she could see and have eye contact with everyone. "We're thrilled to have you as guests for our Sterling Silver Tea and promise to fill your teacups as well as fulfill your expectations."

There were smiles and light applause from the guests.

"Of course, that begins with the lovely tea you're drinking right now," Drayton said as he stepped forward to join Theodosia. "It's a silver needle tea, a white tea from China that's subtle and slightly sweet."

"Your luncheon today," Theodosia said, "starts with triple citrus scones—flavored with lemon, orange, and grapefruit—along with our homemade Devonshire cream. For a second course we'll be serving tea sandwiches of chicken salad on homemade pineapple nut bread. And your third course, your entrée, will consist of grilled sea bass with capers in lemon sauce and a side of spring peas. For dessert, our award-winning chef has whipped up a Lady Baltimore cake as well as her famous pineapple dream dessert."

Drayton cleared his throat. "A pineapple, as most of you know, is the traditional symbol of hospitality in Charleston. Early sailors brought pineapples back from foreign lands and displayed them on their front porches to signify they'd returned safely. Charleston hostesses also graced their dining room tables with pineapples as a symbol of hospitality and care."

"Thank you, Drayton," Theodosia said. "And now . . ." She picked up a tiny silver bell and rang it. "Lunch is served."

Haley and Miss Dimple suddenly appeared with trays heaped with scones while Drayton grabbed two steaming teapots and made the rounds. The scones were a major hit, as were the tea sandwiches. But the grilled sea bass was the pièce de résistance.

"I need this recipe," Brooke demanded.

"I'll get it from Haley," Theodosia said.

"Me, too," said Jill. "For the sauce as well as the fish."

"I second that," said Linda. "Or is that third?"

"You know what?" Theodosia said. "I'll put it on our website."

"Bless you," said Echo. "I'm not much of a cook, but I'll for sure give this a whirl."

By two o'clock it was all over but the leftovers. Their guests had eaten, sipped, conversed, and shopped their little hearts out. (*You see*, Theodosia told herself, *it's a good thing I loaded up the highboys with extra tea tins, tea towels, honey, jam, and tea cozies.*)

And with Miss Dimple minding a finally emptied-out tea room, Theodosia, Drayton, and Haley crowded into the kitchen to gulp leftover tea sandwiches for their very late lunch.

"Yum," Drayton said. "These chicken salad sandwiches are extra good today."

"They're always good," Haley said.

"I try to pay you a compliment and what do I get? Sass." But Drayton said it with a faint smile on his face. Then, as Haley started for the back door, "Just a minute, young lady, where do you think you're going with that last piece of cake?"

"Oh," Haley said. She stopped in her tracks and turned, showing him the plate with a sliver of Lady Baltimore cake. "Did you want this?" She was suddenly the picture of innocence.

"Yes, unless you're going to . . ." Drayton squinted at her. "Wait, you were about to take it outside, weren't you?" His tone was just this side of accusatory.

"Maybe," Haley hedged.

Drayton turned to Theodosia. "There's a little squirrel that Haley insists on feeding. The little bugger has gotten so friendly and tame that he comes scampering down the alley and practically knocks on our back door."

"Mickey," Theodosia said.

Drayton's eyes fluttered. "You *know* about this?"

"Haley's been giving handouts to Mickey for weeks," Theodosia said. "A little more training and he'll be ready to eat with a knife and fork."

"What's the next step once this rogue squirrel becomes domesticated?" Drayton asked. "Will he be invited upstairs to reside with Haley and her stray cat?"

"Teacake was not a stray," Haley said. "He was abandoned and then rescued. By me."

"Well, Mickey was *not* abandoned," Drayton said. "He reigns over his domain in the great outdoors from a lovely oak tree. Where I hope the furry little fellow intends to stay."

"I'm sure he'll . . ." Theodosia stopped as she heard footsteps approaching.

"Knock, knock," Miss Dimple said as she pushed open one of the swinging doors and peered into the kitchen. Then her eyes settled on Theodosia, and she said, "You have a visitor."

"Okay," Theodosia said, wiping her hands on her apron.

Miss Dimple dropped her voice to a stage whisper and added, "It's that police detective, the big fellow with the appetite to match."

"Detective Tidwell," Theodosia said, a hint of apprehension in her voice.

"I can't imagine what he's doing here," Drayton said.

"I can," Theodosia said.

Hurrying out into the tea room, she saw that Detective Burt Tidwell had already settled himself at a table and made himself as comfortable as his bulk would allow.

"Detective Tidwell," Theodosia said, a smile on her face and a slight lump in her throat. "Welcome." Tidwell headed the Robbery and Homicide Division and served as Riley's boss. She knew that when the big pooh-bah showed up on your doorstep it was a good indication you were in some kind of trouble.

Tidwell shifted in his chair. Today he wore a burgundy jacket the color of bad wine, baggy brown slacks, and heavy black cop shoes. A few more lines had encroached upon his pouchy face, and his hair was curly and nondescript. His stomach still stuck out over his belt buckle even though he *claimed* to be eating healthier. But it was his eyes—steely gray and serious—that held Theodosia's attention.

"Did you stop by for tea?" Theodosia asked. "Or is there another reason for this impromptu visit?"

"I'm here as a favor. Honoring a special request."

"And that request would be . . . ?"

"Would you believe it if I said your boyfriend du jour was seriously concerned about your welfare?"

"Riley?" Theodosia pretended to be surprised. "And he asked you to . . . ?"

"Speak with you? Yes. He's worried that you'll get overly involved in this Orchard House Inn murder business." He paused. "And so am I."

"In that case, he's too late, and ditto for you, Detective, because I'm already involved." Theodosia felt a surge of anger and defensiveness. "As Riley obviously told you, I was the lucky duck who discovered Nadine's dead body."

"And a fine job you did at handling that nasty piece of business. Pushed your nose in where it didn't belong and asked a lot of questions that no doubt irritated Sheriff Burney. Now, we're asking you to kindly step aside so law enforcement can do its job. We believe that would be in everyone's best interest."

"What about Nadine's best interest? Or that of her daughter, Bettina?"

"We're dealing with that."

Theodosia stared at Tidwell for a few moments. Something didn't feel quite right.

"That's it? You came here to deliver a quasi-warning?"

"That's it," Tidwell said.

"No, there's something else going on, something fishy," Theodosia said, suspicion tinging her words. For one thing, Tidwell hadn't tried to con her out of a pot of tea, or as many scones as humanly possible, or a double helping of Devonshire cream to go along with. Considering his almost-manic addiction to sugar, it was strange indeed. Also, he was behaving oddly. A little too formal and, aside from his mild threats, a little too polite.

"What makes you think something's going on?" Tidwell said.

"Because my radar—which has served me well in the past—has started to ping like mad. Which leads me to believe you're not giving me the whole story."

"There is no story."

"Sure there is. Try me."

Tidwell pursed his lips together, stared at her, and sighed. Sat for a minute, then said, "If you must know, there *is* more."

"Like what?" Theodosia said.

He shook his head. "I shouldn't."

"I think you should. I think you owe it to me."

Tidwell glanced around, as if expecting KGB operatives to leap out of one of the highboys. "You dare not breathe a word to anyone."

Theodosia crossed her fingers and nodded. "I wouldn't. I won't."
I'll only tell Drayton.

Tidwell lowered his voice. "The Crime Scene investigators found traces of cocaine in the parlor adjacent to the kitchen."

"Cocaine? Whoa." That revelation slammed into Theodosia like a load of bricks tumbling off the back of a truck. "You're telling me that people were doing *drugs* that day?"

"Possibly."

"Do you know who?"

Tidwell shook his head. "Not yet. But we will. I have faith."

Theodosia held up a hand as her mind began to race. Then a possible scenario spun out and started to click into place. "Or . . . hang on a minute. Do you think some kind of *drug deal* went down in that parlor?" She saw the startled look on Tidwell's face and said, "That's it, isn't it? That's why everybody's underwear is in such a twist. There was some sort of drug deal happening, and Nadine inadvertently blundered into it!"

Tidwell sighed. "That's one possibility we're considering."

Theodosia sat back in her chair. She was shocked but not surprised, if that made any sense. And that little nubbin inside her curiosity zone suddenly strummed with energy. Now there was a motive for Nadine's murder. And a lead of sorts.

"This changes everything," Theodosia said.

Tidwell was on instant alert. "Not for you it doesn't." His face suddenly contorted, and he waved a chubby index finger in front of her. "If there *was* a drug deal—and we're not certain those were the circumstances—it's all the more reason for you to back off!"

"Sure, okay, I get it," Theodosia said in an amenable tone.

"I mean it," Tidwell said.

"Okay, relax, I hear you. Just cool your jets, okay?"

He stared at her.

"Sorry, where are my manners?" Theodosia smiled sweetly at him. "Let me grab you some scones and a pot of tea."

"That would be . . . lovely."

But as Theodosia walked away from the table, all she could think was, *Drugs. This is big-time. Something people are definitely willing to kill for.*

Detective Tidwell noshed his scones, drank his pot of tea, and continued to make a pest of himself. After a final warning about not getting involved, he finally (mercifully) shuffled out the door. That's when Theodosia pulled Drayton aside at the front counter.

"I have to tell you something," she said in whispered tones.

Drayton raised an eyebrow. "A secret? Something related to Detective Tidwell's impromptu visit?"

Theodosia nodded. "The Crime Scene techs discovered traces of cocaine."

Drayton gave a shocked double-take expression complete with arched eyebrows, wide eyes, and shoulders that jerked spasmodically. "What? On Nadine?"

"No, traces of cocaine were found in the adjacent parlor at the Orchard House Inn."

"What does that mean exactly?" Drayton pulled down a tin of peppermint tea and set it on the counter with a hard *thunk*.

"According to Tidwell, the pervading theory is that Nadine might have witnessed some sort of drug deal."

"You think that's what happened?"

"Stay with me on this," Theodosia said. "If Nadine *did* witness a drug deal—and it does seem possible—then she was probably killed because of it."

"Merciful heaven." Drayton suddenly looked drained of energy.

"If Nadine *was* an eyewitness to a serious drug crime, then the stakes had been raised so high that the perpetrators pretty much had to keep Nadine quiet. Permanently quiet."

"Gulp."

"It also tells us something else." Theodosia held up two fingers. "It means there were two people involved."

Comprehension dawned on Drayton's face. "The buyer and the seller."

"Exactly."

"Sweet Fanny Adams," Drayton said. "Now we're looking for *two* killers? That sounds doubly difficult." He drummed his fingers against the wooden counter. "No, make that doubly *dangerous*."

10

❧

Some forty-five minutes later, Theodosia decided to stick Detective Tidwell's warning on the far back burner and set off for a talk with Simon Nardwell, Nadine's erstwhile boyfriend. Or, according to Bettina, the man Nadine had dated a few times. Maybe Nardwell would have a few ideas about why Nadine had been murdered? Although, if Nadine had stumbled into a dope deal, maybe he was clueless.

In any event, Theodosia got in her Jeep, drove a few blocks to Cumberland Street, parked in a sunny spot, and found his shop.

It turned out to be a narrow redbrick building sandwiched between two others and fronted with a single large window that had white plantation-style shutters on each side. Across the window, in gold letters done in old-timey typeface, were the words ANTIQUE GUNS AND COLLECTIBLES. And underneath that in smaller type, SIMON NARDWELL, PROPRIETOR.

Antique guns, pistols, and derringers sat in the front window display, nestled cozily on green velvet fabric. Sunlight winked off a small derringer with rosewood grips. A Frontier-era pepperbox derringer looked old but wicked, as if it still had a few deadly tricks.

Knowing she had nothing to lose, Theodosia pushed the button that said RING FOR ADMITTANCE and, when the door buzzed loudly, stepped inside.

There were two people in the shop. A customer who looked to be in his early sixties and Simon Nardwell, who was younger but not by much. He aimed a smile at Theodosia, the kind of smile that said *I'm busy and will get to you as soon as I can*, and went back to talking to his customer.

That was fine with Theodosia. It gave her time to study Nardwell and look around the shop. The shop itself was small and old-fashioned, wall to wall with locked wooden cases that featured rounded glass tops. Inside each case were dozens of antique guns, pistols, muskets, and derringers. Hanging on the walls were sepia-tone photos of men brandishing weapons and bird hunters showing off their dogs and game. The place smelled of Windex, cordite, and Hoppe's gun oil.

Nardwell looked exactly like his shop. Slightly stoop shouldered, old-fashioned, and dressed in a three-piece tweed suit that sagged on his thin frame and had a slightly moth-eaten air about it.

No wonder Delaine referred to him as Simon Ne'er-do-well.

On the other hand, Nardwell was pitching his heart out with the earnest yet well-worn patois of a used-car salesman.

"This one's a real beauty, a Scottish-made percussion pistol with a .50 caliber bore," Nardwell said.

"Authentic?" the customer asked.

Nardwell scratched at the barrel with a finger. "See here? It's marked 'Edinburgh.'"

Theodosia listened with half an ear as she wandered around the shop, peering inside the glass cases. Here was a French flint-lock pistol, looking polished and new, as if it had never been fired. She stopped in front of another case and studied a pair of Civil

War pistols. They were Colt army guns, good-looking pistols, but with a deadly glint to them. She could just imagine one hanging on the belt of a grim-faced cavalry officer as he led his troops into battle. Into certain death.

"What's the price on this one?" the customer asked Nardwell as he hefted a Remington revolver and sighted down the gun barrel.

"That one's twelve hundred" Nardwell said. "But I could do eleven-five."

"And if I pay cash?"

"Eleven even," Nardwell said quickly.

"Sold," the customer said.

Theodosia smiled to herself. Cash meant the gun sale wouldn't appear on the books. Cash meant Nardwell was part of the enormous underground economy that the feds were always railing about but could never seem to put a stop to.

Of course it also meant that Nardwell could be dishonest as hell. And if someone was dishonest, was it that much of a stretch to murder? Theodosia wasn't sure.

Nardwell counted out the cash his customer offered him, then wrapped the gun in a piece of suede cloth and placed it in a small wooden box. He handed the package over to his customer and said, "I hope you enjoy your new weapon."

Then the front door banged shut and Nardwell was suddenly standing in front of Theodosia. "Help you?"

"Hello there," Theodosia said.

Nardwell rested his hands on top of a glass case and said, "You're interested in an antique pistol?" When she didn't answer right away, he said, "Would this be for you or is it a gift?"

"Actually, I'm here on a kind of fact-finding mission."

"Oh?" Nardwell looked curious.

"Concerning your friend's murder."

A nervous hand finger-walked up his tie. "You mean . . . ?"

"Nadine."

Hearing her name spoken elicited a sorrowful look from Nardwell. "A wonderful woman," he said in an almost whisper. "Such a shocking turn of events."

"You have my condolences."

"Thank you. I couldn't quite believe it when I heard the news."

"You were contacted by the police?" Theodosia said.

"The sheriff who's overseeing the investigation," Nardwell said. "Sheriff Burney."

"Yes, that's the officer."

"I'm sorry," Theodosia said. "I know we've never met before, but I understand you were close with Nadine, and I knew her fairly well, too."

It was a little bit of a white lie, but in a case like this Theodosia figured it wouldn't hurt. Might even help.

"After I talked to the sheriff Sunday evening, her sister, Delaine, also called me with a few more details. I could hardly believe my ears." Nardwell's brows pinched together, and his mouth turned down in an unhappy frown. Theodosia wasn't sure if he was upset about Nadine's death or unhappy that she'd brought up the subject and reopened his wounds.

"I'm sure Nadine's death came as a terrible shock to you."

"When a tragedy hits you out of the blue like this it kind of turns your world upside down."

"You must have cared for Nadine very much," Theodosia said.

"We genuinely enjoyed our time together even though we didn't date all that long."

"What's all that long?" Theodosia asked.

"A month . . . no, it was probably more like two months." Nardwell shook his head. "Nadine was . . . a lovely and spirited lady. I actually think that if we'd had more time together, our relationship might have blossomed." Now he pulled a white hankie from his jacket pocket and wiped a tear from his eye. "If only we'd had more time."

Theodosia couldn't decide if Nardwell was a terrific actor or if he was genuinely upset. Maybe both.

But Nardwell did appear lost in a kind of hazy sadness, so she allowed him a few moments to recover.

Then Nardwell gazed at her with a questioning look and said, "Your interest in Nadine's murder is what?"

"You're acquainted with Nadine's daughter, Bettina."

A slight bob of his head. "We've met."

"She asked me to get involved."

"Involved how?" Then a sort of understanding dawned on Nardwell's face. "Oh, you're investigating the murder? Working with the police?"

"More like nosing around and asking a few questions. As a private citizen, of course."

"Ah. Well, then, you've got your work cut out for you."

"Excuse me?" Theodosia wasn't sure what he was referring to.

"I just meant that Nadine's death—her *murder*—sounds like a genuine mystery. I mean . . . who shoots a person in the back of the head like that?" A note of hysteria edged into Nardwell's voice. "If you ask me, it's almost like a gangland killing."

"Interesting," Theodosia said. She hadn't looked at it that way. Maybe Nadine hadn't been an innocent bystander after all. Maybe she'd been involved in something unsavory. Scandal, bribery . . . a cocaine deal?

"Delaine told me that the sheriff didn't have any suspects as yet. Or clues for that matter," Nardwell said.

"I don't think Sheriff Burney has settled on any specific suspect yet, but I do believe he has fairly good instincts."

"That was my impression as well," Nardwell said.

Theodosia decided to address the elephant in the room.

"You have a remarkable collection of firearms," she said.

"I've been collecting and selling antique firearms for as long as I can remember. Almost thirty years." Nardwell's jaw tightened as he focused a hard gaze on Theodosia. "This isn't a social call, is it? Or a visit to extend your condolences." His tone was suddenly crisp and to the point. "You're interested in me because Nadine was shot to death and because I have a gun collection."

"The thought had crossed my mind."

"Well, kindly erase it if you will. When I spoke with Sheriff Burney, he told me that Nadine was probably shot with a 9mm pistol." Nardwell spread his arms wide. "As you can see, my firearms are all of an antique nature. Nothing as modern as that."

"Right," Theodosia said. She decided to drop the bombshell. "You do know there were narcotics involved, don't you?"

"What!" Nardwell looked genuinely shocked. "You're not serious."

"Traces of cocaine were discovered in an adjacent room."

"That's . . . bizarre!" Nardwell cried. "Nadine would never . . ." He choked on his words, waved a hand in front of his face, recovered, and said, "Nadine was murdered at a fashion event, and I understand those types of people are known to use drugs. They have a reputation, you know."

"Actually, I plan to question Nadine's partners," Theodosia said.

"Well, for sure talk to Harvey Bateman. He's what you'd call the senior partner, the money man."

"You're saying Bateman's the major investor in Lemon Squeeze Couture? I thought Marvin Chauvet was."

Nardwell ticked a finger in her direction. "According to Nadine it was Bateman."

"Did Nadine share much information with you about Lemon Squeeze Couture?"

"Early on she showed me a few sketches, some fabric samples, things like that."

"How about marketing plans?" Theodosia asked.

"She might have mentioned something." Nardwell shrugged. "Maybe online sales? A website?"

"Anything else you can think of?"

Nardwell lifted a hand to his head and ran it through his sparse hair. "I seem to remember something about a blog she was planning to write. Style updates, that sort of thing."

"As far as you know, Nadine was all in on this, right? As a business partner and fashion influencer?"

"She said it was the best opportunity she'd ever had. I know she once dabbled in real estate and had worked in a few retail shops in New York, but Lemon Squeeze Couture really seemed to capture her interest. I remember taking her to dinner one night early on and she was all excited about working with the two partners. She called them angels who brought serious venture capital to the table."

"By any chance were you also an investor?"

"Me?" First Nardwell looked stunned, then his expression switched to amusement. "Hardly. I know zilch about the fashion industry. Besides . . ." He reached down to lovingly stroke a pistol. "All my money's tied up in antique weapons."

Theodosia gazed at his extensive collection. "And they're popular? There are still serious collectors out there?"

"The interest seems to be growing. Every day I receive inquiries from all across the country. From all over the world."

"That's wonderful," Theodosia said. "I mean that your business is so prosperous."

Nardwell gazed at her, as if knowing there were more questions.

Theodosia was ready to oblige him.

"Getting back to the drugs. Do you know if Nadine used drugs, was ever involved with drugs?"

"Are you asking me if she *took* drugs?"

"Did she?"

"Maybe an aspirin now and then if she . . ." Nardwell stopped. "But of course you're asking about drug-drugs. Hard drugs." He seemed confused.

"More like using illegal drugs." Theodosia wondered if his confusion was genuine or conveniently faked.

Nardwell's eyes moved back and forth rapidly, like a Kit-Cat Klock that had lost its spring. "Oh no, I doubt that Nadine would ever get involved in something like that!" He looked horrified.

A knock sounded at the front door and they both turned to look. It was the FedEx guy standing outside holding a couple of packages.

"One minute," Nardwell said as he reached beneath the counter and hit a buzzer.

There was a loud BRIIING and then the FedEx guy pushed open the door.

"Fred," Nardwell said. "Looks like you've got some deliveries for me."

"Two packages," Fred said. "One you need to sign for."

Nardwell fumbled for his glasses as Fred set the two packages on the counter.

Theodosia slid forward and gave them a casual glance.

One package had a return address that said Hamburg, Germany. The other package was from San Lorenzo, Ecuador.

"And I've got one to go out. Two-day delivery is fine." Nardwell slid his package to Fred as Theodosia craned her neck. It was addressed to someone in Miami.

Once Nardwell had done his business and the FedEx guy was out the door, Theodosia said, "Okay, thanks for your time. If you can think of anything else . . ." Theodosia dug in her wallet and handed him one of her business cards.

Nardwell studied it. "The Indigo Tea Shop, I've heard of that."

"Stop by sometime and we'll set you up with a pot of tea and a scone."

"That sounds lovely. Let me give you one of my cards, too."

Theodosia took his card and said, "Okay, thanks again." She was halfway to the front door when Nardwell held up a hand and waved to her.

"There is something I just remembered," he said.

Theodosia turned and slowly walked back to him. "What's that?"

"I don't know how important it is . . ."

"At this point anything could be of help," Theodosia said.

"It has to do with finances. Nadine mentioned to me that Lemon Squeeze Couture was taking out key partner insurance on the various players. So with her passing—her death—I'm assuming the two remaining partners will receive a fairly serious cash payout."

"How serious a payout?"

"That I don't know. But it might be interesting to find out, don't you think?"

Theodosia did indeed.

11

The afternoon was warm and sunny with cerulean blue skies that seemed to stretch all the way up to the troposphere. Theodosia rolled down her window as she drove along, enjoying the fine spring weather. This part of Charleston, known as the French Quarter, was a romantic neighborhood filled with historic churches, town houses, art galleries, and shops. There were new restaurants, too, many serving the low-country cuisine that was starting to catch on all over the country.

Turning onto King Street, Theodosia drove past Keelhaul Seafood Bar, the Barsteller Inn, and Slippery Grounds Coffee before she saw the sign up ahead for Chauvet's Smartwear. She slowed down as an idea popped into her head.

Should I stop in? Hmm, and do what? Ask Marvin Chauvet a few probing questions? Maybe under the guise of talking about Friday's catering gig? Sure, I'll do that if I can find a parking spot nearby.

Theodosia found a spot. She fed a quarter into the meter and strolled toward the front door. As she passed the display windows, she peered at sleek black lacquer mannequins that were all dressed conservatively but expensively.

Inside was more of the same. Elegant, expensive clothing and accessories for both men and women. In fact, the place fairly reeked of money and class. A plush green carpet (the color of money?) fairly tickled underfoot. Heart pine paneling covered the walls, and small sitting areas featured cushy furniture. Everywhere were racks of beautiful women's clothing and antique armoires stuffed with sweaters, scarves, and lingerie. There was a jewelry counter and a display of hand-tooled Italian leather bags. A few steps up on the mezzanine was the men's department. More displays of clothing—jackets, tuxedos, leather jackets, and casual wear for golf, tennis, and sailing. It was clubby and exclusive-looking with antique golf clubs, fly rods, and tennis rackets hung on the walls. Theodosia noticed that the decor included several tasty oil paintings done in dark tones and rich with crackle glaze.

A friendly-looking saleswoman in a killer camel skirt suit greeted her immediately.

"Good afternoon, how may I help you?" The saleswoman was attractive and mid-thirties, with blond hair pulled back in a low chignon. Oliver Peoples glasses highlighted her lovely oval face, and her feet were shod in butter-soft caramel-colored stilettos. She looked sleek and serious, like a classy librarian.

Theodosia smiled. "Actually, I just stopped by to speak with the owner."

"I'm sorry, but Mrs. Chauvet is in a meeting right now."

Theodosia was slightly taken aback. "Excuse me, I thought Marvin Chauvet was the owner."

"Yes, well, he is the husband." The saleswoman's bright smile suddenly tightened.

"But Marvin Chauvet has offices here?"

"Not at the moment."

Theodosia glanced around. "Somehow I was assuming that his Lemon Squeeze Couture line was headquartered here."

"I'm afraid that's a separate entity, quite distinct from this business."

"Really." Theodosia stood there, considering what to do next. "So the businesses are separate," she said, almost as an aside to herself.

"They are indeed," the saleswoman said. "But I can give you Mr. Chauvet's phone number if you'd like."

"Please. That would be terrific."

The saleswoman went behind a counter and scribbled a number on the back of a business card. She came back out, handed the card to Theodosia, and smiled. She obviously approved of Theodosia's sea green silk T-shirt, linen blazer, Rag & Bone jeans, and Tod's loafers.

"I jotted Mr. Chauvet's number on the back of my card." She paused. "I'm Bernice Waverly. If I can ever help you with anything— wardrobe curating, styling for a special event—be sure to let me know."

"Thanks," Theodosia said. "I'll do that."

Driving back to the Indigo Tea Shop, Theodosia's brain rumbled with newfound facts and a few itchy questions.

Did Mr. and Mrs. Chauvet have totally separate businesses? It certainly looked that way. Or maybe financial considerations were in play so they'd agreed to keep the two companies completely autonomous? Did that mean they led separate lives as well? Or, worst-case scenario, could they be in the throes of a nasty divorce? Maybe they were duking it out while they each tried to hang on to their individual income streams.

Or how about this: What if Marvin Chauvet wasn't the raconteur and world-beater businessman that everyone thought he was? What if his wife had kicked him out of the business because he was a dud? And what if Chauvet had borrowed money to help get Lemon Squeeze Couture off the ground? Launching a new business was costly—and there were always unexpected expenses—so did that mean he was flat broke now?

Hmm.

If that were the case, would the murder of Nadine have actually *earned* money for Chauvet? After all, Nardwell had just told her that key partner insurance was in play.

Or could Marvin Chauvet be the dope dealer that Nadine had walked in on? And thus he'd killed her in order to preserve his dirty little secret.

As Theodosia pulled into her parking space behind the tea shop, she also wondered if Lemon Squeeze Couture could be one big Ponzi scheme? Maybe Chauvet and Bateman had hustled up a bunch of investors (like Nadine, backed by Delaine), suckered them in with a fancy line of bull, and then pocketed most of the money. Perhaps they'd ginned up a line of clothes that wasn't intended to sell at all, then weeks or months from now they'd claim bankruptcy?

Or was fashion simply a good cover-up for dope dealing? Was Chauvet a cocaine freak? And was Bateman in on it? Could they be the same guys that Riley was looking for? The ones that the so-called lowlifes from Florida were supposedly going to do a deal with?

Theodosia hurried in the back door of the tea shop, dumped her purse on her desk, and threw on a long black apron.

Miss Dimple was still there and turned to greet her with a broad smile.

"You're back," she said. "I was just about to take off, unless you or Drayton need me for something." She dropped her voice. "We've only got a few customers left."

"We're good," Drayton said, glancing at Theodosia. "Aren't we?"

"You go on home, Miss Dimple, and we'll see you on Thursday, okay?" Theodosia said.

"For your Irish Cream Tea. That should be a jolly bit of fun, too," Miss Dimple said.

"Thank you, dear," Drayton said as Miss Dimple grabbed her coat and hurried out the door. Then he turned to Theodosia and said, "You've got that slightly breathless look. Have you learned something?"

"Tons," Theodosia said, slapping her hands down on the counter. "It turns out that Simon Nardwell has unrequited love for Nadine even though he's basically married to his gun collection."

"Somehow that doesn't surprise me. The question is, is Nardwell the dope dealer who pulled the trigger?"

"Could have been, I guess. But there are more than a few strange wrinkles to this case."

Drayton picked up a steaming teacup, took a leisurely sip, and said, "Do tell."

So Theodosia unloaded on him. Told him about the key partner insurance Nardwell had mentioned. About Nardwell knowing he was under semi-suspicion because of his gun collection. About her worry that Chauvet and Bateman could be operating a major Ponzi scheme. And also about Marvin Chauvet not being involved in Chauvet's Smartwear.

That was the real shocker for Drayton. "So *Mrs.* Chauvet is the one in charge of the shop?"

"It would appear so," Theodosia said.

"Impressive," Drayton said. "And that's not a reference to Mrs. Chauvet, even though I'm positive she's one smart cookie. I mean it's impressive that *you* were able to glean so much good information."

"The problem is I picked up lots of incriminating details, but nothing substantial. Nothing that would make you point a finger at one person and say, 'That's the lunatic who shot Nadine.'"

"But they're still all good theories and leads," Drayton said, giving a philosophical nod. "So what do you see as our next step?"

"Maybe try and talk to Harvey Bateman, the so-called money guy. Ask him a few tough questions and see if he squirms."

"An excellent idea. When would you do that?"

"I'll give the Lemon Squeeze office a call right now."

Theodosia disappeared into her small office and plopped herself down behind her desk. She gazed at the mess and half-heartedly began to straighten it. Stacked a bunch of tea magazines, swept a bunch of invoices off to one side, dropped a scatter of pens into a chipped Haviland cream pitcher she used as a holder. Then she dug out the card Bernice Waverly had given her and dialed the number.

There were six long rings, a hollow click, and then the answering machine came on.

It was a woman's voice with a friendly but businesslike message that basically said, *Nobody home.*

Theodosia wandered back into the tea room.

"Nobody there," she told Drayton.

"They must be busy with Charleston Fashion Week events. I image there are lots more fashion shows to attend as well as meetings with buyers and critical PR pitches to the trade. They're probably hanging out and hustling the brand."

"Maybe we should try to cash in on that. Drop by the Echo Grace informal modeling and see if we can pick up the rumor du jour."

Drayton tapped his watch. "May I remind you that Nadine's visitation is also tonight?"

"I know. And I still can't believe how speedy Delaine was in making all the arrangements."

"That's how she rolls. A virtual tornado."

"I'm okay with a little speed and hustle; I just hope things aren't moving too fast for Bettina. The poor girl might need a little more time to sort out her mother's death."

"I hear you," Drayton said. He stood there for a few moments, then said, "So, what's the plan? If there is one."

"Let's clean up the tea shop and hit that fashion show," Theodosia said.

They were rinsing out the last teapot when they heard a clunk and felt a whoosh of cool air. Two seconds later, the door whapped open all the way and Riley came rushing in. He was wearing a light blue polo shirt tucked into a pair of khaki slacks topped with a navy blue blazer. Theodosia knew that under that blazer he wore a Bianchi shoulder rig with his Glock 22 tucked inside.

"Hey!" Theodosia exclaimed. "I didn't expect to see you today." She was delighted that he'd dropped by.

"I took a chance," Riley said, "hoping against hope I could grab some of your leftover goodies." He smiled at Theodosia, then gave a solemn nod in Drayton's direction. "What you'd call . . . takeout?"

"I think we can manage a scone and a couple of sandwiches," Drayton said. "Give me a few minutes to scrounge through our larder." He spun on his heels and disappeared into the kitchen.

Theodosia rose on her tiptoes, gave Riley a quick kiss, and said, "You must be working tonight. Going on another stakeout."

"Mmn," Riley said. "Not so fast." He reached out, encircled Theodosia with his arms, and pulled her close for a second, lingering kiss. When he finally released her, he said, "Yes, very nice indeed." Then his mellow mood seemed to shift.

"What?" she said. "Something wrong?"

"This case I'm working is driving me slightly nuts."

"The drug deal? Trying to get a handle on the local buyers?"

"It's frustrating because nothing's happening. I'm thinking we might have gotten some bad intel from the OC unit."

"That's . . . ?"

"The organized crime unit."

"But crime tends to be *dis*organized, doesn't it?" she asked.

"Very funny," he said. "But we also got some poop from a couple of informants." Riley rolled his eyes. "Still, they're no great shakes when it comes to being reliable, either."

"Tidwell dropped by to see me this afternoon," Theodosia said.

"Oh yeah?"

Theodosia saw right through Riley's casual demeanor. "Don't you dare pretend to be surprised when I know you were the one who put him up to it." She placed both hands on her hips for added emphasis.

"I'm afraid Detective Tidwell doesn't take orders or even advice from the likes of me. He's his own man."

"Right. Sure. Anyway, Tidwell happened to mention *another* drug deal. The one that possibly went down during my Limón Tea. The one that probably got Nadine killed."

"Tidwell told you about that?" Riley looked skeptical. "About what the Crime Scene techies found?"

"I wormed it out of him. So, it's looks as if a possible drug deal did take place."

"Maybe."

"But what's really starting to worry me is . . . could the two drug deals be related? The one you're staking out and the one that Nadine might have gotten mixed up in?"

"No. No way." Riley shook his head. "There's not a single shred of evidence that says they're linked in any way, shape, or form."

"You're sure."

"Positive."

"Okay, just checking."

"Theo, listen to me. Tidwell was dead right about you backing away from Nadine's murder. You need to let Sheriff Burney conduct his investigation as he sees fit . . ."

Drayton suddenly emerged from the kitchen, an indigo blue bag dangling from one hand. Haley was a step behind him. She wore her white chef's jacket, had a toque perched atop her head, and was cuddling her cat, Teacake, in her arms.

Drayton thrust the bag at Riley and said, "Here you go, Detective: takeout for a stakeout."

"Ooh, a stakeout," Haley exclaimed. "That sounds so exciting!"

Riley managed a half-hearted smile. "You try sitting in a foul-smelling impounded Ford Taurus for hours on end. With nothing better to do than listen to the crackle of a police radio and drink cold coffee."

"Sorry, Officer Grumpy, I didn't mean to bring up such a sore point," Haley said.

"That's not the part that gets sore," Riley said, which made Haley giggle. Then he turned serious. "This supposed drug deal has been a tough thing for the department. Even though the DEA has asked for our cooperation, these dealers might be ghosts. They might never materialize. And even if they do, how are we going to gather enough evidence so we can bust them?"

Haley gazed at him with guileless blue eyes and said in all sincerity, "Maybe you could try calling the psychic hotline?"

12

Even though Theodosia and Drayton had only met Holly Burns, the owner of the Imago Gallery, once before, she greeted them profusely, as if they were old friends.

"Welcome, beautiful people," Holly Burns gushed in her throaty, slightly burned-out voice. Pulling Theodosia close, she gave her a quick swipe on the cheek, then turned and did the same to Drayton. Holly was anorexic thin, a tad past forty, and had long black hair that swirled about her like a dark cloud. Tonight she was dressed in an Echo Grace silver-gray silk bomber jacket with matching pajama pants. There were so many statement necklaces looped around her neck that she jangled like spurs when she moved.

"Wonderful to see you again," Theodosia murmured, hoping Holly's fuchsia lipstick hadn't left a smear.

"You, too! You, too!" Holly fluttered her hands as if to physically push them into the gallery. "You see that good-looking hunk standing behind the bar? That's my boyfriend, Phil, who's pinch-hitting as a bartender tonight. Now go. Drink. Mingle. Marvel at the clothes. Enjoy!" she gushed.

"I'm not sure those ideas are all compatible," Drayton murmured under his breath as they shouldered their way into the crowded gallery.

Like many contemporary art galleries, the Imago Gallery favored strict minimalist decor. That is, white walls, gray industrial carpeting, and pinpoint spotlights overhead to highlight the photos and paintings that were on display. There were also large white cubes that held contemporary metal sculptures, as well as a pair of chairs—very modern and cheeky—made out of bent metal tubes that were covered in fuzzy black fabric. Crouching low on the floor as they did, the chairs reminded Theodosia of giant black spiders straight out of a horror flick. Maybe something to avoid.

Tonight the works of art on the walls felt complementary to the event. Lots of large abstract expressionist paintings with slashes of bright color as well as black-and-white photos that were moody and slightly ethereal.

A frizzy-haired, denim-clad DJ sat at his soundboard, twisting his dials and bobbing his head, lost in his own little world as he blasted out earsplitting rock music. Tall, thin women, almost like human mannequins, wore Echo Grace fashions as they wandered through the crowd, looking haughty and slightly bored. Clearly, the informal modeling was well underway.

"Bar," Drayton said in Theodosia's ear, trying to override the music. He pointed in the direction of a small bar that was doing a brisk business. "Care for a glass of wine?"

Theodosia nodded as they elbowed their way through what was mostly an artsy, fashionista crowd.

"Two glasses of white wine, please," Drayton said to Phil the bartender. He slipped a five into the glass tip jar and nodded when Phil winked at him. Then he grabbed the two wines and handed one to Theodosia. At that exact moment, Echo Grace came rushing over, clutching a flute of champagne, almost spilling it on them.

"If it isn't my favorite tea people!" she cried.

"We're probably the *only* tea people here," Drayton said, but his words carried a good-natured lilt.

"I'd say a victory toast is in order," Theodosia said as she held up her glass. "To a talented designer and another fantastic fashion show."

"Hear! Hear!" Drayton added.

They all three clinked glasses.

"Your clothes," Theodosia said, as three models sauntered by, "are making me positively delirious. I mean . . ." She tipped her glass at a model in a lemon-colored dress. "They're all so frothy and delicious."

"Gauzes are really my jam right now," Echo said. "They're challenging to work with but also lots of fun." She herself had on a long diaphanous dress that'd been dip-dyed into ombre layers of caramel, gold, and wheat. A belt bag made of recycled tan leather and encrusted with turquoise and lapis stones was cinched about her tiny waist.

I would kill to have a waist that small, Theodosia thought. Then a waiter came along with a tray of canapés, and she picked out a lovely goat cheese goody covered in crushed pistachios.

When a group of chattering fans closed in on Echo, the designer gave a helpless, hapless wave goodbye and let herself be pulled away.

"This is turning out to be fun," Theodosia said. "I thought it might be kind of a chore, but now that I'm here . . ." She turned to Drayton who was gazing past her shoulder at someone.

"I see Arnold Fisher over there," he chuckled. "Though I never thought an antique dealer would be part of the fashionable café crowd. Give me a minute, will you? I want to go over and say how do."

As Drayton hurried away, Theodosia took a sip of wine and looked around the gallery. That's when she also spotted a familiar face.

It's Billy—no, Bobby—one of the cameramen from Channel Eight News.

Bobby was cradling a video camera in the crook of his arm and had a coil of black cord looped over one shoulder. Behind him was his lighting and sound guy, Trevor.

Theodosia walked over and touched his arm to get his attention. "Bobby . . ."

Bobby turned, instantly recognized her, and said, "Theodosia. Long time no see. Hey, you remember Trev, don't you?"

"I do," Theodosia said. "Nice to see you both again." She'd met Bobby and Trevor a few months earlier when one of their team members, a female reporter, had been brutally murdered.

"How are you doing, Bobby?" Theodosia asked.

"Oh, you know, can't complain. There's always plenty of news to keep us hopping from one story to another. Crime, celebs, city events, political dustups, the same old same old." Bobby had curly dark hair, olive skin, and wore a battered leather jacket that looked like it had come through World War II. Trevor, his blond and blue-eyed soundman, wore a hoodie and jeans. He was skater-boy cute and had the earnest gawkiness of a teenager even though he was in his mid-twenties.

"Are you here to film the show?" Theodosia asked. "The informal modeling?"

"Yeah, the station is putting together a half-hour special on Charleston Fashion Week, and they want to feature as many local designers as possible. So I've been bouncing all around town filming all sorts of fancy shows, which, it turns out, is actually pretty fun duty." Bobby ducked his head. "Lots of free food and good-looking models."

"I'm sure," Theodosia murmured. Then, "You've worked at the station for a few years now, right?"

Bobby winked one eye closed. "Um . . . almost four years."

"And you do freelance camerawork as well?"

"Industrial films, some commercials . . . why? You got something in mind?"

"Really just a question. I was wondering if you knew a film guy by the name of Eddie Fox. He's the owner of Foxfire Productions."

Bobby was already nodding his head. "Are you kidding? Sure. Everybody in the business knows Fast Eddie. He started out working at Channel Six. Then, when he got his butt canned, he went out on his own. I hear he's doing okay, won some big award."

But Bobby had said something interesting that caught Theodosia's ear. "Eddie Fox was fired because . . . ?"

"Not for lack of talent, because Fox is actually a fairly skilled shooter," Bobby said. "He always got his story and managed to make it *look* good, whether his slant was tearjerker, upbeat, or just plain hard news. No, the problem wasn't with his work; it was that Eddie liked to dip his nose into the white stuff a little too much."

"You're telling me Eddie Fox is a cokehead?"

"Big-time."

"You know this for a fact?" Theodosia asked.

"Well . . . yeah." Bobby watched as a model in a flowing pink and green tunic and formfitting leggings strolled past them. He followed her with roving eyes and an interested smile, then turned back to Theodosia. "Fox was involved in that shooting last Sunday, right? At your tea party? At least that's the scuttlebutt I heard in the newsroom."

"He was there to film the fashion show, yes," Theodosia said.

Bobby was no dummy. "Is Fox, like, a suspect?"

"Probably everyone is at this point," Theodosia hedged. "But anything you can tell me about him would be helpful."

"You mean to clear him? Or pin the hit on him?"

"Could go either way."

"I don't know what Fox is up to now, but . . ." Bobby glanced around, then dropped his voice. "Have you ever heard of the High Life Club?"

"Never, what is it?" Theodosia asked.

"It's this loosey-goosey private social club that was formed by a bunch of kids who were born with silver spoons in their mouths. Or, in some cases, coke spoons in their noses. They're basically rich kids in their twenties and thirties who love to party."

"Rich kids," Theodosia said. "You're telling me Eddie's a rich kid?"

"He used to be, anyway. Don't know what his financial situation is now. Daddy was a partner in a big-time hedge fund. Anyway, Eddie was part of that group, hanging out with the heirs and heiresses apparent. You know, the mailbox money crowd, the lucky ones who receive nice fat dividend checks each month."

"So the party never has to end," Theodosia said.

Bobby gave a crooked grin. "I used to wish my life could be like that. Now I'm not so sure."

At quarter past six Theodosia grabbed Drayton and said, "Come on, we have to take off for Nadine's visitation."

As they drove over in her Jeep, she told him about her conversation with Bobby the cameraman.

"You're telling me that Eddie Fox snorts cocaine?" Drayton said. He sounded only somewhat surprised.

"That's what Bobby said."

"And traces of cocaine were found at the Orchard House Inn.

So Eddie could have easily been inside." Drayton was silent for a few moments as they coasted down Bay Street. It was full-on dark now, and colorful neon lights from Elmo's Oyster Bar and Batavia Jack's House of Blues reflected off their windshield. "Is it possible that Eddie was the one who murdered Nadine?"

"I suppose it's possible," Theodosia said. "I mean, the fact that he's a user and traces of cocaine were found nearby is one heck of a coincidence."

"But you're not big on coincidences."

"No, I'm not."

Drayton drummed his fingers against the dashboard. "Still, it's interesting. So what are you going to *do* with this information?"

"Mmn . . . that's still up in the air."

"Knowing Fox uses cocaine points directly to his character. Well, a character flaw, anyway."

"It's also circumstantial evidence," Theodosia said. She turned from Bay Street onto George Street and tapped her brakes lightly. "Where is this doggone place, anyway?"

"What are we looking for again?"

"Oswald Brothers Funeral Home. I looked it up online, supposed to be a red stone building that's over one hundred years old."

"Not familiar with it," Drayton said. Then, he pointed and said, "Oh, is that the place? I do know it. Started out as a funeral parlor, became a private home, then it was the First Security Bank for a while. Now it's come full circle."

Oswald Brothers was a redbrick monstrosity—too many balustrades, columns, and pediments. A Romanesque-style castle where a modern-day witch might reside.

"Kind of creepy," Theodosia said. She hooked a right, drove through a portico where she imagined old-fashioned horse-drawn hearses had once passed, and ended up in a small parking lot that was already packed with cars.

"This is not exactly A-list real estate," Drayton said. "And did you see how the Oswald Brothers sign was outlined in blue neon? That kind of tackiness is not reassuring."

"Maybe it's not as bad as it looks," Theodosia said as she turned off her engine and listened while it slowly ticked down.

"Uh-huh."

"After all, Delaine was under a lot of pressure, so this is probably all she could line up in the short run."

Theodosia made no move to get out and go in and neither did Drayton.

Finally, Theodosia grabbed a black jacket from the seat behind her and said, "It's probably not that terrible."

Drayton drew a deep breath, clapped his hands against his knees, and said, "I suppose we'd best find out."

Oswald Brothers Funeral Home wasn't terrible, but it was still a dreary, down-at-the-heels funeral parlor. The expansive lobby had outdated wine-colored carpeting, overstuffed chairs covered in sedate florals, and ponderous end tables that held de rigueur boxes of industrial-strength tissues. The smell of overripe flowers permeated the chill air along with a subtle hint of chemicals.

"Somebody could benefit from the skills of a decorator," Drayton whispered as they signed the guest book using a ballpoint pen with a pink plume stuck on the end of it.

"Or a lifestyle guru," Theodosia said.

"Or deathstyle," Drayton snickered. "As well as some room deodorizer."

They nodded at a professionally serious black-suited funeral home employee who directed them through a swag of black velvet curtains and into Slumber Room A.

Where—WHAM!—everything suddenly changed.

13

Theodosia's initial impression was that it was like going from the dregs of steerage to the grandeur of first class on the *Titanic*. Or Alice falling down the rabbit hole. Because after the dreary atmosphere in the lobby, they were suddenly greeted by a team of white-jacketed caterers who proffered glasses of wine and trays full of hors d'oeuvres. Across the room, a slick-looking string quartet played sprightly, upbeat music. And a well-dressed crush of people milled about as if they were attending a cocktail party. Which they kind of were.

But the pièce de résistance was the shiny white coffin at the front of the room, flanked by flickering pillar candles and marble statues of winged angels. If that wasn't enough of a showstopper, Nadine's open coffin was surrounded by an undulating ocean of white orchids. And hanging above her coffin was a frothy bunting of lace with a photo of a smiling Nadine stuck smack-dab in the middle. Or, as Theodosia thought with a grim smile, stuck dead center.

The deceased Nadine was dressed for eternal slumber in a pale peach dress with her fingernails (Theodosia was pretty sure they were press-on nails) painted a matching peach. Interestingly enough, her blond hair also carried a peach tinge. To the left of her coffin was a gilded birdcage with two blue parakeets cheeping away.

"Can you believe this setup?" Theodosia whispered to Drayton.

"There's so much pomp and pageantry I feel like I just walked into the stage version of *Evita*," Drayton said.

"Or a Busby Berkeley musical," Theodosia said as she clutched his arm to keep from laughing. It *was* an immensely over-the-top display. On the other hand, she knew that nothing was ever too extreme, too embellished, or too overdesigned for Delaine. Or, in this case, for Delaine's dead sister.

Delaine spotted them immediately and rushed to greet them, taking tiny, quick steps in her towering stilettos.

"Theo!" Delaine squealed. "And Drayton. Thank you so much for coming." She seemed upbeat and chatty and, instead of wearing funereal black, was dressed in a hot pink wrap blouse and matching slacks. A plump pearl pendant surrounded by diamonds dangled around her neck, and she had on matching pearl earrings. Theodosia guessed the pearls had to be at least 14mm.

"Looks like a lot of people showed up for the visitation," Drayton said to be polite.

"Yes, well . . ." Delaine gave an offhand wave. "I did a bit of phoning around and some subtle arm-twisting if you want to know the truth. No sense putting on a lavish production like this and having it go to waste."

"Lavish," Theodosia repeated, to underscore Delaine's words.

"I wanted this to look more like an interesting *salon* than a visitation," Delaine said.

"I think you accomplished your goal," Drayton said. He was doing a masterful job of keeping a straight face.

"Of course we'll reuse all the flowers at tomorrow's funeral," Delaine said. "And the birds are rented." She peered speculatively at Theodosia. "You're coming tomorrow, aren't you? You, too, Drayton?"

"We'll be there," Drayton assured her.

Suddenly, Delaine let out a surprised squeal and said, "Bless my heart, can you *believe* who just walked through the door?"

Theodosia turned to see Simon Nardwell. He glanced about, looking tentative and slightly lost, then gratefully accepted a glass of wine from one of the waiters.

"It's Simon Ne'er-do-well," Delaine said with a pussycat grin.

"I had a meeting with Mr. Nardwell just this afternoon," Theodosia said.

Delaine lifted her gelled eyebrows in surprise. "You're poking your nose into my sister's death because of his gun connection?"

"That's one reason," Theodosia said. "The more important one is because Bettina asked me to."

"Poor Bettina. She's beyond sad," Delaine cooed.

"She has a right to be," Drayton said.

"Actually, Nardwell seemed quite upset by Nadine's death," Theodosia said. "He confided in me that he wished he and Nadine could have had more of a future together."

Delaine put a hand to her mouth to cover a genteel snigger. "You're joking, aren't you?" She batted her eyes like a frantic moth against a screen door. "Tell me that was a joke."

"No joke," Theodosia said.

"I don't mean to speak ill of the dead, but . . ." Delaine lowered her voice because she was going to anyway. "Nadine was one of those women who was constantly looking to trade up."

Theodosia blinked. Had she heard correctly? "You mean trade up to a better caliber of boyfriend?" To her the idea sounded calculating and nasty.

"Lord, yes," Delaine said. "Come on now, you don't really *believe* Nadine would have been deliriously happy with a frumpy shopkeeper like Nardwell, do you? A middle-aged man in dreary brown suits who gets his jollies communing with dusty old firearms?"

"When you put it that way, he doesn't sound like a prize catch at all," Theodosia said. "But, to get back to what you were saying . . . Nadine had traded up . . . to someone else?"

Delaine gave a slow wink. "She said she had."

"Do you know who the lucky suitor was?" Theodosia was hoping for a name.

"Unfortunately, I don't. Nadine was *très* coy when it came to her personal life."

"Marvin Chauvet alluded to the fact that Nadine might have been cozy with Eddie Fox," Theodosia said.

"Eddie, huh? Well, there you go." Delaine glanced over in the direction of Nadine's coffin and gave a bitter nod. "Put another notch in the old girl's belt."

Bettina was sitting by herself on a black tufted chair near her mother's coffin, looking as if she'd lost the most important and beloved person in her life. Which she probably had.

Theodosia leaned down and said in a soft voice, "Bettina? How are you holding up, sweetie?"

Bettina turned red-rimmed eyes on her. "I'm not," she said. "This has been the most traumatic thing I've ever been through."

Theodosia sat down next to her and took the girl's hand in hers. She knew she could utter platitudes such as *time heals all wounds* or *everything happens for a reason*, but she figured they wouldn't help. They hadn't been any help to her when her own mother had died. But maybe if she sat here, squeezing Bettina's hand, her physical presence would offer some small measure of solace. She hoped it would, anyway.

After a minute or so, Bettina sighed deeply and leaned her head against Theodosia's shoulder.

"Thank you," she whispered. "All Aunt Delaine does is talk, talk, talk. It's nice that you can just *be*. I appreciate it."

Theodosia nodded.

"Look at all these people," Bettina said, as mourners continued to file past her mother's coffin. "I don't even know most of them. It makes me feel . . . empty inside."

"Still, they've come to honor your mother," Theodosia said. "Honor her memory. And, in their own way, to honor you."

Bettina frowned as she pondered Theodosia's words. "I suppose," she said. Remaining quiet for a few more moments, she asked, "Theo, are you still investigating?"

"Of course I am, honey. That's what you want, isn't it?"

"More than anything." Bettina cleared her throat and forced herself to sit up straight. "You do realize that many of the key players are here tonight, right?"

Theodosia bit her lip. She knew what Bettina was referring to. Someone responsible for her mother's death—someone who had been close to Nadine—could be right here at the visitation, masquerading as a sympathetic mourner.

"That's why I'm here, too," Theodosia whispered. She put an arm around Bettina, kissed her on the forehead, and said, "Time to go to work."

Bettina blinked back tears and whispered, "Bless you."

Bettina was right, Theodosia decided. A lot of the players *were* here tonight. Harvey Bateman and Marvin Chauvet had strolled in just minutes after she and Drayton had arrived. Eddie Fox was across the room, grabbing a glass of wine and chatting up one of the female servers. Simon Nardwell was standing in a corner, looking awkward and out of place. There were also a lot of guests and media people who'd been at the ill-fated Limón Tea last Sunday. And she'd yet to meet Mark Devlin, the freelance fashion designer, but figured he was probably here as well. Somehow she'd have to find him and wangle an introduction.

Theodosia decided to start with Marvin Chauvet, since he was the one closest to her. She walked up to him, a pleasant smile on her face, and said, "I stopped by Chauvet's Smartwear this afternoon."

"Oh yeah?" Chauvet rocked back on his heels and jingled the loose change in his pocket. Tonight he was wearing a navy blue summer-weight cashmere sweater with khaki slacks dotted with little images of fish. Dolphins maybe, or marlin.

"And, surprise surprise, I was told you don't have an office there."

"No, we leased space over near the Dock Street Theatre." Chauvet gave a chuckle. "The artsy-fartsy part of town."

Chauvet didn't seem one bit concerned that Theodosia was questioning him about his current office locale. In fact, he seemed perfectly at ease. So . . . maybe the man had nothing to hide? Maybe he and Mrs. Chauvet were simpatico? Still, she was hesitant to drop him from her suspect list. Maybe she could push him a little harder and see how he reacted.

"Will Nadine's passing leave a gaping hole in your organization?" she asked.

Chauvet gave a shrug. "Not really."

"Even though this is Charleston Fashion Week with so much going on?"

"Delaine's stepped in rather nicely, even though she still had to shoehorn in all these funeral arrangements. The good thing is, she has excellent contacts in the media and also managed to hook us up with some buyers we hadn't been able to get close to before."

"So you haven't missed a step?" Theodosia said.

"Not really." Chauvet gave a polite, noncommittal nod, said, "Excuse me," and walked away.

Hmm.

Theodosia looked around, saw Eddie Fox, and decided to lay a few questions on him. After all, she'd since learned a few things about his lifestyle.

"I understand you're a card-carrying member of the High Life Club," Theodosia said to Fox as her opening gambit.

That surprised Fox. "What?" he said. Then regained his composure. "Oh, *that.*" He wrinkled his nose in a partial sneer and shook his head. "Don't I wish. Unfortunately, my gonzo partying days are long gone. Now I'm a regular working stiff always on the lookout for a paying gig."

"And you're a well-respected filmmaker."

"I just wish awards came with a nice fat check. Unfortunately . . ." Fox took a sip of his wine and said, "Just out of curiosity, where'd you hear about the High Life Club?"

"Idle talk around town," Theodosia said. She saw Echo Grace waving at her from across the room and waved back.

Fox peered at her closely. "Are *you* a member?" The idea seemed to intrigue him.

"Hardly. Especially since my main focus is on tea."

"That's not what I've heard."

"What have you heard?" Theodosia asked as Echo Grace, accompanied by a smiling Delaine, suddenly edged in to join them.

"I heard that you've been asking questions all over town," Fox said, his voice starting to grow louder. "Concerning Nadine's murder. What's the deal, anyway?" As his voice carried, he started to attract attention from the people around him. "Are you some kind of crime groupie or amateur detective?" He jerked his arm, practically spilling his wine.

"Are you serious?" Delaine suddenly cried in a burst of static. "Theodosia happens to be Charleston's *number one* private investigator!"

Which made Echo grin and caused Fox to take a surprised step backward.

"What?" Fox said as more people, cognizant of Delaine's verbal outburst, were drawn to them.

Delaine put an arm around Theodosia's shoulders and hugged her so close she was swept up in a cumulus cloud of Chanel No. 5.

"Theo is our very own Nancy Drew!" Delaine announced loudly. "Our Trixie Belden, if I may. She's made a solemn, pinky-swear promise to Bettina that she'll look into my dear sister's murder."

"You mean actually investigate?" Fox said. He seemed gobsmacked by the idea.

Thanks a lot, Delaine, Theodosia thought. *Thanks for blabbing the news all over town.* Now the small crowd watched her with growing curiosity.

"Of course, the murder!" Delaine cried. "Theodosia's an absolute *whiz* when it comes to scoping out killers. She's done it before and she can do it again." Then Delaine dimpled prettily at Fox and waved a hand in front of her face as if she'd developed a sudden case of the vapors and was about to pass out. "Mr. Fox, I see you and I are both out of wine. Could I impose on you to escort me to the bar for a refill? I'm afraid all this excitement has left me feeling quite overwhelmed."

"I . . . well, yes," Fox said.

"Sheesh," Echo said as she watched Delaine and Fox wander off together and their crowd of onlookers slowly dissipated. "I don't know which one of those two is crazier."

"They might just be the perfect match," Theodosia said.

"Narcissist meets egotist."

"Exactly."

"To change the subject to something a little less bizarre, I hope you had fun at our informal modeling today," Echo said.

"Are you kidding? I told you I was gaga over every single one of your pieces and I meant it," Theodosia said.

"Yeah, they're all kind of perfect in their own way, aren't they? Soft, filmy, a little bit romantic but with a rock and roll vibe, too. You can wear them to the office or toss them in a suitcase for a fun weekend getaway." Echo gave a mischievous grin. "Or wear them to a tea party."

"I particularly loved the suede jacket with the feathers."

"Ostrich," Echo said. Then she glanced over at Nadine's coffin and her face assumed a serious expression. "I never knew anyone who was murdered before, did you?"

"A few people," Theodosia said. "Unfortunately."

"This is a first for me, and it kind of weirds me out."

"Did you know Nadine well?"

"I'd have to say we were starting to become fairly good friends," Echo said. "Strange as it may seem, women's fashion—at least here in Charleston—is mostly male dominated. There are a few female shop owners like Delaine and that shoe designer, Heidi Glynn, but all the designers and really successful fashion houses are either run by men or owned by men. So I've been trying to make it a point to hang out with other women in the industry so we can support one another. I figure it's the only way we can stay competitive."

"You're probably right," Theodosia said.

"Those two guys over there . . ."

Theodosia looked over at Marvin Chauvet and Harvey Bateman.

"Harv and Marv," Echo continued. "They're really trying to push the crap out of their Lemon Squeeze Couture line. They think there's big money to be made."

"Is there?" Theodosia asked.

"The athleisure trend will stay popular for a while, sure. But I'm more interested in getting out ahead of the next trend." Echo made a wavy up-and-down motion with her hands. "You know, try to be like a porpoise flitting along the bow of a ship."

"Staying out in front," Theodosia said, intrigued. "So what *is* the next big trend?"

"I think it's going to be high-low."

"Sounds like a card game."

Echo laughed and aimed an index finger at her. "Good one. But no, in this context high-low means fashion juxtaposition. Like wearing inexpensive jeans with a fabulous designer sweater. Or pairing an exquisite full-length skirt with a plain old sweatshirt and then adding a jeweled statement necklace."

"I think I do that all the time," Theodosia said.

"There you go," Echo laughed. "You're already on trend!"

"My, my," Delaine said, walking back to them with her full glass of wine. "Aren't we having fun." Her green eyes glittered. "Are you going to let me in on your private joke?"

Echo waved a hand. "We're just jabbering about fashion."

"Delaine," Theodosia said, "you haven't introduced me to Mark Devlin yet."

"The designer? You haven't met him? Well, come on." Delaine looped an arm through Theodosia's and pulled her away.

Echo gave a little finger wave as they walked off. "Play nice, you two."

"This," Delaine said rather breathlessly, as she parked herself in front of a tall, dark-haired man, "is the illustrious designer Mark Devlin."

Devlin wore a cream-colored sweater with loose-fitting slacks that looked as if they might be Egyptian cotton. His hair was pulled into a samurai topknot, and he had a silver piercing over his left eyebrow. He smelled vaguely of sandalwood and wore leather sandals.

"Mark, sweetheart," Delaine said. "This is the tea lady I told you about. Theodosia Browning."

"Nice to meet you," Theodosia said, shaking hands with him.

"Adore tea," Devlin said. He raised a hand in a theatrical gesture, and Theodosia immediately thought, *Drama queen.*

"Especially Japanese green tea," Devlin continued. "It's so calming and Zen."

"We serve several varieties of green tea at the Indigo Tea Shop," Theodosia told him. Devlin was interesting in that he looked like some kind of guru. A design guru? Or maybe he was just a garden-variety poser.

"I'll be sure to stop by your tea shop sometime," Devlin said. "You're located where?"

Delaine smiled brightly. "Theo's on Church Street. Just down from St. Philip's."

"From what Delaine's told me, it seems you single-handedly designed the Lemon Squeeze Couture line," Theodosia said to Devlin.

"Harv and Marv had a lot of fun ideas for the brand. And once they laid out their vision, as well as their marketing and merchandising strategies, it was kind of a slam dunk." Devlin turned eyes back on Delaine. "I know I told you this before, but I'm very sorry about your sister. Here . . ." Devlin peeled a brown bead bracelet off his wrist and handed it to Delaine. "These are *juzu*— Japanese prayer beads. Please accept them for your peace and comfort."

"Thank you," Delaine said, fingering the beads, but not really looking at them. "It's been a tough situation. But I have to say I'm ready to move forward. And to work with *you*."

"There is that," Devlin said.

"And of course we've got the Lemon Squeeze Couture Fashion Show coming up in a couple of days," Delaine said. "We'll finally be showcasing the *entire line*, not just bits and pieces on a shared runway with other designers."

"When's that happening?" Theodosia asked.

"Thursday afternoon. At Cotton Duck."

Which is probably why you rushed the visitation and funeral, Theodosia thought to herself. *Business first, family second.*

"I'm looking forward to styling the models," Devlin said to Delaine. "Working with some of the accessories in your boutique. Should be interesting."

"Mr. Devlin?" A young woman was suddenly standing at his elbow. "Excuse me . . . I don't mean to bother you . . ."

Devlin turned. "You already did," he said. Eyebrows raised, his demeanor was suddenly haughty and a little unkind.

"I'm sorry, really sorry, to interrupt, but Mr. Bateman would like a word with you," the woman said.

Devlin sighed heavily. "Now?"

"If it's okay with you." The young woman fidgeted, clearly nervous and uncomfortable.

"Whatever," Devlin said. "Theodosia, this is Julie Eiden, our intern. Julie, do something constructive for a change and entertain Theodosia while I go talk to the old man, will you?"

Julie turned frightened eyes on Theodosia as Devlin slipped away.

"I'm off, too," Delaine said. "Got to hobnob with the guests."

Which left Theodosia standing there with the intern.

"Julie?" Theodosia said. The girl was petite and elfin, early twenties, with reddish-blond hair, hazel eyes, and a pointed chin. She wore her nervousness like a cloak. "Are you okay?"

"Um . . . I guess," Julie said. "I didn't expect to be here tonight, and then Delaine told me I had to come. To help out, I guess, though there isn't a whole lot for me to do."

"No, probably not. Delaine tends to have things buttoned up."

"Just like her sister."

"So how's the internship going?"

"It's okay," Julie said.

"Just okay? Then again, I suppose the learning curve on developing and marketing a brand-new clothing line would be fairly challenging."

"No, it's not that," Julie said. "It's more the personalities involved."

"I've met the two partners," Theodosia said. "And I have to tell you, those types of men can come across strong."

"So can Mr. Devlin."

As Julie said Devlin's name, Theodosia glanced across the room at him. Interestingly enough, Devlin was waving his arms at Harvey Bateman as if trying to drive home a point. Whatever it was, Bateman wasn't buying it. His face was red as a Roma tomato as he glowered at Devlin. Then, he poked a finger just inches from Devlin's face and shouted, "A deal's a deal. Take it or leave it!"

Interesting, Theodosia thought. The more she saw of these people, the more she realized this team was fraying at the seams. The excitement of a fashion launch should have them all jumping for joy. Instead, they were at one another's throats like slavering dogs.

And now this—an actual shouting match between Harvey Bateman, the money guy, and Mark Devlin, the designer.

Who didn't seem one bit Zen anymore. Perhaps he needed his prayer beads back?

14

Does that happen a lot?" Theodosia asked Julie. "The fighting?"

Julie hunched her shoulders together. "You have no idea. The thing is . . . Mr. Devlin designed most of the Lemon Squeeze Couture collection. Which was a gigantic amount of work. I mean, like, twelve-hour days. And then because he did all the sketches, he had to supervise the fabrication and production. So now he thinks he should be paid a whole lot more money." Julie hugged herself protectively. "This has been an ongoing battle ever since I came on board."

"And I'm guessing it's not even close to being resolved," Theodosia said.

"I don't think it will ever be. Mr. Bateman is awfully tight with money."

Theodosia studied Devlin, who was still arguing with Bateman but had now assumed a haughty attitude.

"So Devlin is one unhappy camper?"

Julie twisted her hands together, looking even more uncomfortable. "He goes off on these wild tangents. I guess he thinks his creative persona deserves to be catered to. On the other hand, he's not nearly as fierce as Mr. Bateman."

Theodosia sensed a problem brewing. "Bateman's got a bad temper?"

Julie drew a deep breath. "Mr. Bateman is . . . well, let's just say you don't want to be around him when he's in one of his ugly moods."

Theodosia sensed that Julie had more to say. "Has Bateman ever had one of his ugly moods around you?" she asked.

Red blotches appeared on Julie's face and tears glistened in her eyes. "Yes," she said in a shaky whisper.

This struck Theodosia as rather ominous. "Bateman doesn't actually get violent, does he?"

Julie swallowed hard. "He's been known to. I heard . . . well, it's really more of a rumor . . . that Mr. Bateman slapped a girl who used to work for Lemon Squeeze."

"Do you know who the girl was?" Theodosia wondered if it might have been Nadine.

Julie shook her head. "No. I guess she was fired before I came on."

"Julie," Theodosia said, putting a hand on the girl's shoulder. "You don't have to put up with that kind of toxic workplace. You don't have to be subjected to angry outbursts and intimidation, or take crap from anyone."

Julie nodded and shook a hank of hair out of her face. "That's what I keep telling myself. The problem is . . . I'm just a lowly, unpaid intern trying to gain some practical experience. I can't apply for a *real* job until I can list something tangible on my résumé."

"You're positive you want to work in fashion?"

"It's all I've ever dreamed about," Julie said. "Based on my sketches and a BA in fashion merchandising from the University of South Carolina, I was able to ace out two dozen other people to get this internship. Is it the ideal situation? No. But I'm determined to stick it out for the experience. Besides, where else am I gonna work?"

"Let me think about that," Theodosia said. "See if I can come up with a few ideas."

Thirty minutes later, Theodosia and Drayton were speeding down Tradd Street, back in their Historic District neighborhood.

"That had to be the strangest visitation I've ever attended," Drayton said. "Makes me wonder what's in store for us at tomorrow's funeral."

"Maybe they'll load Nadine's casket onto a horse-drawn carriage?" Theodosia said.

"Or rent the birds for a second day."

"Cheap, cheap," Theodosia quipped. Then, "Did you get a chance to meet Mark Devlin, the designer?"

"No, but someone pointed him out to me."

"What was your impression?"

"That he looked like a groupie for the Dalai Lama."

Theodosia turned onto Archdale, one of the fancier streets, and rolled down her window, the better to take advantage of the warm spring weather. "Pretty out tonight," she said. Spring had finally made its glorious appearance in Charleston. Gardens were in full bloom, and everything felt fresh and wonderful.

Drayton caught her mood.

"Look how elegant and peaceful the big homes are," Drayton said. "I love driving by at night and catching glimpses of libraries and parlors and grand dining rooms through a crack in the curtains. It's like a wonderful old-fashioned stereopticon."

"Don't remember those," Theodosia said.

"Neither do I. But it's a fanciful image."

"Vintage-y," Theodosia said. "Like this whole part of town."

"You see that corner house? The Queen Anne style with the wraparound porch? That's the old Porter home, built in the mid-eighteen hundreds by Alexander Porter, owner of a clipper ship line."

"You could serve as the duly appointed historian of the Historic District," Theodosia said.

Drayton smiled. "I thought I already was."

Theodosia felt herself relax as she drove along. With the scent of magnolias and crepe myrtle riding on the wind and a faint skim of fog starting to drift in from the Atlantic, everything felt dreamy and ethereal. Old-fashioned wrought iron streetlamps were encircled with a slight haze, and the air felt rich as silk.

"Want me to swing by and pick you up for the funeral tomorrow?" Theodosia asked as she pulled to the curb in front of Drayton's house. He lived in an impeccably restored brick home that had been built by a Civil War doctor.

Drayton sat in the dark for a few moments before he said, "Do we have to go?"

"We pretty much promised Delaine that we'd be there."

"Okay, tomorrow, then. Around eight-ish?

"Eight-ish it is."

Theodosia drove home, enjoying the night, listening as the velvet, lilting Jamaican voice of Celeste oozed out of her CD player. It put her in a perfect relaxed mood.

Parking her Jeep in the alley, she walked through the wooden gate into her backyard, her very own slice of heaven. Wind whispered through the fanciful bonsai tree that Drayton had trimmed for her, and goldfish circled lazily in their small pond. A tangle of wisteria perfumed the air, and down the block came the gentle coo of a mourning dove.

Theodosia didn't notice the scrap of paper tacked to her back door until she reached for the doorknob.

What's this? A flyer from a tree service? Maybe a charity looking for donations? But why would they put their notice on my back door?

Then she saw the jagged handwritten scrawl and her heart jumped a beat. And when she read the message, that beat turned into a fast timpani solo.

The note read, *Back off if you know what's good for you!!*

Theodosia's first inclination was to be shocked and a little scared. Because this was clearly a threat. And scrawling those words with two exclamation points instead of one meant someone was trying to drive home their message. Hard.

Then, as she stepped inside her house, locked the door (checking it twice), and really thought about the note, she started to calm down. And the curiosity gene that was so ever-present in her DNA kicked in big-time.

Because somewhere, somehow, she must have struck a nerve. Somebody that she'd talked to or rubbed shoulders with in the last few days—maybe even tonight—was feeling stressed and nervous.

And nervous people are often guilty people.

Had she unknowingly stumbled across Nadine's killer? If so, who could it be?

Harv or Marv, one of the Lemon Squeeze Couture partners? The film director Eddie Fox? The gun guy Simon Nardwell? How about Mark Devlin, the designer guy? Or any number of people who'd attended the visitation tonight and overheard Delaine raving that Theodosia was the second coming of Nancy Drew.

Oh my.

In a way, Theodosia was tickled because it reaffirmed the fact that she was on the right track.

But the big question now was—what to do about this threat? Keep investigating because the trail seemed to be heating up? Call Riley and tell him about the note—and risk that he'd warn her away? Or do nothing for the time being?

The one thing she didn't want to do was bow out of this investigation. She was too involved, too vested. Most importantly, Bettina was counting on her.

Theodosia slowly became aware that Earl Grey was standing in the kitchen, gazing at her with inquisitive eyes.

"Did you hear somebody at the back door?" she asked. "Not just now, but earlier tonight?"

Earl Grey did a full-body doggy shake, starting with his nose and working his way down to the tip of his tail. Then he looked at her and said, "Rrwr."

"Yeah. Someone was pretty sneaky, huh? Putting a note on the outside door. Okay, you're a good boy because you didn't let anybody come inside. That in itself warrants a treat."

"Rwuh?"

"The peanut butter kind? Sure."

While Earl Grey munched his treat, Theodosia walked into her dining room and stared at herself in the antique mirror that hung above her Sheraton sideboard. She reminded herself that she'd learned a few things today. And maybe the most critical nugget of information she'd gleaned was Eddie Fox's drug use. The fact that he was a card-carrying cokehead made him a super suspect. And this was information she *could* share with Pete Riley. And if Riley thought the coke angle was worth pursuing, then he might press Sheriff Burney to take Fox in for questioning. And make him sweat.

Is it too late to call Riley?

She glanced at her antique French bronze clock and saw it was just ten thirty. Excellent.

Theodosia quickly dialed Riley's personal cell phone, hoping he had it with him instead of just working off his police radio. She was in luck.

"Yello."

"Are you busy?" Theodosia said. "Because I need to talk to you."

"Hey, it's not as if I'm doing anything important in the realm of crime fighting," Riley said. "I'm basically sitting in the dark staring at a bunch of boat docks. Just in case." He drew a breath. "So what's up, cupcake?"

"I went to one of the fashion shows earlier today. Actually, it was right after you stopped by the tea shop."

"Did you have a nice time?" Riley asked.

"Let's say I had an interesting time, because I learned something that could relate to Nadine's murder."

"Which is?"

"I talked to Bobby, one of the cameramen from Channel Eight, and he told me that Eddie Fox had been fired from another TV station . . ."

"Because of his drug use. Yeah, we know all about that."

"You do?" Theodosia was slightly taken aback.

"You may find this hard to believe, Theo, but we *are* the Charleston Police Department. As such, the Robbery and Homicide Division *does* conduct investigations."

"In other words, you've already interviewed Eddie Fox."

"Not me, personally, but Sheriff Burney did share a transcript with us. One of his investigators conducted a fairly extensive interview with Fox."

"So he's not a suspect?"

"I didn't say that."

"So Fox *is* a suspect?"

Riley blew out a long breath, and Theodosia could picture him sitting in a cramped car, brow furrowed, frustration bubbling up, wondering how he was going to get her to back off.

Finally, he said, "Theo, in the interest of public safety, you really shouldn't be involved in this case."

"Really?" she said. "That's the card you want to play? In the interest of public safety?"

"Okay, let's switch it up and say it's for your *personal* safety."

Theodosia clutched her phone so hard her knuckles turned white. If Riley only knew about the note she'd found on her door.

Was she going to tell him about it? Should she tell him?

Oh no. Absolutely not. Well, not yet, anyway.

15

As if Theodosia hadn't had her fill of fashion-conscious mourners last night, here she was, sitting in St. Michael's Church, one of the oldest of Charleston's many churches, at the corner of Meeting Street and Broad, waiting for Nadine's funeral to begin. And even though Drayton wasn't exactly pleased to be here, he was a class act as he sat next to her wearing a charcoal gray three-piece suit.

Theodosia leaned in close to him and said, "I never got a chance to tell you about Julie."

Drayton hesitated for a moment, then whispered, "Who's Julie?" Drayton was uncomfortable talking in church even though mourners were still filing in and there was chatter all around them.

"The intern at Lemon Squeeze Couture."

"Do you mean the small reddish-haired girl who looked like she's afraid of her own shadow?"

"That's the one. Anyway, she told me that Harvey Bateman has a nasty temper."

"How nasty?"

"Apparently, Bateman has a short fuse and goes off on people at a moment's notice," Theodosia said. "Julie said he's insulting and demanding, and isn't afraid to get physical."

Drayton frowned. "What's he done?"

"Supposedly, Bateman's thrown coffee cups, raised his hand in a threatening gesture . . ."

"And this leads you to believe . . . what?"

"That a guy who threatens female interns or employees might not think twice about shooting someone if his livelihood were in jeopardy."

"You think Bateman shot Nadine because his livelihood was threatened? You think *he's* the one connected to the cocaine?"

"Maybe. I don't know, but I intend to find out."

"This amateur investigation is becoming a lot more dangerous than I expected."

Theodosia nodded. She figured it would be dangerous. After all, they were talking murder, drugs, big money, and titanic egos. With all that going for them, what could possibly go wrong?

Actually, she just needed one thing to go right.

At nine o'clock on the button, the organist struck her first chord on the ancient organ. And with a somber hymn wafting out over the mourners, Delaine walked down the center aisle clutching an ornate silver urn. She was accompanied by Bettina, a couple of distant cousins she wasn't particularly fond of, and Janine, her faithful, overworked assistant from Cotton Duck.

"That's it? No fancy casket like last night?" Drayton asked.

"Maybe it was rented just for show," Theodosia said. "Like the birds."

Drayton didn't laugh out loud—he was too polite for that. But his mouth did pull into a pucker.

What Delaine *did* spring for was a gospel choir. A full-on, purple-robed group of two dozen men and women who filed into the sacristy at the precise moment she set her sister's urn on a small table next to a podium.

The gospel choir kicked things off by singing "Swing Low, Sweet Chariot," then segued into a snappy version of "How Great Thou Art."

As the choir sang, Theodosia craned her head to see who was sitting in the pews up front. Predictably, it was the Lemon Squeeze Couture gang—Marvin Chauvet, Harvey Bateman, and Mark Devlin. Julie the intern was a couple of rows back from them. And behind her was Simon Nardwell.

When the choir finished, the minister, a tall, balding, kind-faced man, stepped up to the podium and introduced himself as Reverend Chait Burwell. He welcomed the mourners to what he called a "celebration of life."

Theodosia stared at the stained glass window behind the altar as she listened to the minister speak. The window depicted St. Michael slaying a dragon, and it was a wonder—an original Tiffany. St. Michael looked sure and confident of his victory over evil as he stood there with his sword raised. Theodosia's thoughts began to wander, and she wondered if they'd enjoy a similar type of victory in finding Nadine's killer. She didn't want to literally slay whoever it was, but she did want to bring him—or her—to justice. Good should triumph over evil, right? In the real world, not just on church windows.

Drayton stirred next to her. The minister had finished, and now Delaine had taken his place at the podium. He raised a single eyebrow as if to say, *This should be interesting.*

Turns out it was beyond quirky.

Delaine unfolded a piece of paper, pulled her face into a sad smile, and said, "Here's a quick little poetic gem I know my dear, departed sister would have adored. I think it captures her spirit perfectly." And then she read:

> Don't mourn for me now,
> Don't mourn for me never,
> I am going to do nothing
> For ever and ever.

Delaine gazed out at the stunned faces and open mouths and said, "Isn't that sweet? Doesn't that sound like Nadine's true outlook on life?"

"How wildly inappropriate," Drayton whispered to Theodosia.

"But typical Delaine," Theodosia whispered back. "You should know by now that she doesn't do morbid."

"Or anything close to religious."

Luckily, the moment was resurrected by Bettina, who walked to the podium, smiled sadly at the mourners, and read Psalm 25, which began with "To you, O Lord, I lift my soul." She had a lovely speaking voice and, with so much emotion involved, touched the hearts of everyone in church.

Marvin Chauvet got up, looked disinterested, and said a few words. Which, to Theodosia, sounded like generic platitudes. Your basic she'll-be-sadly-missed, blah, blah, blah.

There was a final number from the gospel choir, and then the minister stepped to the podium, adjusted the microphone, and invited everyone to a post-funeral brunch at the Lady Goodwood Inn.

"Are we going?" Drayton asked. He glanced at his antique watch, frowned, and tapped the crystal. "Do we have time?"

"Are you serious?" Theodosia said. She watched as Eddie Fox jumped out of his pew and aced out Simon Nardwell so he could walk down the aisle with Delaine. "I wouldn't miss it for the world."

* * *

The Lady Goodwood Inn, a lovely brick edifice with tangles of green ivy curling up the sides of the building, was one of Theodosia's favorite places. She'd hosted teas there as well as attended garden shows, bridal showers, and wedding receptions. Both she and Drayton enjoyed friendly relationships with their guest services and catering directors.

Theodosia parked her Jeep in the circular drive that led to an entrance fronted with a half dozen white Doric columns and a dark green canvas awning. Palmetto trees stood guard on each side of the main door; bougainvillea plants spilled out of red ceramic pots. They nodded to the liveried doorman, breezed through the main lobby, hooked a left, and headed down a wide hallway.

"Where do you think the brunch is being held?" Drayton asked. "The Rose Room or the Solarium?"

"Has to be the Rose Room," Theodosia said. "It's the showiest spot."

Drayton nodded. "Of course. That would be Delaine's preference."

And there was Delaine, standing at the entrance, looking a little unsettled but welcoming everyone and distributing air-kisses like fairy dust.

"Theo, Drayton!" she exclaimed. "Thank you for coming." She put a hand on Drayton's arm, pulled him close, and said, "You know, if I'd had more time I could've planned a destination funeral. I hear those are so on trend right now."

"A destination funeral," Theodosia repeated, deadpan.

"Where to?" Drayton asked.

Delaine shrugged. "I understand the Turks and Caicos are lovely this time of year."

"Indeed," Drayton said, in a strained tone. He looked around, spotted a large silver teapot, and headed off in that direction.

Theodosia, on the other hand, stepped into the Rose Room, saw Julie Eiden, the intern, hand a clutch of papers to Eddie Fox, and decided to make the two of them her immediate business.

She approached them just as Julie said, "It's the updated schedule from the postproduction house. The final edit is set for Monday."

"Yeah. Good," Fox said, folding the papers and jamming them into his jacket pocket. Then he spotted Theodosia and said, "Hey, tea lady, how's it going?"

"Not bad for a funeral," Theodosia said as Julie scooted away.

"Do you know her well?" Theodosia asked, nodding after Julie.

"Julie? I've only dealt with her a few times. But, from what I can see, the poor kid's getting the short end of the stick."

Theodosia wanted to know more. "How so?"

"Take it from me, Harv and Marv are no picnic to work for." His eyes darted sideways and he pursed his lips.

Theodosia searched his face. "Was there something else? It seemed as if you were about to . . ."

"Say more?" Fox dipped his chin and lowered his voice. "Well, yeah. The thing is, when Nadine was with the company . . ."

"Yes?" Theodosia slowly drew out her word.

"Whenever we sat down for a production meeting, Nadine acted as if she hated Julie."

"Are you serious?"

"Heck yeah. I once saw Nadine lay into Julie because she brought her the wrong kind of sandwich from the deli." He shook his head. "It was something really stupid . . . like rye bread instead of whole wheat. I don't remember what exactly, but I do know Nadine was super picky. And nasty. But that was Nadine's thing. She was always horrid to Julie no matter how hard the poor kid tried to please her."

"And now there's no Nadine," Theodosia said. She had a sudden, strange thought, immediately dismissed it, then let her brain circle back to it. What if Julie, pushed to the breaking point by Nadine's cruelty and nattering, had finally hit the wall? What if Julie had grown to hate Nadine as much as Nadine hated her? And then murdered her?

Interesting idea. Crazy idea. But wouldn't that mean Julie had been involved in cocaine? She certainly didn't *look* like a druggie or a party girl. But these days, who could tell?

Drayton tapped Theodosia on the shoulder. "Excuse me?"

She turned. "Yes?"

"Hey," Fox said. "It's Mr. *GQ*. All dressed up in his funeral suit."

Drayton ignored him. "We need to eat and get back to the Indigo Tea Shop ASAP."

"Excuse me," Theodosia said to Fox. "The buffet line calls."

"See ya guys," Fox said as he headed for the bar.

"This looks delicious," Drayton said as they picked up their plates and started down the buffet line. Charleston's culinary landscape embraced influences from Europe, Africa, France, and the Caribbean, so dining out was always an adventure—whether it be the lush ambiance of the Charleston Grill or the gracious hospitality of 82 Queen.

"Farrow and shrimp hash," Theodosia said as she ladled a helping onto her plate. "Yum."

"Plus Charleston-style oysters Benedict," Drayton said. "Your basic fried oysters and poached eggs on a toasted English muffin."

"And I have to try some of this French toast stuffed with apples and topped with whipped cream."

"Couldn't be as good as Haley's."

Theodosia placed a piece of French toast on her plate. "I'm more than willing to do a taste test."

"Okay, and here's some braised okra. We really should sample that as well."

"Agreed."

Plates filled, Theodosia and Drayton wove their way through the maze of tables over to where Delaine and Bettina were seated.

Delaine, who had passed on the brunch in order to smoke a cigarette and sip a glass of white wine, immediately pounced on them.

"What did you think of the funeral?" she asked.

"It was lovely," Theodosia said.

"Mm-hmm," was Drayton's comment.

"Did you like my poem?"

"I think all the readings were quite apropos," Theodosia said.

Delaine gave a twitchy smile. "Bettina's selection was lovely, yes? A bit churchy and preachy, but nicely done." She reached over and patted the girl's hand. "You did good, sweetie."

Bettina focused a gaze on Theodosia and gave a rueful smile, as if to say, *What can you do? She's family and I'm stuck with her.*

Theodosia was working her way through her shrimp hash, when, nearby, voices suddenly rose a couple of decibels—as if a disagreement or argument had broken out. And then, in another instant, all hell broke loose as aggressive shouts escalated to a fever pitch.

Definitely not indoor voices. Now what's going on?

Theodosia looked across a sea of tables and saw Eddie Fox waving his arms wildly and shouting at Marvin Chauvet who was still seated. Fox, who'd adapted a threatening posture, was haranguing Chauvet about something—and there seemed to be no sign of letting up. Then, just as suddenly, Chauvet, who'd obviously had enough, let out a primal scream and jumped to his feet so fast his chair toppled over with a loud BANG.

That grabbed everyone's attention. Heads turned, chairs were moved discreetly for better viewing.

"What did you say?" Chauvet demanded in a loud screech.

Confronted, Fox didn't miss a beat. In a forceful voice, he shouted, "I said you can't make a silk purse out of a sow's ear!"

"How dare you," Chauvet shouted. "Especially when you know how much blood, sweat, and tears we've poured into this line. The fact of the matter is, I need film footage. *Better* footage than you've given me so far!"

"I'm working on it!"

"No, you're not. You're diddling around and handing me excuses. How long do you think I'm going to tolerate your ineptitude and lazy work ethic? We need decent footage *now*."

"You'll get it!" Fox screamed.

"Try harder," Chauvet screamed back, his face turning bright crimson.

Drayton spun in his chair and said, sotto voce, "Does it feel like we're at a hockey game instead of a funeral luncheon?"

"Gracious," Delaine said. "Those two are *always* trying to rip each other's throats out." She shook her head dismissively. "And with our big show happening tomorrow, you'd think those two could simply grit their teeth and suck it up."

"They probably both have a valid point," Drayton said.

Delaine waved a hand dismissively. "Whatever." And helped herself to another glug of wine.

But Theodosia was slightly unnerved. The entire crew surrounding Lemon Squeeze Couture seemed to have come unhinged. Chauvet was furious with Fox, Fox was disgusted by Chauvet, Harvey Bateman only loved money, and the designer, Mark Devlin, was dismissive of everyone. And then there was Julie Eiden, who, heaven forbid, might have snapped over Nadine's nasty treatment of her. And let's not forget Simon Nardwell, who owned a pile of guns.

Any one of these miscreants could have killed Nadine. Any one of them might possibly be involved in a cocaine deal. So what to do? Questioning these people was like pulling teeth.

Theodosia looked across the table at Bettina, who was dabbing her eyes with a hanky. And her heart went out to her.

But I have to try and sort things out. Because I promised Bettina.

"Excuse me," Theodosia murmured. She got up from her table, walked over to where Harvey Bateman was sitting, and said, "Mr. Bateman, could I have . . ."

Bateman shook his head and turned away, basically ignoring her. Then he stood up, hurried across the room to where Julie Eiden was talking to one of the caterers, and started yelling at both of them.

Doesn't that just beat all?

Theodosia glanced around the room, saw Simon Nardwell, and thought, *Nardwell. I could take one more shot at him.*

But Nardwell either saw her coming or had pressing business. Because no sooner had she headed in his direction than he jumped up from the table, hunched his shoulders, and sprinted out the door.

Strike three. Theodosia stood there, knowing there wasn't much more she could do.

16

When Theodosia and Drayton arrived back at the Indigo Tea Shop, it was midmorning. And Theodosia was heartened to see that Haley and Miss Dimple had everything well in hand. Guests looked happy; the aroma of tea and baked goods filled the air.

At least something's going right.

"We did a super simple morning cream tea," Haley hastened to explain. "Just two options. A pair of apricot-rosemary scones with Devonshire cream and a fruit cocktail, or a single scone served with strawberries and balsamic vinegar plus a wedge of warm Brie cheese sprinkled with toasted pine nuts. I plated everything in the kitchen so it was easy-peasy for Miss Dimple to serve, no multiple courses to fuss with."

"And the tea?" Drayton asked.

"Miss Dimple brewed pots of ginger green tea and jasmine dragon," Haley said. "Did a pretty fine job, I think."

"I *hope* I did," Miss Dimple said. "I also tried my hand at brewing a pot of Drayton's British blend."

"Tricky," Theodosia said. She knew that particular tea, a

hearty blend of Chinese and Ceylonese black teas, had to steep a little longer.

"How'd it turn out?" Drayton asked.

"It was so popular I just brewed a second pot. Why don't I pour you a cup and you can taste for yourself," Miss Dimple said. She stepped behind the counter and carefully filled a small red-glazed Chinese teacup. "Here you go."

Drayton took a sip and seemed to ponder the brewing.

"Well?" Miss Dimple looked alarmed, as if she were facing a firing squad.

"Delicious!" Drayton proclaimed.

"Hallelujah," she said.

Because the morning had slipped by so quickly, lunch suddenly loomed on the horizon. Theodosia and Miss Dimple rushed around the tea room, clearing dishes, resetting tables, filling sugar bowls, and putting out fresh pitchers of cream and plates of lemon slices.

"Have you had any more brainstorms concerning our various suspects?" Drayton asked as Theodosia slipped behind the front counter.

"Only one," she said. "And it concerns Julie the intern."

Drayton stood on tiptoes and grabbed a tin of Keemun tea. "What about her?"

"Is it possible . . . that Julie killed Nadine?"

"Sweet dogs!" Drayton exclaimed, practically slamming the tin down against the counter. "Now you suspect that poor waif of a girl?"

Theodosia gave a shrug. "From what Eddie Fox told me, Nadine absolutely detested Julie. And now that I think about it, those feelings could have extended both ways."

"*Detest* is an awfully strong word."

"So is *murder.*"

Drayton picked up his tea tin and popped off the lid. "You really believe that an intern pulled the trigger on Nadine?"

"She could have."

"We're talking cold-blooded murder here. Is Julie capable of that?"

"If she was dealing drugs and got caught red-handed, then sure. And the fact that Nadine had been so horrid to Julie gave her an added impetus to kill two birds with one stone. Literally speaking, that is."

Drayton peered at her. "With so many suspects on the docket, what's your master plan? How do you intend to crack this case?"

"Not sure," Theodosia said. "I need some more time to think about it."

"While you're thinking, can we please take a few minutes to iron out the details for Saturday's Tea Trolley Tour?"

"Can it wait until after lunch? Or, better yet, once we finish today's luncheon service, I could pop over to the Featherbed House B and B and talk to Angie in person. See what her plans are for their part in the Tea Trolley Tour. Then you and I can put our heads together . . ."

"Well, hello!" Drayton suddenly boomed out. He was staring past Theodosia's shoulder at whoever had just come in the front door.

Theodosia turned to see who the newcomer was and found herself pleasantly surprised.

"Lois!" she cried. Lois Chamberlain was a good friend and bookshop owner from down the street who'd endured a tragic personal loss as well as a devastating fire a month or so ago. After dealing with her problems, haggling with her insurance company, and hunting around for empty retail space, Lois had landed back on Church Street.

"Are you here for lunch?" Theodosia asked. "Can you stay awhile?"

"Give us all the news?" Drayton added.

"I'm afraid it's strictly takeout for me today," Lois said. "I'm busier than a moth in a mitten right now, putting the finishing touches on my new bookshop."

"If it's takeout you want, we're happy to oblige," Drayton said as he took off for the kitchen.

Lois paused to grab a breath. "Theo, you have to come and see my new shop!" Lois was in her late-fifties and a retired librarian with a love for books. She was short, a little stocky with a cherubic face, and wore her long salt-and-pepper hair in a single braid down her back. Today she was dressed Lois-style, which meant an embroidered top, jeans, and sensible shoes. A bulging book bag was slung over one shoulder. Books stuck out as well as a skein of yarn and knitting needles.

"I can't believe you were able to find another space right down the block from us," Theodosia said.

"I almost signed a lease for an empty shop around the corner," Lois said. "Then the stars aligned, the angels sang their vespers, and the space next to Boyet's Camera Shop suddenly became available."

"The spot where the fancy sheet and comforter shop was located, right?" Theodosia said. "With the cute little upstairs loft?"

"That's it exactly. The sheet and comforter lady moved to a storefront on Queen Street because she needed more room," Lois said. "More pouf space, I guess. Anyway, I sure lucked out!"

"It'll be great to have you back on Church Street where you belong."

"I have to say I've missed the old neighborhood."

Drayton emerged from the kitchen carrying an indigo blue bag. He set it on the counter, poured a cup of tea, snapped on a cover, then pushed it all toward Lois.

"There you go, Lois. A scone, two prosciutto and cheese tea sandwiches, and a cup of Earl Grey."

"Thanks so much, Drayton," Lois said. "How much do I . . . ?"

Drayton held up a hand. "Please. It's on the house."

"Thank you so much!" Lois grabbed her lunch and turned to Theodosia. "Do you have a few minutes to come take a look?"

"Can you handle things okay, Drayton?" Theodosia asked.

"Natch," he said. "You go have fun while I toil away. Just be back in time for lunch, okay? Which gives you all of five minutes."

Theodosia did have fun. She walked with Lois down Church Street to her brand-new space where a newly hand-lettered sign graced her front window. It said *Antiquarian Books.*

Lois stuck her key in the lock and opened the door. "Come on in and have a look around."

"Ooh, it's all done up in fresh Sheetrock and painted so it's got that new shop smell," Theodosia exclaimed as she stepped inside.

"Fresh as a daisy thanks to my new landlord. And isn't it cute?" Lois said.

She'd brought in an antique library table to use as a front counter, hung Tiffany-style lamps from wooden ceiling beams, and laid Oriental carpets on the floor. Just-built wooden bookshelves were half-stocked with books, while boxes full of books were stacked everywhere.

"It's going to be wonderful," Theodosia said. She couldn't imagine how she'd feel if she lost the Indigo Tea Shop in a fire. The tea shop was her baby, her life's blood. How difficult it would be to start over. How difficult it must be for Lois.

"This place will look even better when all my boxes are unpacked and the books finally shelved," Lois said.

"I'm loving it already," Theodosia said as she glanced around. "This shop's a tad smaller than your old one, yes?"

"I look at it this way," Lois said. "I'm rightsizing instead of downsizing."

"You sound like one of those corporate raiders. Never apologize for firing half the company; just chalk it up to smart business practices."

Lois cocked a finger at her. "Exactly."

Theodosia wandered through the space. The shelves already carried crisp new labels that read FICTION, HISTORY, MYSTERY, COOKING, LOCAL LORE, ROMANCE, CHILDREN'S, BUSINESS, and RELIGION.

"I love this spiral stairway that leads to your loft," Theodosia said, going halfway up the stairs to look around. "It's got a cozy, magical feel."

"Like a secret place you want to explore to your heart's content," Lois said.

"What books are you going to put up here?"

"It'll be half children's books and half mystery."

"Sounds apropos."

"And I plan to . . ." Lois stopped mid-sentence as the bell over the front door jingled merrily. "Will you look at this, an actual customer."

Mark Devlin walked in and quickly glanced around. His eyes immediately landed on Lois, who was standing front and center. He hadn't yet noticed Theodosia.

"Lois?" Devlin said. Today he was dressed in ripped jeans, a Gucci T-shirt, and boots that looked as if they'd been hand-tooled in Morocco.

Lois smiled. "That's me."

"I'm the guy who called earlier? To see if you had that book on Christian Dior? The fashion book?"

"I have it," Lois said. "But, like I told you on the phone, it's used."

"That's okay," Devlin said as he stepped up to the counter. Then he spotted Theodosia as she came down the staircase. "Well, hello there," he said with a broad smile. "Fancy seeing you here."

"Mr. Devlin," Theodosia said.

"Mark. Call me Mark." Then, "Oh, this is the street where your tea shop is located, isn't it?"

"We're three doors down."

"If only I had time to stop by for lunch. Unfortunately, I have a business appointment."

"Perhaps another time," Theodosia said.

"Here's that Dior book," Lois said. She dropped the oversized book on the counter with a loud THUNK. "Good thing you're not paying by the pound."

"How much do I owe you?" Devlin asked.

"Twenty," Lois said, sliding the book into a paper bag.

Devlin handed Lois a twenty-dollar bill, thanked her, then gave Theodosia a little salute as he left with his purchase. "Like you said, another time."

"Sure," Theodosia said. Then to Lois, "I'd better get back to the tea shop and help serve lunch."

"What's Haley got on the docket for today?"

"I have no idea," Theodosia said as she watched out the window as Mark Devlin jumped into a dark blue SUV and pulled away from the curb. And wondered—was it possible that Devlin was the missing link in this case? Could this self-assured, slightly effete designer also be a drug dealer and the one who'd pulled the trigger on Nadine? He had that prima donna arrogance that creative people so often possessed. But then so did many cold-blooded killers.

17

Turned out Haley had come up with quite a few delightful offerings for today's luncheon menu: ham and cheese scones, apple and walnut muffins, Earl Grey tea bread, chicken and fruit salad, crepes with crab stuffing, and roast beef and cheddar cheese tea sandwiches. There were also butterscotch brownies and lemon bars for dessert.

"Did you get a load of Haley's crepes?" Drayton asked Theodosia as she tied her apron on. He was timing and brewing six different pots of tea with the ease of a magician working the main stage at Caesars Palace. The Indigo Tea Shop was suddenly crowded—almost every table occupied—and Theodosia was glad Miss Dimple had agreed to stay and help out.

"Saw her making crepes but didn't taste them," Theodosia said.

"I snuck a quick nosh and I'm here to tell you those crepes are light as air and her crab filling is blissful. Fresh-caught blue crab in a sinfully rich béchamel sauce. Really, one of my all-time favorites."

"I hope there's some left over."

Drayton shook his head. "Doubtful."

And he was right. Once lunch service was over, Theodosia tiptoed into the kitchen, hoping to score one of Haley's crepes. Wasn't happening.

"I just sent the last order out," Haley told Theodosia. She made a sad face and said, "Sorry." When Theodosia didn't immediately respond, she added, "But I could whip up another batch of crepe batter if you want."

"No, that's okay," Theodosia said. "Just be sure to give me the recipe."

"Count on it."

Theodosia eyed the butcher-block counter where baking racks held cooling goodies. "But we have extra scones, right?"

"Lots. You know me. I always bake an extra dozen or two."

"Good. Because I want to take a half dozen scones to Angie."

"You going over there pretty soon?"

"Right now."

The Featherbed House B and B was a charming landmark located two blocks from the Indigo Tea Shop. It was an enormous old house built of brick and clapboard that had been added onto over the years—an extra wing here, an annex there—and turned into a cozy but luxurious inn. Wicker furniture and lazy swings graced a wide front porch; a second-floor balcony was perfect for sunning. Looking up at the structure from the street, a third floor offered a virtual wedding cake display of decorative turrets, finials, and balustrades.

Inside, the cozy lobby featured red and yellow chintz sofas and chairs, handwoven fabric rugs, and a redbrick fireplace. In keeping with its namesake, the Featherbed House was chock full of plush geese, ceramic geese, carved geese, and metal geese. Geese were even embroidered on sofa cushions and stood guard as four-foot-high sculptures. A myriad of geese paintings hung on the walls.

As Theodosia stepped across the lobby, Angie Congdon glanced up from her perch behind the high wooden reception desk. She looked adorable as always with curly blond hair cascading down onto her shoulders. She wore a serene expression on her face and was dressed in a pink ruffled blouse and short denim skirt.

Angie's face lit up when she saw Theodosia.

"Miss Theodosia. What brings you to my parlor?"

Theodosia held up the bag filled with scones.

"Be still my heart," Angie said. "Those are scones, right?"

Theodosia nodded.

"Did Haley also pack a container of her famous Devonshire cream?"

"Is the sky blue?"

"Just checking."

"And I'm here to double-check on plans for the Tea Trolley Tour," Theodosia said. "You know how Drayton always likes to have everything nailed down."

Angie came out from behind her desk. "Speaking as a compulsive type A, I can definitely identify."

"I think I already mentioned that I plan to be on the first leg of the tour when it stops at the Dove Cote Inn."

Angie nodded. "Where they'll serve morning tea and scones to the trolley guests."

"Right, then I'll hop on the trolley for a short tour of the Historic District, with our second stop here for lunch."

"Where, knock on wood, the very capable Drayton and Haley will have their exquisite food and tea ready to go."

"And where I'll be playing tea hostess."

Angie held up a finger. "There's been a change in plans concerning that."

"Uh-oh."

"No, it's all good. Better than good. Now you can mostly take it easy during the luncheon."

Theodosia chuckled. "That would be a first."

"I'm serious," Angie said. "You don't have to do your usual table-hopping and tea introduction thing because I've lined up some amazing entertainment. At least I consider it entertainment."

"I'm intrigued. What have you got up your sleeve?"

Angie beamed. "Would you believe informal modeling throughout the entire luncheon?"

"Seriously?" This *was* good news for Theodosia. Took a load off.

Angie nodded. "I decided, pretty much on the spur of the moment, to partner with the Charleston Fashion Week people."

"Smart."

"Actually, Brooke Carter Crockett was the one who steered me in that direction. She knows this great designer . . ."

"I'll bet it's Echo Grace!" Theodosia exclaimed.

Angie was both surprised and pleased. "You *know* her?"

"Kind of. Well, I fell in love with Echo's clothes, anyway. They're gorgeous and amazing. Your guests won't just be entertained, they'll be enthralled."

"Looks as if I made the right choice—with a little help from Brooke, that is. Oh, and when I spoke to Echo she suggested we bring in another designer as well. A woman by the name of Kiki Everhart who creates these elegant one-of-a-kind clutch purses, hobo bags, and leather cuffs. The bags are basically stitched-together swatches of brocade fabric, most of it vintage, that are embellished with faux gems and use fancy drapery cords as drawstrings. She calls her line Hart Song."

"Sounds fabulous."

"I've seen the bags and they are," Angie said. "Of course, I still have a few logistics to work out. And I'm praying that this tea will go smoother than your Limón Tea did last Sunday." Angie's face took on a commiserating expression. "I read all about it in the *Post and Courier* and I'm so sorry that happened to you." She reached out and gently touched a hand to Theodosia's shoulder.

"Thank you. But it didn't so much happen to me as to poor Nadine. Her death—her murder—was a crushing blow to Delaine and Bettina."

"I wish I could have attended the funeral this morning, but we had a huge group check in at the last minute. A bunch of birders from Kentucky. They're here to visit the Ravenel Caw Caw Interpretive Center and hopefully spot a fulvous whistling duck or two."

"Well, good luck to them," Theodosia said. "I've been to that center, and the rarest bird I spotted was an indigo bunting."

Angie gave a sly smile, lightening the mood. "Is that your official tea shop bird?"

Theodosia grinned back at her. "Good one."

When she returned to the tea shop, Theodosia thought some more about Julie Eiden as she cleared tables and reset them for afternoon tea. And how much Nadine had hated that poor girl.

But swirling around in her mind was the million-dollar question—had Julie also hated Nadine? Had Julie gotten fed up with Nadine's hostility and simply snapped? Experienced a complete mental breakdown, a total lapse in judgment? Or had Julie seen an opportunity in the making and simply murdered Nadine?

But as Theodosia continued to kick her ideas around, the idea of Julie as a gun-toting, stone-cold killer began to feel a bit improbable. Mostly because she came across as soft-spoken and a little mousy.

So who else could have put a gun to Nadine's head and pulled the trigger?

Actually, there *was* another quiet, mild-mannered person

who'd been peripherally involved in Nadine's life. And that was Simon Nardwell. The man *looked* innocent, acted as if he was devastated by Nadine's death. But what if Nardwell wasn't what he appeared to be? Maybe he was a passive-aggressive type. A man who held it all inside until—*boom*—he finally blew his cork.

Theodosia thought about the packages Nardwell had received the day she'd visited his shop. Could a fusty middle-aged antique weapons dealer also be a well-connected drug dealer? He could be.

Or could he?

Theodosia racked her brain to remember the return addresses on those two packages. Okay, one was from Germany. She remembered that okay. The other package was from . . . where? She thought hard but couldn't quite pull it up. Oh well, the address probably wouldn't have led anywhere . . .

Ecuador. That's where it was from. A town called San something. What was it again? San Leandro? No, I think it might have been San Lorenzo.

Pleased that she'd been able to conjure up the name, her curiosity suddenly rising to a fever pitch, Theodosia decided to do a little primary research on San Lorenzo. She got on her computer, clicked along, read a few articles . . .

What she found shocked her.

Really? Whoa.

Feeling apprehensive as well as tingling with excitement, Theodosia got up from her desk, walked halfway down the back hallway, and said, "Drayton, could you pop in here when you have a minute?"

"What?" he said, looking up from where he was putting the final touches on a takeout order. He pushed his half-glasses up on his nose and said, "Okay, yes. Soon as I'm finished here."

When Drayton wandered into her office a few minutes later, Theodosia said, "I'd like you to take a look at this." She surrendered her desk chair to Drayton and waited while he skimmed the article she'd pulled up on her computer.

Drayton stared at the screen, blinked, and said, "This article says that San Lorenzo, Ecuador, is one of the cocaine trade's main dispatch points. For drugs coming out of Colombia." He gave her a questioning look. "Highly informative, but how is it relevant to us?"

"Simon Nardwell received a package from San Lorenzo yesterday."

"Probably a coincidence," Drayton said.

"What if it isn't?"

"Then we . . . hold on a minute." He rubbed the back of his hand across his chin. "I see an ominous twinkle in your eye and feel suspicion oozing out of that crafty brain of yours. What exactly do you have in mind?"

What Theodosia had in mind was a creepy-crawl through Nardwell's shop. Best-case scenario, they'd pick a lock, go inside, and look around. Of course, it wasn't certain they'd be able to get inside.

When she told Drayton her idea, his answer was a resounding, "No!"

"Why not?"

"Because what you're proposing is breaking and entering."

"Not exactly," Theodosia said as she quickly rethought her idea.

"What's *not exactly* about it?"

"I just realized that, since Nardwell sells valuable guns, he probably has secure locks on all his doors as well as a serious alarm system."

"Thank goodness," Drayton said. "Saved by the proverbial alarm bell."

"So what I have in mind is poking around."

"Define *poking around.*"

"Looking in the back alley, searching through his trash," Theodosia said.

Drayton rolled his eyes. "A dumpster dive. I *knew* it."

"So what do you think?"

"I hate it."

Theodosia gazed at him. "But you'll do it? Yes or no?"

"No," Drayton said. Then, when he saw the look of disappointment on Theodosia's face, he said, "Okay, maybe I could help. But certainly not in my good suit."

Theodosia looked at her watch. "It won't be dark for another couple of hours, so we've got some time. Tell you what, after we finish afternoon tea I'll drop you at your house so you can change into something less spiffy. Then I'll run my errand and come back for you."

"Dare I ask what errand this is?"

"Probably best not to."

18

The errand Theodosia had in mind was taking a quick run out to Orchard House Inn. She'd already phoned Andrea Wilts, the owner, and gotten a resounding okay. There were no major banquets or events scheduled for tonight, only a few bed-and-breakfast guests, so Theodosia's popping in would be no big deal.

Theodosia took US 17 out of the city, hit Highway 171, then turned south on Highway 700 where she crossed the slow-moving Stono River and found herself on the largest of the barrier islands known as Johns Island. She drove a narrow, twisty road that took her past small country churches known as praise houses, the Sunnyside Goat Farm, and charming roadside markets with names such as Honey Acres and Rosemary Creek Farm. This was where onions, peas, squash, zucchini, sweet potatoes, and collards were grown, and you could pick your own strawberries in season. Every so often there'd be a small seafood market, almost like a cute little shanty, advertising fresh-caught grouper, shrimp, oysters, or blue crabs.

There were more rivers out here, too. Plus acres of marshes and cypress swamps, all rich habitat for deer, alligators, foxes, mink, bald eagles, and coyotes. In a few places, where the narrow ribbon of road dipped into low-lying areas, puffs of ground fog gave the impossibly dark green wetlands an ominous and slightly ethereal feeling.

As the dying rays of the sun skittered off her rear window, Theodosia turned down a lane edged with tamaracks and stopped in front of the Orchard House Inn. Viewed from the front it was a lovely old plantation home complete with columns and a wraparound porch. Lights glowed warmly from within, and she could see a half dozen or so people holding wineglasses as they queued up to a table that held appetizers and a wheel of cheese. She drummed her fingers against the steering wheel, then drove around to the back of the building and parked outside the kitchen door.

A few seconds later, Andrea peeped out a back window. She'd been waiting for her.

"You made good time," Andrea said as she opened the door and welcomed Theodosia into the inn's warm and well-lit kitchen.

"Not much traffic tonight," Theodosia said.

"There rarely is midweek."

"It smells wonderful in here." Plates were set out on the counter, great aromas were coming from the oven.

"We're serving baked squab and root vegetables tonight," Andrea said. "Simple but heartwarming. And a little showy." She paused. "So. You said you wanted to take a look around?"

"Just in the parlor and the cooler. Well, I guess here in the kitchen, too."

Andrea gave a shiver. "The scene of the crime. I'm trying not to let the whole weird thing bother me, but it does feel as if this place is somehow tainted. Maybe I should burn sage or something."

"Please don't worry unnecessarily," Theodosia said. "Your inn is so quaint and charming that I'm sure any bad feelings will dissipate in no time at all."

"Hope so," Andrea said. She turned, led Theodosia through

the kitchen, and pushed open the door to the parlor. "Well, here it is. This is where the Crime Scene techs found traces of cocaine. If that's what you're interested in—and I'm guessing it is. But, as you can see, it's all been cleaned up."

"I'm mostly trying to get a basic impression," Theodosia said as she looked around. In fact, everything appeared the same as last time she'd been here. Two dark blue velvet sofas with tufted backs, two floral wing chairs, a gleaming mahogany cocktail table, an octagonal-shaped gaming table with four captain's chairs tucked around it, and a large wooden sideboard. Probably, when the inn was filled to capacity, this room was used as a second spot to serve wine, cheese, and appetizers.

"If you don't mind, I need to check on my guests," Andrea said. "Pour seconds on wine."

"No problem," Theodosia said. "I'll be a few minutes at most and then I'll be out of your hair."

Theodosia waited until Andrea had left, then walked to the middle of the parlor and looked around. Tried to imagine a drug deal going down here—if that's what had actually happened. Two people, a buyer and a seller, negotiating a price. Or maybe the price had already been agreed upon and this was just a handoff?

And then Nadine walked in and spoiled it all. Paid the ultimate price for her snooping.

So a serious drug deal. Worth killing for to keep it all hush-hush.

Theodosia let that notion settle around her for a few moments, then turned, pushed through the swinging door, and walked back into the kitchen.

It was a kitchen to die for. And, as Theodosia grimly reminded herself, Nadine had. There was a six-burner Wolf stove, counter space galore, stainless steel shelving that held all manner of pots and pans. A roomy kitchen where two or even three people could work without getting in each other's hair. It would be heaven to have a kitchen like this for the Indigo Tea Shop. But whenever

Theodosia broached the subject of a possible move to a larger space, both Drayton and Haley vehemently opposed it.

"Hello?" came a voice at her shoulder.

Theodosia was so startled she not only jumped, she clapped a hand to her thudding heart.

"Apologies, I didn't mean to scare you," Andrea said. "I just wanted to check on my squab and see if you needed anything. Or had any questions."

"No, I'm . . . I'm doing fine," Theodosia said, fighting to get her heart rate under control. "In fact, I was just about to take a look inside the cooler."

"After the Crime Scene unit wrapped up their investigation on Monday, we moved things around in there. Plus, we just got a shipment of raw oysters and blue crabs for a community dinner we're hosting tomorrow night."

"But it's okay to go in?" Theodosia gazed at the formidable stainless steel door.

"Oh sure, look around to your heart's content," Andrea said. "But I have to warn you, it's plenty cold in there."

"Okay."

Andrea took a peek inside the oven, gave a satisfied nod, and said, "Call if you need me." And disappeared again.

Theodosia had come prepared. She slipped on a cardigan sweater, opened the door to the cooler, and stepped inside. A light came on, and instinctively, she looked down to where she'd first discovered Nadine's dead body. Scanned for remnants of blood that had been smeared across the floor. But of course that had all been cleaned up. Probably by one of those professional cleaning companies that dealt with hazardous waste.

Sad to think of Nadine as hazardous waste.

Just as Andrea had said, there were boxes marked MACKEN-ZIE'S CRAB CO. and a large wooden crate holding several mesh bags filled with bumpy gray oysters. Almost forty pounds' worth.

There were several boxes of lemons as well, a few cartons of eggs, and bundles of meat.

Ordinary. Not that much to see.

For some reason, Theodosia had thought she might arrive at some brilliant deduction if she came back here and poked around. Or, in her mind's eye, she'd be able to envision the murder more clearly. Nadine, the killers, a confrontation, the gun being fired.

Wasn't happening for her.

Disappointed, Theodosia made a slow three-hundred-sixty-degree turn. Looked up, looked down. Decided this had probably been a fool's errand.

And that's when she felt something—a tiny bump—under the toe of her left shoe. She took a step back, looked down, and saw a small metal spring, maybe an inch long, with a tiny hook at each end.

It reminded Theodosia of the end of a miniature bungee cord. Could Haley have used some kind of small cord to help keep the lid on one of their portable coolers? Or maybe on a container of Devonshire cream? That was probably it, she decided as she picked it up, then dropped the spring into her sweater pocket. But she'd check with Haley just to make sure.

A globular yellow moon dangled in a blue-black sky as Theodosia and Drayton rolled down the alley behind Simon Nardwell's gun shop.

"This is such a bad idea," Drayton said. For the last half hour, ever since Theodosia had stopped by to pick him up, he'd been trying to dredge up excuses to skip out of this. None of them had budged Theodosia in her determination.

So here they were, pulled up next to a hulking green dumpster that had BUDDY'S SANITATION stenciled on the side in flaking yellow paint.

Theodosia hopped out of her Jeep; Drayton climbed out reluctantly. It was dark as pitch in the alley with a tangle of power lines overhead. A dog barked a block away, a long, baying *yi-yi-yi*, then went silent. A car with a bad muffler sputtered by over on King Street. Then the night grew quiet.

"Got some disposable plastic gloves here," Theodosia said.

Drayton sighed, accepted a pair, pulled them on, then looked up and down the alley. "What do we do now?"

"Let's try opening the lid," Theodosia said. She walked over to the dumpster, gripped the lid, and muscled it upward. There was a loud creak, then the lid rose on pneumatic hinges and tilted back. The smell of days-old garbage drifted out.

"Nasty," Drayton said. "What do you think is in there?"

Theodosia peered over the ledge of the dumpster and into the dark interior. She snapped on a small flashlight and aimed the beam. "I see a pizza carton from Luigi's Pizza, so there's probably a half-eaten olive and pepperoni in there. Plus, there's a bunch of cardboard boxes and some empty wine bottles."

"The wine no doubt consumed with the pizza," Drayton said. For some reason he was dressed as a commando. Black slacks, a dark green military-looking sweater complete with epaulets.

"There are two apartments above Nardwell's shop, so the residents probably make use of this dumpster as well."

"Lucky us. Say there, what's that you're doing?"

Theodosia had stuck a toe into an indentation on the side of the dumpster and was hoisting herself up onto the edge.

"You're not actually *going* in there, are you?" Drayton sounded horrified.

"I just want to excavate the top layer." Theodosia ducked down, practically disappearing into the darkness. All Drayton could see was the top of her head. Then she let out a muffled cry of "Stand back!"

Sheets of cardboard, bottles, pizza cartons, and junk suddenly rained down into the alley.

"You're emptying it out?" Drayton cried. He was waving his arms, looking a little frantic.

"The better to see what's what in here. It's so doggone dark."

"It's dark out here, too," Drayton said. He shifted from one foot to the other, unwilling to root through the trash.

"Did you see any FedEx boxes come flying out?" Theodosia asked.

"No."

"Are you looking?"

"Not really."

Theodosia popped her head up like a gopher. "Turn on that mini flashlight I gave you and see what's what."

"What exactly should I be looking for? Give me a hint," Drayton said as he dug in his pocket for the flashlight.

"Like I said, a shipping box. And any packing material that may have been stuffed inside."

"Why?" He snapped his light on and began to poke through the debris.

"If we find it, we can send it to a lab and have it tested."

"For drugs?" Drayton said.

"That would be the general idea," Theodosia said.

"Okay, I see some brown wrapping paper."

"Excellent. And I just spotted the corner of a FedEx box. It's wet and a little crumpled, so I need to kind of ease it out . . ." There was a squishing sound and then a limp FedEx box sailed out of the dumpster and into the alley. It landed with a hard splat at Drayton's feet, spraying droplets onto his shoes and slacks.

"Cleanup on aisle three," Drayton said.

"Look at the return address. Does it say San Lorenzo?" Theodosia asked.

Drayton bent forward and jabbed at it gingerly. "It says San Loren. The rest of the word is missing."

"Which means we found the right box," Theodosia cried as she climbed back out of the dumpster.

"You're really going to have this tested?"

"Sure."

"You're going to ask Riley to haul a pile of stinky garbage into the police forensics lab? Where they will drop everything and test for drugs?"

"Hmm. That might be a bit awkward." Theodosia thought for a few moments. "Tell you what, we'll shove it in a plastic garbage bag and tuck it away for safekeeping. Then, if the police start to focus on Nardwell, we can introduce the box as evidence. You know, to help seal the deal."

"Where exactly do you intend to store this magnificent trove of evidence?"

"In your garage?"

"Because I have so much extra room?"

"Mostly because you don't have a car," Theodosia said.

"My stars," Drayton said. "I've been shanghaied again." He gazed down at his shoes. "And all I have to show for tonight's work is a spatter of red sauce on my loafers. Honestly, your Mr. Nardwell eats meatball sandwiches for *lunch*?"

"Not everyone can have a refined palate like yours, Drayton."

"Is that a jab?" Drayton asked. "On the surface it sounds like a compliment, but it's really a jab, isn't it?"

"No, Drayton," Theodosia said. "It's simply the truth."

Theodosia was still keyed up when she arrived home, so she changed into a sweatshirt, leggings, and tennis shoes. Then she snapped a leash on an excited Earl Grey and headed out for a run.

They jogged down Meeting Street for about four blocks, taking it easy, warming up, blowing out the carbon. At Water Street, Theodosia and Earl Grey turned left and picked up the pace. They sprinted past the Old Market, which was closed for the night, danced past Rainbow Row, and then ran down a block where several of the homes dated back to the Colonial period. Theodosia loved the fact that Charleston, with its historic homes, churches, civic buildings, parks, and narrow alleyways, was basically a living museum. In fact, almost every other building she passed had some sort of commemorative plaque.

Including Philadelphia Alley, one of Theodosia's favorite places.

Dark, secretive, and lined with row houses, the alley dated back to 1776 and had once been called Cow's Alley. Probably because cows had originally grazed there.

Stepping lightly down the narrow alley, Theodosia was mindful of the cobblestones underfoot, stucco walls, hidden doorways, and lush canopy of trees overhead.

Wind chimes sang faintly, and there was a smoky aroma in the air, as if someone might be grilling a late supper in one of the walled gardens.

Smells good. Reminds me that I haven't eaten yet.

Just past a towering wall of bricks that had been stained terra-cotta red, Theodosia turned a corner.

And there they were. Two dark shapes. Quick, furtive, moving fast in her direction.

Meaning to harm me?

Theodosia had a smart, instant-flash-to-the-brain reaction. She turned, tugged on her dog's leash, and started to run.

Earl Grey had other ideas.

Instead of fleeing alongside Theodosia, he dug in his heels and spun around, ripping the leash clean out of her hands. A low growl rose from his throat as he lowered his head and lunged at the two shadowy figures. It was an aggressive move, clearly out of character for the normally docile Earl Grey. But he'd been startled badly, just as his dear human had.

"Earl Grey!" Theodosia cried. She skidded to a stop, turned to look back over her shoulder, and shouted, "Earl Grey, come!"

But no.

Confronted by the snarling, aggressive dog, the two figures were suddenly in full retreat. They started down the dark street, Earl Grey hot on their heels and gaining with every step. Seconds later, the dog's haunches bunched and he launched himself at one of the figures. Snapping his jaws hard like an angry crocodile, he found purchase on their right pants leg, just below the knee. As Earl Grey pulled the figure to a screeching, skidding halt, he spun them around in a frenzied half circle and chomped down hard.

Whoever he'd grabbed did a crazy, frantic, one-legged dance, trying desperately to shake Earl Grey off. All the time making a high-pitched *ee-ee-ee* sound. Dog and figure spun wildly, tangling for another few seconds, then Earl Grey released his grip and ran back to Theodosia.

"Good boy," she said, grabbing his leash and giving him a well-deserved pat on the shoulder. "Good guard dog." She wondered if the two mysterious figures—they were gone now, disappeared down the block—had intended to harm her. Could they have been shadowing her? Or were they opportunistic muggers simply looking for an easy target?

In either case, they were stupid, she decided. *Especially since I had a dog with me. A good guard dog who will always protect me.* Then she stood up, gave her dog another pat, and headed for home.

Coming up her back alley, just breezing along now, she was surprised to see lights on in the mansion next door to her. She knew the lawyer who owned it hadn't returned from England yet, so maybe the property had been leased to someone else? Theodosia hoped that wasn't the case. She didn't want to deal with any more crazy neighbors.

Or any crazy street drama.

Home again, doors securely locked, Theodosia felt both tired and a little revved up from her strange adventure. She grabbed an apple, a hunk of Swiss cheese, and a bottle of Fiji water out of the fridge and went upstairs while Earl Grey lapped thirstily from his dog bowl.

Post shower and snack, Theodosia changed into a snuggly nightgown and thought about the two muggers again. Had they been waiting for her? Or had they been a couple of tweakers out to try and grab some fast cash? It had been so dark she really hadn't gotten a good look at them. Too bad.

Sighing, putting them out of her mind, Theodosia turned and surveyed her bedroom suite. She'd been thinking about changing the lighting. Maybe get a slightly stronger floor lamp for her reading alcove and switch out the two small lamps on her dresser for something more elegant. She'd seen a pair of Chinese ginger jar lamps in an antique shop on King Street a week ago. They might be just the ticket. But only if she could afford them.

Flopping onto her bed, Theodosia grabbed her laptop and checked her e-mail. There wasn't much. A notice from her Jeep dealership for twenty bucks off an oil change, a note from a tea shop in Beaufort saying they wanted to reorder some of Drayton's house blends, and an invitation to a show of miniature portraits at the Gibbes Museum of Art.

And one e-mail from an address she didn't recognize.

Curious, she clicked on that one and frowned as a weird graphic appeared on her screen. A red swirl—a kind of whirlpool—that spun around then suddenly dissolved into hundreds of tiny pixels to reveal . . .

My face? What is this?

It was a photo of her face all right, staring directly out at her.

And, bizarrely, it had been superimposed on a tiny, cartoonlike body. The little arms waved helplessly as arrows suddenly appeared out of nowhere and flew at her, piercing her body, her head, her eyes. It was a terrifying image but fascinating at the same time. Theodosia couldn't look away; it was as if she were a mongoose being taunted and hypnotized by a wily cobra.

Why was this happening? Who would send her a video like this?

Could it be Nadine's killer? Teasing me? Once again warning me to back off? Had it been sent by the two people who accosted me tonight?

She studied the video again. Putting something like that together demanded some technical skills.

Theodosia's first thought was Eddie Fox. After all, he had the cameras, computers, studio, and all the film and video know-how in the world. He could have knocked out this piece of crap in about five minutes flat. Of course, so could any computer-savvy teenager.

Really, she wondered, was Fox trying to taunt her? Enrage her? Did that mean that Fox had killed Nadine? And now that she was hot on his trail, getting dangerously close to exposing him, had he suddenly decided to up the ante and play a game of cat and mouse?

Theodosia pushed her laptop aside and flopped against her pile of pillows. Or was it someone else?

She thought about the possibilities, mulled them around every which way she could imagine. Marvin Chauvet? Harvey Bateman? Or how about Mark Devlin? He was a talented designer. Maybe he knew how to bang out a down and dirty animation and send it to her.

Send it to me. Where did this rotten thing come from, anyway?

She hunted around, trying to determine the sender's address, but it was no use. Probably, she decided, the sender had been tricky and used a resender. Or maybe even two of them. Possibly a resender that was offshore. If that was the case, there wasn't a snowball's chance in hell that she could ever trace it.

Doggone. This is too crazy for words. No, it's actually spooky-dangerous.

Theodosia slipped under the covers, still thinking, worrying, about the people in the alley and the weird e-mail that had slithered its way into her nice, neat life. Finally, she turned off the light, closed her eyes, and decided this was something better faced in the cold, clear light of day.

But it was a long time before she was able to fall asleep. And even then her dreams were troubled.

19

❧

"I got the weirdest e-mail last night," Theodosia said to Drayton. It was Thursday morning at the Indigo Tea Shop and they were buzzing about, setting up for another busy day. Haley was rattling pans in the kitchen as teakettles whistled and burped out hot puffs of steam.

"What?" Drayton said as he measured scoops of orange pekoe into a blue-glazed teapot. "A missive from Delaine?"

"No, not from Delaine. It was a strange, almost threatening video."

"Almost threatening?"

"Okay, threatening, it *was* threatening. In fact, maybe I should show it to you."

Drayton looked up, brows beetled together. "Now?"

"If you could."

Fussing under his breath about all the things he needed to do, Drayton followed Theodosia back to her office. He plopped down in her desk chair while she picked through her e-mails, then played the video for him. When it was done—the video lasted only ten or twelve seconds at most—Drayton leaned back and said, "Creepy."

"Still, production values aren't that terrible, so I wondered . . ."

"What?" Drayton spun around to face her. "You think you know who sent it?"

"My initial thought was Eddie Fox. Just because he knows his way around cameras, filmmaking, and the Internet."

"If you're right, then he's warning you to back off the investigation."

"If he's warning me, then he's probably guilty," Theodosia said. "Play it again, will you?"

Theodosia played it again.

"Whew," Drayton said. "It is awfully menacing. Do you intend to show this to Riley?"

"Are you serious? If he knew there was an active threat against me, he'd handcuff me and ship me to Outer Mongolia where no one would find me in a million years."

"Better the Canary Islands," Drayton said. "I watched a PBS film about them and, let me tell you, those puppies are remote."

"I'll keep that in mind," Theodosia said. "Just in case." She wondered if she should tell Drayton about the two figures that had popped out at her last night. No, maybe not. If she told him, then he might really get worried and spill the beans to Riley. Then where would she be?

"So what are you going to do about this . . . this crazy e-mail thing?" Drayton flipped a hand at the computer screen.

Theodosia shook her head. "I don't know. Maybe see if I can figure out how to trace it."

"Is that doable?"

"Not for me. I'm not that computer savvy. But I might know someone who could."

"But maybe you don't want to know," Drayton said. "Or shouldn't know. Maybe this investigation is too much of a hot potato and you—really, the both of us—should bow out."

"I hear you. But . . ."

"Yes?"

"We made a promise to Bettina."

Drayton's shoulders collapsed. "There is that."

They went back to work then, setting tables, brewing tea, huddling with Haley over her morning offerings (which turned out to be English crumpets, apple bread, and cinnamon muffins) as well as her menu for today's Irish Cream Tea.

Customers came and went, Miss Dimple arrived at ten, and Theodosia continued to puzzle over the e-mail even as she chatted away, acting as if she didn't have a care in the world. Though she had many.

"I have a question," Miss Dimple said.

Theodosia was standing at the counter, waiting for a pot of Formosa oolong from Drayton. She turned to the diminutive Miss Dimple and said, "Yes?"

"When you say elevenses, what exactly do you mean by that?"

"Drayton," Theodosia said. "Do you want to address Miss Dimple's question?"

Drayton pushed his slightly steamed-up glasses onto his nose and said, "In the UK, elevenses is a term for a midmorning tea break, sometimes thought of as a second breakfast that's enjoyed around ten thirty or eleven."

"Kind of like what we're doing here," Miss Dimple said. "Like a morning cream tea."

"That's it exactly." Drayton smiled, as if he'd just thought of something else. "And if you think back to your Paddington Bear stories, you'll remember that Paddington often took his elevenses at an antique shop on Portobello Road run by his friend Mr. Gruber."

"I *do* remember that," Miss Dimple said. "I loved those stories. And I love all the marvelous tea lore that you folks dole out. Working here is so fun and enlightening."

"Of course it is," Drayton said as he turned back to his tea brewing. "Now, I must focus."

"Oh," Miss Dimple said.

"Don't mind him," Theodosia said. "Drayton's starting to edge into panic mode. He gets that way every time we have an event tea. Between you and me, I think he enjoys it." She stuck her hand in her pocket, found the tiny spring she'd picked up last night, and set it on the counter. Something to ask Haley about later.

"Me panic? No way," Drayton said.

"Drayton," Miss Dimple said. "You need to learn the fine art of chilling out. Especially since event teas seem to be your stock-in-trade."

"People," Drayton said. "We need to be *working.*"

By the time eleven thirty rolled around, the Indigo Tea Shop was practically empty. Morning customers had come and gone, which meant Theodosia could kick it into high gear and get everything set for their Irish Cream Tea.

"So the white linens with the green shamrocks, right?" Miss Dimple said as she pulled them out of the cupboard.

"Works for me," Theodosia said.

"And we've got a full house today?"

"We had six unsold seats at nine this morning, then we got a couple of last-minute calls, so now we're completely booked."

"The luck of the Irish," Miss Dimple joked.

"Whatever it is," Theodosia said, "I'm happy for it."

She went to her cupboard, surveyed her various sets of dishes, and pulled out the Irish Rose pattern by Donegal Parian.

"That's such a sweet pattern," Miss Dimple said.

"I just hope we have enough plates."

"Let's do a quick count."

Turns out they made it. With two plates left over.

"Whew," Miss Dimple said. "That was close." She surveyed the tables carefully and said, "The Gorham silver pattern you chose is wonderful. So shiny and elegant. Now . . . what else?"

"We can't have a proper Irish Cream Tea without a few more touches of Ireland," Theodosia said. "So I took the liberty of ordering a few stems of genuine bells of Ireland from Floradora. Which I think will look perfect in our Belleek porcelain vases."

Miss Dimple snapped her fingers. "I'm on it."

But Theodosia wasn't finished yet. She also added white pillar candles to the tables along with several ceramic sheep, Irish harps, and shamrocks.

"The tables look adorable," Miss Dimple said when she came back with her carefully arranged flowers. Are you also going to do that extra fun thing where you put out favors for your guests?"

Theodosia dug into a brown paper sack, came out with a handful of gold-wrapped chocolate coins, and tossed them onto the tables.

"Like a pot of gold at the end of a rainbow," Miss Dimple exclaimed. "Your guests are going to be charmed."

And charmed they were. A gaggle of ladies wearing hats and gloves began showing up at ten minutes to twelve, looking happy and expectant. Then cooed as soon as they stepped into the tea room and saw how adorable it looked, how terribly authentic everything was.

Theodosia continued to greet everyone at the front door, then handed them off to Miss Dimple who led them to their seats. There was a brief flurry as two entire tables were taken up by

Mable Price, president of the Broad Street Flower Society, along with eleven of her membership. Then there were the regulars and a few first-time guests as well.

Both Delaine and Echo Grace showed up, Delaine in a kelly green skirt suit with a white blouse and flouncy bow. Echo wore a shimmery beaded top with flowing slacks in colors that seemed to change from peach to orange and back to peach again. Like a delicious rainbow.

"I can't believe you're here today," Theodosia said to Delaine. "Especially since your big fashion show is happening later this afternoon."

"Yes, yes, well, the show's producer basically kicked me out of my own shop." Delaine shrugged. "There wasn't all that much for me to do since I know next to nothing about lighting, sound, or constructing runways."

"Except to put in your two cents' worth," Echo joked.

"Obviously," Delaine said.

Drayton hurried over to greet them both. "So nice to see you ladies," he said as Delaine stepped forward, grabbed him by his lapel, and administered a quick series of air-kisses. Then he pulled back and said, "Delaine, you seem to be feeling some better."

Delaine wrinkled her nose. "You know me, I'm not one to dwell on the dreary things in life."

"How's Bettina doing?" Theodosia asked. She knew Delaine didn't like being reminded of death, but figured Bettina was still plenty heartsick.

"She's okay, I guess," Delaine said. Then her shoulders stiffened and her eyes turned wary. "I suppose you're still looking into things?" She'd pronounced the word *things* in a disgusted tone of voice as if she were referring to dung beetles.

"I am. But it's kind of slow going," Theodosia said.

Delaine pulled a lipstick from her handbag and dib-dabbed a

swath of carnelian red across her lips. "I'm not surprised." She clicked the lid back on, then said in a quiet voice, "I sincerely hope you don't rock the boat too much."

"By that you mean . . . ?"

"Coming to the show today and pestering Harv and Marv with lots of silly questions when this is their *big* day." Delaine's right eyebrow rose and quivered. "After all, you wouldn't want to endanger *my* position as brand ambassador, would you?"

"Perish the thought," Theodosia said, which made Echo grin.

"Frankly, I think it's wonderful that you're looking into Nadine's murder," Echo said to Theodosia. She nudged Delaine and said, "You've got a real friend in Theodosia." Then to Theodosia again: "I hope you keep at it. I hope you break this case wide open."

"Believe me, there's nothing I'd like better," Theodosia said.

"Well, you *are* talking to just about *everyone*," Delaine said.

"Not quite. I'm having trouble getting a handle on Harvey Bateman," Theodosia said. "He's the one guy I haven't been able to have a conversation with."

"From what I've heard, Bateman's quite the entrepreneur," Echo said. "Besides being a partner in Lemon Squeeze Couture, he buys and sells overstock and remaindered clothing and also has something to do with a liquor wholesale business."

"Really," Theodosia said as the two women moved off. *Liquor business.* For some reason, that struck a chord with her. She remembered Simon Nardwell's comment the other day about Nadine's murder reminding him of a gangland killing. And wondered—was Bateman involved in organized crime? Was he the one wild card she should be watching closely?

Theodosia mulled over the idea as she welcomed her next couple of guests. Then she shook off her worries and forced herself back to the here and now. She could think about stupid Harvey Bateman *after* the Irish Cream Tea.

With renewed enthusiasm Theodosia greeted a lovely-looking blond woman in her mid-forties who was dressed in a snappy tweed jacket and caramel-colored leather pants.

Interestingly, the woman grabbed Theodosia's hand and said, "You don't know me, but your tea shop comes highly recommended."

"Thank you, that's wonderful to hear," Theodosia responded.

Then the woman gave a warm smile and said, "I'm Meriam Chauvet. The owner of Chauvet's Smartwear."

"Marvin Chauvet's wife," Theodosia said, a little surprised.

"Something like that, yes," Meriam said, a hint of mischief in her voice.

Theodosia was momentarily at a loss for words. Then she recovered and said, "Welcome. We're delighted to have you join us today."

Meriam Chauvet gestured at two women who were standing behind her. "And I brought along a couple of friends as well."

"The more the merrier," Theodosia said, telling herself she just *had* to have a few words later on with Meriam Chauvet.

20

When all their guests had settled in their places, when Drayton and Miss Dimple had served up steaming cups of tea, Theodosia stood in the middle of the tea shop and welcomed their guests.

"It's lovely to see all of you today for our springtime Irish Cream Tea—and I do thank you for coming. Since you're probably eager for lunch—and to see what our chef has dreamed up—I'm delighted to give you the rundown."

There was a spatter of applause and then Theodosia continued.

"Today's luncheon will begin with Irish soda scones served with Irish creamery butter and your choice of strawberry preserves or orange marmalade. The scones will be followed by a bowl of house-made potato-leek soup. For our main course, we'll be serving baked brown sugar salmon with sides of caramelized asparagus and heritage tomato salad. And the tea you're sipping right now is Irish Breakfast Tea from Simpson and Vail."

Drayton stepped in next to her. "And I'll be ready with as many refills as you'd like," he said.

"Of course there's dessert," Theodosia said.

"Which for now shall remain a surprise," Drayton said.

"So please enjoy your luncheon and we bid you *slainte*," Theodosia said. "Which means good health!"

The luncheon went off without a hitch. The scones were oohed and aahed over, soup spoons scraped soup bowls clean, and the brown sugar salmon elicited almost a dozen requests for the recipe. Thrilled by its popularity, Theodosia ducked into her office and printed out the recipe. With a stack of copies, she delivered them into eager, outstretched hands.

As Theodosia made her way around the tables pouring refills, Meriam Chauvet turned to her and said, "Everything has been wonderful. And your staff is so genteel and precise."

"We try to create a relaxed, flawless experience for our guests," Theodosia said.

"I wish we could do the same at our store. Unfortunately, staffing always seems problematic. It's difficult to find people who understand retail as well as know how to build customer relationships."

Theodosia took a chance and said, "Have you ever thought about hiring Julie Eiden?"

Mrs. Chauvet gave her a curious look. "Who's that?"

"Julie's an unpaid intern who works at Lemon Squeeze Couture right now. But I happen to know she's looking for a full-time paid position. She's young, smart, and knows her way around fashion."

"Sounds as if you think highly of her."

"I've only met Julie a few times, but she kind of oozes common sense. Fashion sense, too."

"If I stole this young woman away from Marvin, he'd be completely unhinged." Meriam tapped a manicured finger against her lower lip as a smile spread across her face. "It would be absolutely delicious."

"There you go," Theodosia said. "You can solve your staffing problem and tweak your husband all in one fell swoop."

Dessert was served with fanfare. Drayton carried out an Irish apple cake and held it aloft, making sure everyone got a good look at it.

"What's that on top?" one woman cried.

"Streusel topping," Drayton said.

"I want to know what's *in* that cake," another guest asked.

"A lethal concoction of butter, cream, sugar, flour, eggs, apples, and oats," Drayton said. "Not to be outdone by the tangy custard sauce we're about to drizzle on top of it."

Anticipation ran high as the cake was whisked back into the kitchen where Haley had two more Irish apple cakes waiting. When all the pieces were cut, plated, and judiciously sauced, they were delivered to the guests, who dug into their desserts with gusto.

As Theodosia made the rounds, refilling teacups, Drayton commanded everyone's attention by doing a recitation of an Irish poem:

When Irish stew is bubbling and the soda bread is hot
And the Irish tea is steeping in a little Irish pot,
When the room is warm with laughter
And the songs are bright and bold
And there's poetry and magic in the stories that are told,
Isn't it a blessing, isn't it just grand
To know the heart and soul of you belongs to Ireland.

Applause rang out with such exuberance that Drayton's face flushed bright pink. Then he took a quick bow and exited stage left.

It was the perfect ending to a perfect tea luncheon. But, of course, the guests didn't just jump up from their chairs and skedaddle. They circled through the tea shop, greeting friends and shopping their little hearts out. Grabbed tea towels, tins of loose tea, jars of honey, and everything else that was fun and tea related.

Surprise, surprise, even two of Theodosia's grapevine wreaths were snatched off the wall and sold. One wreath decorated with miniature pink teacups and woven with pink ribbons and pink straw flowers, the other a much larger wreath with full-sized teacups, silk flowers, curling ribbons, and small silver tea charms.

"I'd say this has been a wildly successful event for us," Drayton said to Theodosia. They were both standing behind the counter, he tallying up final bills and cashing out the last of the customers, she securing a bone china teacup in Bubble Wrap.

"Anytime we have an event tea it helps fluff the bottom line," Theodosia said.

"Well, consider it fluffed to the tune of more than eleven hundred dollars. I know we have to minus out food costs and overhead, but still . . ."

Theodosia squeezed his arm as she snicked past him. "Still . . . it's darn good business."

Headed back to her office, Theodosia had a bee in her bonnet and an idea whirring in her brain. Ever since Echo had mentioned Harvey Bateman's involvement as a liquor wholesaler, she'd been even more curious about him. And even though curiosity had killed the proverbial cat, Theodosia was generally in the mood to take a few risks. So she dialed Riley's number, hoping to entice him into giving her a small assist.

After their opening hey-how-are-you's, Theodosia got right to the point.

"You know I've been snooping around, asking questions about the Lemon Squeeze Couture partners, right?" she said.

"I'd rather not know what you're doing behind Sheriff Burney's back," Riley said. "Whatever it is, it's probably illegal."

Theodosia took a deep breath and continued. "The thing is, I've come across some information concerning Harvey Bateman."

There was silence for a few moments, then Riley said, "What would that be?"

"I learned that Bateman has his sticky fingers in the wholesale liquor business."

"And you want to know—what?" Riley asked.

"Whether it's true or not," Theodosia said.

There were a few more seconds of silence where Theodosia swore she could hear Riley's wheels turning.

Finally, he said, "I suppose it wouldn't hurt to check. I've got a buddy in the OC division, so let me see what dirt I can dig up and call you back."

"You're the best," Theodosia said.

"No, Theo, this is no ordinary gimme," Riley said in a faux-serious voice. "For this information you're going to owe me big-time. I'm talking a fancy dinner featuring your famous pork tenderloin with Carolina Reaper sausage and mustard sauce. And a good bottle of wine to cap it off."

"Okay. Deal."

Back in the tea shop, Theodosia grabbed a plastic tub and began clearing dishes off tables.

"You don't have to do that," Miss Dimple said. "I can manage."

"I know you can. I just like to, you know, keep busy."

Miss Dimple smiled. "I've noticed that."

Five minutes later, true to his word, Riley called back.

"What did you find out?" Theodosia asked. "Does Bateman have a record?"

"Well, you were right," Riley said, though he didn't sound particularly happy about it. "I don't know how you figured this out—and I probably don't want to know—but Harvey Bateman has been kind of a bad boy."

"Tell me," she said.

"He was arrested six years ago under the Interstate Commerce Act."

"What does that mean exactly?"

"Seems Bateman was caught bringing in a truckload of liquor that didn't have the appropriate paperwork and tax stamps. Uncle Sam frowns on that sort of thing, and the South Carolina Department of Revenue regards it as a major no-no."

"So what happened?"

"Bateman slipped out of it. He must have a damn good attorney because he's been able to get out of a few other things. Let's see, there was a fuzzy charge concerning guns, handguns not long guns, but the prosecutor dropped the charges because there wasn't enough evidence."

"Guns," Theodosia said. "That's kind of interesting. Why wasn't there enough evidence?"

"No witnesses, I guess," Riley said.

"No witnesses or witnesses afraid of reprisals?" Theodosia asked.

"I don't know. Listen, Theo, it looks as if this guy Bateman is one bad dude. Even though he claims to be in the fashion business now, which seems fairly benign, you don't want to go poking around him."

"I'll be careful, I promise."

"That's not the answer I want to hear," Riley said. When she didn't respond, he said, "I mean it. You need to stop any kind of investigation right now."

"Then will *you* look a little deeper into Bateman's activities?" Theodosia asked.

"Yes, I will."

"Promise?"

Riley sighed. "Theo, you're incorrigible."

"I know. Sorry."

"And don't forget about the pork tenderloin dinner you owe me."

"Dinner. Right."

"What was all that about?" Drayton asked as she hung up the phone.

"It seems Harvey Bateman has a record," Theodosia said.

"You mean a *criminal* record?" Drayton's brows rose like a pair of furry caterpillars. "What on earth did he do?"

"Something concerning illegal liquor and guns."

"Holy Hannah, that sounds serious."

"As if Nadine's murder wasn't serious enough?"

Drayton popped a lid off a tin of tea and said, "You know what I mean."

"Okay, sorry. I didn't mean to be snappy."

"No, that's okay. It shows that you care. That you're concerned. Just please don't be more concerned about others than you are about yourself."

"Words to live by," Theodosia said.

Miss Dimple sidled up to the counter and handed Theodosia a sheet pan stacked with strawberry scones. "Compliments of Haley. But do you think we'll get much of a crowd this afternoon for tea?"

"There are always a few folks who wander in," Theodosia said.

"Here's one now," Drayton said as the front door opened.

They all turned to watch as Bill Boyet sauntered in. He was the proprietor of Boyet's Camera Shop down the block and a semi-regular at the tea shop. Boyet was in his early fifties and husky, with pink cheeks and sparse white hair. Today he wore khaki slacks with a navy golf shirt tucked in.

With a big grin on his face, Boyet continued to the counter

and said, "Any plans to stage another one of your murder mystery teas? Because I'm happy to take a dive and play victim again."

"We're probably going to do another one real soon," Theodosia said. "Since our last one . . ."

"Murder at Chillingham Manor," Boyet filled in.

". . . was so popular," she finished.

"You even remembered the name," Drayton said.

"Because I had so much fun playing the dastardly Lord Bledsoe." When Drayton pursed his lips, Boyet said, "No, really, it was a blast. I never got to do playacting of that caliber before."

"Then we'll have to give you a starring role in our next production," Theodosia said as she began stacking scones in the glass pie saver.

Drayton poured out a cup of tea and slid it across the counter to Boyet. "Assam tea work for you?"

"Absolutely," Boyet said. He lifted his cup, took a hearty sip, and set it back down. "Good. Bracing." He slid his hand sideways, saw the metal spring sitting on the counter, and picked it up. "Which one of you is into drones?" he asked.

At which point Theodosia looked up from her scones and said, "*What?*"

21

❧

"Drones," Boyet said as he fingered the metal spring. "Because it's not every day you find a gimbal spring just lying around."

"What, pray tell, is a gimbal spring?" Theodosia asked. Her heart had skipped a beat, and she felt a tickle of anticipation. Was this a clue? Then she asked the all-important question. "You say it's a part from a drone?"

Boyet held the spring up between his thumb and forefinger. "Yup, it's small but critical because it helps stabilize the wings." He raised it to eye level. "You really didn't know?"

"We do now," Theodosia said. But her thoughts were firing on all eight cylinders. A drone, who used a drone? Had Eddie Fox mentioned shooting film with a drone?"

And now a semi-interesting connection had just tweaked her curiosity yet again. She'd discovered this gimbal spring in the cooler at Orchard House Inn. So did that mean Fox had been inside the cooler? Or had wandered around the inn? And if he had, was he the one who'd pulled the trigger on Nadine? And did that mean he was involved in some sort of cocaine deal? It felt like serious evidence was beginning to pile up.

Which is exactly what Theodosia said to Drayton once Bill Boyet had left.

Drayton was semi-amused. "Ten minutes ago you were hot for Harvey Bateman. Now you're back on the Eddie Fox bandwagon."

"I'm fairly sure that Eddie Fox used a drone when he shot that bird documentary."

"So you think *he* was the one who shot Nadine."

"Yes. Well, *maybe* yes. They were supposedly having some kind of affair. Maybe Nadine got too needy. Or . . ."

"Or what?" Drayton asked.

"Or something else happened?"

"Are you asking or telling?"

"I'm not sure."

Drayton poured a stream of hot water into a Brown Betty teapot, then pushed it across the counter to Miss Dimple. "The black currant tea for table five," he said. "But let it steep for at least three minutes." Then he turned back to Theodosia. "You're making this extravagant leap just because you found a teensy little metal part? A part that could have come from anywhere? That someone—even one of us—could have inadvertently kicked into the cooler?"

"The gimbal spring is like a clue," Theodosia said. "Well, not *like* a clue, it *is* a clue."

"If you say so. The question is, what do we do with it? How do we run with this?"

"I think we need to dig into Fox's business a whole lot more."

"How?"

"I don't know. But my hunch is we'd best pussyfoot around him. He's a fairly smart guy, and we don't want to tip him off."

"I'm of the mind that we should *confront* Fox head-on," Drayton said. "Go ahead and ask our probing questions and try to ascertain if he really does make use of a drone for filming."

"Because if he's clueless about drones, then he might not be our guy?"

"Right."

Theodosia thought for a few moments, then said, "We'll be seeing him at the Lemon Squeeze Couture show in about"—she looked at her watch—"an hour and a half."

"True, but Delaine's shop is going to be a madhouse and Fox is going to be busy. You can bet that Marvin Chauvet and Harvey Bateman will be riding him like a rented mule when it comes to filming the show."

"Maybe we could drop by Fox's studio tonight," Theodosia said, unwilling to let the subject drop.

"Might work if you can arrange it," Drayton said. But he didn't sound all that convinced.

Just as Theodosia was clearing dishes from the last table, Holly Burns from the Imago Gallery came bouncing in. She brushed back her mass of dark hair, sniffed the air, and seemed to find it most agreeable. Then she turned and gestured to a man who'd trailed her in.

"Holly," Theodosia said, "I'm afraid we're closing the shop in about fifteen minutes. But if you're okay with a fast cuppa and a scone, we can surely accommodate you."

Holly raised both hands and made scrubbing gestures in the air. "No, no. No tea is necessary. I came here with a request."

"And a guest," Drayton said, leaning across the counter and nodding at the man who'd accompanied Holly.

"Excuse my goofball manners," Holly said. "Theo, Drayton, this is Jeremy Slade. Jeremy, this is Theo, the tea lady I told you all about, and her tea sommelier, Drayton Conneley."

Jeremy Slade was tall and lean, with slicked-back dark hair, a long face, and flat gray eyes. He wore round John Lennon glasses that caught the light and was dressed from head to toe in black. He looked, Theodosia thought, like a hip funeral director.

Only he wasn't.

"Jeremy's my new partner," Holly burbled.

"Silent partner," Slade added. His voice was low, a little gravelly.

"Right," Holly said. "He's an art lover of the first magnitude . . . well, you tell them, Jeremy."

Jeremy Slade shrugged. "I have a double major in art history and economics from Columbia and an MBA from Wharton."

Holly grinned. "Pretty impressive, huh?"

"I'd say so," Drayton said.

"You said silent partner," Theodosia said.

"Jeremy is one of the brainy cofounders of Arcadia Software. But as a sideline, he's also decided to invest in the Imago Gallery, which has suddenly given us a healthy infusion of cash."

"Sounds like you plan to expand the gallery," Theodosia said.

"More like attract a higher caliber of artist," Slade said.

"And allow us to do more advertising and art openings," Holly added.

"Very enterprising," Drayton said.

"Anyway, to announce what we're internally calling Imago 2.0, I was wondering if you'd cater a tea for us," Holly said.

"We'd love to," Theodosia said, warming to the idea immediately. "Were you thinking of having it at the Imago Gallery or . . . ?"

"Not the gallery. Since the weather's so nice, I was thinking more of an outdoor event," Holly said.

"Maybe a park or hotel courtyard," Slade said.

Holly nodded. "Someplace where we can set up good-sized easels to showcase the work of our new artists. You know how in Paris there are all those wonderful artists who display their work down by the Seine?"

"Yes, I've seen that," Theodosia said.

"That's the vibe I'm looking for. Very Parisian."

Theodosia thought for a few moments. "Have either of you heard of Petigru Park?"

Holly and Slade both shook their heads.

"It's a fairly new park," Theodosia said. "Not far from the yacht club. The land was recently donated to the City of Charleston, and the Park Board has initiated a community beekeeping project there, along with a lovely chunk of parkland set aside for native grasses." She paused. "It's a gorgeous property and might just be the perfect venue for your event—if we can get a permit, that is."

"Petigru Park sounds fantastic," Holly said. She turned to Slade, her enthusiasm contagious. "Don't you think?"

"I think it's a fine idea," Slade said. "Unexpected, what you'd call out of the box."

"And the bees," Holly said. "I love that angle. We could actually do a beekeeping theme."

"I was thinking more like a honey theme, since it's going to be a tea party," Theodosia said. "We could serve honey cream scones, honeyed ice tea, that sort of thing."

"My dear, you are totally brilliant!" Holly cried.

"What's your timing on this?" Drayton asked. He'd already opened his notebook and had a pen in hand.

"I'm thinking maybe a month, month and a half from now?" Holly said.

Drayton jotted a note. "I do believe we can fit you in."

"Drayton!" Theodosia ripped off her apron and hastily slipped into a white knit jacket. "Come on. The Lemon Squeeze Couture show starts in, like, twenty minutes." She'd been running around like a crazy woman, arranging tables just so, sweeping the floor.

She liked to be ready for the next morning, which always seemed to arrive a little too early.

"Do we really have to go?" Drayton asked.

"Yes, we have to go. We promised Delaine. Besides, Bettina will be there. If anything, we have to show the flag for her."

Drayton's lips moved, producing a low grumble.

"Lately, whenever I mention Delaine's name, you say '*Do I have to?*'" Theodosia said.

"Do you have to what?" Haley asked as she came bopping out, dressed in jeans and a black leather jacket.

"Go to Delaine's show," Drayton said. He eyed Haley and said, "I think I'd rather go where she's going."

"On the back of a motorcycle?" Theodosia said. "With Haley's new boyfriend?"

"Oh. No," Drayton said, as a sudden throaty roar sounded out on the street.

"There's Ben now," Haley said as she scrambled out the front door. "Hey guys, have fun at the fashion show."

"Tell you what," Theodosia said to Drayton. "We'll get there late." She glanced at her watch. "Well, we're going to be ridiculously late as it is. And we'll try to leave early. How would that be? I mean, a fashion show can only last . . . what? Ten, fifteen minutes at best?"

"Please," Drayton said. "This is Delaine we're talking about."

They were fashionably late. Then again, so were all the other guests. As well as the show. The big event was scheduled to kick off promptly at four, but the lighting over the elevated white runway still wasn't perfect, the DJ had taken his own sweet time to show up, and there were electrical issues that had to do with too many power cords and overloaded circuits. Which meant Delaine's boutique was bursting at the seams with anxious fashionistas, press, photographers, invited dignitaries, special customers who expected (and demanded!) front-row seats, and a few fashion groupies who'd managed to sneak in without benefit of invitations.

Worse yet, they'd all been drinking. Delaine had twisted the arm of a wine merchant down the street and talked him into delivering thirty cases of white wine at cost. So now everyone was on their third glass, which ratcheted up the excitement, anticipation, and noise level even more.

"This is awful," Drayton said as he and Theodosia squeezed their way up to the bar.

"It's a fashion show," Theodosia said. "It's bound to be a little crazy and pretentious."

"Going to be tough to talk to anybody."

"Yes, it is."

Theodosia gazed over toward the runway where a stringy-haired blond guy was screaming loudly about his overhead lights. About how they weren't twirling or dimming or twinkling properly. Harv and Marv were trying to calm him down, though Harvey Bateman didn't look a bit calm himself. His face was beet red and he was pointing at Mark Devlin, the designer, who was also shaking his head.

And then there was Delaine.

She careened up to them on four-inch spiky heels and said, "Can you believe this? It's a madhouse!"

Drayton gave a commiserating nod as the bartender slid two drinks across the counter to him.

"Give me another one, too," Delaine said to the bartender. She wore a skintight turquoise jumpsuit with a sparkly line of trim down the arms and legs.

"Take it easy," Theodosia cautioned. "You've got to get on-stage later and do your thing."

"Please," Delaine said. "This is only my third drink."

"Fourth," the bartender said as he handed over her wine.

Delaine shrugged. "Whatever."

"How's Bettina?" Theodosia asked. "Where's Bettina?"

Delaine made a broad gesture, spilling some of her wine. "She's in back. Trying to hurry things along." Then she took a sip and pushed her way back through the crowd.

"I'm going to try and talk my way backstage," Theodosia said to Drayton. "To check on Bettina. Why don't you locate our seats?"

"I'll give it a shot," Drayton said. "But don't hold your breath."

Murmuring a string of "excuse me"s, Theodosia elbowed her way to the back of the store and poked her head around a black curtain. Luckily, Bettina was right there, talking to the show's producer, a short woman with spiky hair who was wearing a black nylon jumpsuit. She was also wearing a headset and talking to somebody named Nellie, while carrying on a cell phone conversation and consulting her clipboard.

Bettina saw Theodosia and waved her in. "Theo," she exclaimed. "You came!"

Theodosia gave Bettina a kiss on the cheek and said, "Of course I did." Then, "It looks as if you're up to your eyeballs in drama."

"We are," Bettina said.

The models were lounging around, blissfully talking on their phones while makeup artists tried to aim brushes at constantly moving heads. The producer began shouting at the top of her lungs, calling for someone named Beverly. And to top it all off, a guy with a box full of high heels was trying to find a pair that would fit each model's feet. Not an easy task.

"At least working on this show has kept me busy," Bettina said with a wistful expression.

"If it's any consolation, I'm still poking around and asking questions," Theodosia said.

"Do you think you're getting anywhere?"

"Still trying to narrow it down . . . but, yes, I think I might be."

"Then I'll keep praying," Bettina said. "Because I believe in you and really don't want justice to be an old-fashioned concept."

"It's not," Theodosia said. "Please hear me when I say I want justice for your mom as much as you do."

Bettina gazed at Theodosia with something akin to hope. "Even if the killer turns out to be someone close to us?"

Her words hardened Theodosia's resolve. "Especially if it turns out to be someone close to us."

22

Back out in the boutique, Theodosia elbowed her way through the chattering, jostling crowd. Even when there wasn't a fashion show going on, Cotton Duck was jam-packed with shoppers eager to pick up the latest and finest in clothing, lingerie, scarves, and jewelry. Today was no exception. Delaine and her assistant, Janine, had rolled the display racks into one corner and smooshed them all together. But that didn't deter anyone from shopping. The guests were having a field day, pulling out elegant gowns, looping on long strands of pearls, and exclaiming over a new crop of silk summer blouses that looked as gossamer as dragonfly wings.

Even Theodosia couldn't help noticing a green and gold ankle-length silk skirt printed with a tiger-in-the-jungle pattern.

Perfect with a sleeveless black top and black strappy heels.

But today was not the day for bumping up her wardrobe, she told herself as she stalked through the crowd, hunting for Eddie Fox and Harvey Bateman. When her search proved fruitless, she sighed, changed tactics, and headed for the grouping of white enamel folding chairs that had been set up on both sides of the runway.

She found Drayton occupying one of those chairs and guarding the one next to it with his life.

"I can't tell you how many people I've had to shoo away," were his first words to her. "I've gotten so many nasty looks I'm starting to feel like the Grinch."

"Sorry about that," Theodosia said as she sat down next to him.

Drayton turned and leaned toward her, a conspiratorial look on his face. "Did you get a chance to talk to Bateman? Or Fox?"

"I couldn't find either one, let alone get near them."

"Fox just set up five minutes ago. You see his camera gear hunkered there at the end of the runway?"

Theodosia leaned forward and looked. Yes, there he was. Fox was fiddling with a camera set on a tripod and talking to the stringy-haired lighting guy. Maybe things were finally set to go? She glanced at her watch. Time was slipping away. The fashion show had been delayed nearly forty minutes even though guests were now rushing to take their seats.

"Here," Drayton said, handing her a program. "I scored one of these for you."

Theodosia opened the program, read it, and . . . holy guacamole, there were forty different looks being shown today?

"Did you see this?" Her finger tapped the long list of fashions.

"Yes, and I can't believe there are that many variations on what they're calling athleisure clothing. I mean, once you get past a sweatshirt, sweatpants, and maybe a T-shirt, what more is there?"

"I think we're about to find out."

Theodosia watched as Mark Devlin peeked out from behind a shimmering silver curtain. He seemed satisfied that most everyone was finally seated and turned to whisper to someone behind him. Then the overhead lights dimmed and a murmur of excitement swept through the crowd. A voice rumbled over the speakers: "Ladies and gentlemen, please take your seats. The Lemon Squeeze Couture Fashion Show is about to begin."

There was a final scurry for the last seats, and the red, blue, and gold lights above the runway started to whirl. The sound system let out a loud crackle, then high-energy music boomed out.

It was Iggy Pop's "The Passenger," and Theodosia recognized the tune immediately. It was perfect for a fashion show. Exciting techno-rock with lots of hard edges. The models would have a blast walking to this up-tempo beat.

As the music thump-thumped, the first model burst out from behind the silver curtain and strutted her way down the runway, arms moving gracefully, hips swaying. She wore a glittery sequined hoodie, matching shorts, and blade sunglasses.

"You see," Theodosia whispered to Drayton, "there *are* variations on the sweatshirt theme."

The second model, dressed in a skintight neon green jumpsuit, popped out just as the first model hit the end of the runway and spun around in a gravity-defying turn. From then on it was nonstop fashion, music, and action. The Lemon Squeeze Couture line included jumpsuits, leggings, jackets, crop tops, joggers, anoraks, tank tops, and workout shorts. They were done in sequins, silks, neoprene, fleece, cotton, and all manner of stretchy fabrics. And the designs were good. Better than good. They were pieces that Theodosia herself would love to wear.

As the music segued to Nicki Minaj's "Pound the Alarm," Theodosia thought, *Maybe Delaine and her crew are onto something here. Maybe this is the next big thing. Or, rather, a bigger thing than athleisure already is.*

The final two looks brought the crowd to its feet. One was a poufy red silk anorak that, when unzipped, turned into a kind of cozy sleeping bag. The last piece was an ethereal white silk jacket with matching tank top and flowing pajama pants. Not for working out in, but definitely the epitome of luxe loungewear.

Then Harvey Bateman, Marvin Chauvet, Mark Devlin, and Delaine Dish appeared on the runway. They hugged one another, waved to the enthusiastic crowd, and put up high fives. The music rose to a crashing crescendo and a stream of models emerged, taking a final turn on the runway, then intermingling with the Lemon Squeeze Couture partners. It was a spectacle that looked like it was right out of New York or Paris Fashion Week.

"Goodness," Drayton said as the lights came up and the excited crowd began to shift from their chairs to the bar area, where servers waited with trays of appetizers and finger foods. "That was quite dramatic."

"Much better than I thought it would be," Theodosia said. She looked around, saw Julie Eiden, the intern, standing in the back of the room, along with Echo Grace, who gave a little finger wave. Theodosia waved back.

"This might be your one chance to talk to Eddie Fox," Drayton said. Fox was fussing with his camera, handing two flat black cartridges to someone, probably his assistant, and looking generally frazzled.

"I'll give it a shot." Theodosia brushed past a few people who were still seated, made her way to where Fox was standing, and said, "I know you're busy, but do you have a minute to talk?"

He stared at her. "What about?" he asked and turned away.

"It concerns . . ."

"No!" Fox said in an emphatic tone. "This is a bad time, a terrible time." He turned back to his assistant and said, "Bucky, you need to get those SD memory cards to Delta Labs ASAP. You got that? I have to start editing tomorrow."

Bucky nodded back. "Delta. Righto." He opened a camo messenger bag and tucked them inside.

"Mr. Fox," Theodosia tried again.

His eyes rolled toward her. "I said no. I'm in deep doo-doo and now I gotta . . ." He shook his head in frustration, as if a cluster of bees were chasing after him, then hissed, "Why am I even *bothering* with you?"

"I don't know, why are you?" Theodosia asked, stung by his brusque words.

But Fox had turned back to Bucky again. "Guard those cards with your life," he warned. "Or heads will roll."

"He's gone!" Theodosia exclaimed to Drayton when she finally located him some ten minutes later. He'd just munched a piece of shrimp toast and had a cheese-topped cracker in his hand. "I caught Fox's attention, practically begged him to talk to me, and he completely blew me off. Two seconds later he disappeared into the crowd—poof—like some kind of unfriendly ghost."

"He didn't want to talk to you," Drayton said. "Or maybe he was ferociously busy. Maybe he's double-booked or something. Here, have an appetizer. They're excellent." He reached out and grabbed another shrimp toast off the tray of a passing waiter.

"No, it was a snub. I know a direct snub when I see it."

"Not much you can do about it now."

"Oh yes, there is." Theodosia whipped out her cell phone.

"You're going to call him?"

"At his studio, sure."

"He's probably not there yet. Better give him ten minutes or so."

Theodosia fumed, drank a glass of wine, nibbled a few more appetizers, and waited nervously as they were jostled about by the crowd. When she couldn't hold out any longer, she dialed Fox's studio number.

"I'm calling Fox's office," she told Drayton, "to see if we can go over there and try to catch him. Pin his ears back."

A woman answered on the first ring. "Studio," she said in a cheery voice.

"Excuse me," Theodosia said. "I'm trying to get hold of Eddie Fox?"

"You found him. Well, you almost did. Foxfire Productions and Scot Shot Photography share this space. I'm Josie, studio manager for both companies. How can I help you?"

"I need to speak with Eddie Fox. It seems I just missed him at the Lemon Squeeze Couture show. He went flying out of here as soon as he was done filming."

"I can believe that because Eddie ran into the studio, like two seconds ago, then bounced right back out again. Said he had to shoot a spot for Granite Bank—a TV spot—then go scout a location. He's apparently on the lookout for some special type of house."

"Can you tell me where I might find him? It's important I get in touch with him immediately."

"Let's see, I have that information here somewhere." Papers rustled, then Josie was back on the line. "Here it is. He'll be at EmCom for the Granite Bank shoot, then checking out a house just off the Maybank Highway. 1120 Turnbull Road to be exact. But that's not till later. It's kind of a long haul, so I doubt you'd want to meet up with him there. I'm sure Eddie will be back in the studio tomorrow morning."

"I'll figure something out," Theodosia said. "Thank you."

"Now what?" Drayton asked as the after-party swirled around them.

"I just missed him. Now I have to call EmCom."

"What's an EmCom?"

"Emerson Communications. They're a production house and that's where Fox is directing a shoot."

"You think he'll come to the phone?"

"We'll find out."

But when Theodosia called EmCom and finally got someone on the line, she was told that Fox was there, but he was setting up and far too busy to talk.

"Who is this, please?" she asked.

"This is Brenda Dutton, one of the producers."

"I really need to get hold of Eddie Fox," Theodosia said.

"Then kindly do it on your own dime and not mine," Brenda said. "I'm already wrangling four actors, two dogs, a lighting company, and Fat Boyz Catering. Plus, I'll probably have to hold Eddie's hand and coach him on his shots. So goodbye." With that Brenda hung up.

Theodosia hung up, too, and turned to Drayton. "The woman in charge of Fox's shoot, the DP, the director-producer, sounded frantic. I hate to go barging in there . . . we probably wouldn't be welcome."

"What choice is there?"

"Fox is supposedly scouting a location afterward, but he wouldn't be there until nine at the earliest."

"You want to confront Fox while he's scouting a location?"

"I know it's a pain, but that way we'd have him all to ourselves. It'll be difficult for him to duck out."

"Where's this location?"

Theodosia consulted her hastily scribbled note. "Some historic home just off the Maybank Highway."

"And not until nine?" Drayton said. He rolled his eyes skyward, as if looking for divine intervention. When it didn't come, when angels didn't fly down to rescue him, he said, "That means we have a couple of hours to kill."

"We could do dinner," Theodosia said. "My treat. That's if you didn't fill up on appetizers."

"Not likely."

"So what would tickle your fancy?"

Without hesitation, Drayton said, "I'd kill for the crab cakes at Poogan's Porch."

"Done. I'll phone them right now and see if we can score a table on their patio."

23

There was barely a sliver of orange in the western sky when Theodosia and Drayton arrived at Poogan's Porch, one of Charleston's most storied restaurants. Located in an 1891 Victorian home at 72 Queen Street, the place wasn't just famous, it was rich in history. Not only had prominent families lived there, so had a ghost named Zoe and a dog named Poogan. Though to be fair, Poogan was more of a Southern porch dog who'd hung out around the neighborhood. But because he was such a favorite, Poogan's Porch was named in his honor. And, to this day, dogs were welcome in the outdoor dining areas.

But, of course, the real star at Poogan's Porch was the food. The menu was equally low-country cuisine and fine dining. Starters included fried green tomatoes, pimiento cheese fritters, and she-crab soup. Entrées included lump crab cakes, shrimp and grits, Poogan's fried chicken, and Atlantic salmon.

Theodosia dropped a linen napkin in her lap and looked across the table at Drayton as he studied the menu.

"What strikes your fancy tonight?" she asked. "Besides the crab cakes."

"I've changed my mind. I'm going to have the cornmeal fried pickled okra as my starter and the pan-seared scallops as my entrée." He snapped the menu down on the table. "Yes, that's it. How about you?"

"Still debating. No, I *do* know what I want. She-crab soup and the grilled grouper." She leaned back in her chair, enjoying the soft spring evening, flickering candles, dark sky overhead, and sea breeze riffling the nearby palmettos.

"All that seafood calls for a bottle of white wine, don't you think? Maybe the Covey Run Riesling or the Berthier Sancerre?"

"You're the wine expert," Theodosia said. "You choose."

Drayton picked up the wine list, scanned it, and said, "Definitely the Sancerre."

They ordered—food and wine—and when they were finally alone in their quiet, tucked-away spot, Theodosia said, "I feel like we keep running up against a brick wall."

"I hear you," Drayton said.

"Plus, I confess that I keep hop-skipping from suspect to suspect."

"Who wouldn't? They're all a bunch of pudding heads."

Which caused Theodosia to laugh out loud. And feel good about it. Experience a quick release of tension, almost as if she'd been holding her breath and now she could breathe deeply again.

"I know you're focused on Eddie Fox," Drayton said, "but he might not be the killer. What we should do is lay out our suspicions logically."

"Make a kind of list."

"Right. So let's start with Harvey Bateman. He's a mystery man, the one we know least about."

"But we do know that Bateman has a sort-of criminal record," Theodosia said. "And that he's the money man in the Lemon

Squeeze organization so he's obviously got some smarts. After all, he's the one responsible for instituting key partner insurance."

Drayton held up a finger. "And will probably *collect* on it because of Nadine's passing."

"Unless there's some sort of suspicious death clause."

"And Marvin Chauvet?" Drayton said.

"He's kind of an odd duck. The impression I get is that he's separated from his wife, but not divorced. Or maybe they have one of those freewheeling marriages where they each go their own way and do their own thing."

"Do you really believe that?"

"Not for an instant," Theodosia said.

"And Eddie Fox?"

"We're going to deal with him later tonight," Theodosia said. "Talk to him, find out if he ever makes use of a drone while filming."

"The gimbal spring. I'd almost forgotten about that."

They both paused as the server brought their wine, uncorked it with a flourish, and filled their glasses.

"Thank you," Drayton said. He took a sip, gave a small pucker, and said, "Good. Needs to breathe a tad, but we've got time."

"We can't forget about Simon Nardwell," Theodosia said. "Like I told you before, he could be crying crocodile tears."

"What reason would he have to murder Nadine?"

Theodosia took a sip of wine and looked over her glass at Drayton. "Because she kicked him to the curb? Because he was angry at her?"

"The old 'hell hath no fury' argument." Drayton cocked his head to one side. "It's a possibility."

"And then there's Mark Devlin."

"The designer, a man who looks down his nose at his employers and believes he should be the one in charge. Wants to be the big kahuna."

"But you find that dynamic in almost every company," Theodosia said. "There's always one jerk who thinks he's *da bomb.*"

They chuckled as their waitperson set their starters in front of them.

Drayton picked up his knife and fork, took a bite of fried okra and said, "The wild card in all this is the young intern."

"Julie Eiden."

"The girl Nadine was so cruel to." Drayton took another bite and said, "This is all rather complicated. There are lots of little permutations here and there, reasons why someone would want to be rid of Nadine, but nothing major stands out."

"And there's a dope deal to figure in as well," Theodosia said as she took a spoonful of she-crab soup. "It's kind of like disarming a bomb. You snip the wrong wire and it all explodes."

"Heaven forbid," Drayton said.

When they finished their starters, when the rest of their dinner arrived, they made a point of not talking about murder or mayhem or angry people. Tried to enjoy this lovely respite where faint murmurs of conversation drifted in like distant radio signals, where crystal glasses clinked softly and thousands of white twinkle lights strung on the facade of Poogan's Porch sparkled like fireflies in the night.

A perfect evening. Almost.

The drive out Maybank Highway was almost relaxing. They crossed any number of bridges, then zoomed through rolling hills and fields where many of the old rice and indigo plantations had been replaced by new plantation-style homes. Farther out, the Maybank Highway became a two-lane ribbon as they drove through pine forests and swampland, and passed in sight of the Charleston Tea Plantation. It was dark out here with fewer homes and farms.

In places where the narrow road dipped, ground fog swirled in their headlights, adding a spooky, mournful touch.

When Theodosia knew she was getting close, she drove with one eye on the road and one on her iPhone.

"Okay, keep a look out now. Pretty soon we need to make a right turn onto Katy Hill Road."

"We just passed Bear Bluff Road a mile back," Drayton said.

"Then we have a ways to go yet."

"Nice out here," Drayton said. "Open space and room to breathe." He settled back against the seat. "Don't get me wrong—I love Charleston. It's the best city in the entire world."

"Better than Amsterdam? Better than Shanghai?" Drayton had worked in both cities in the tea industry and always spoke fondly of them.

"Oh my, yes," he said. "Charleston is home. What was it Robert Frost said about going home?"

"Don't quote me on this, but I think it was something like 'Home is the place where, when you have to go there, they have to take you in.'"

"That's precisely how I feel about Charleston. It has a warm, welcoming feeling as well as a pulse to it. Yes, we sometimes move slowly, but gracefully so. And there are still a few hidebound traditions, but all in all, we're getting more flexible."

"Don't forget manners," Theodosia pointed out. "We're known for our manners."

"Which will never go out of style, and thank goodness for that. Say, I think this might be our turn up ahead."

Theodosia put her foot on the brake and coasted along. "Can you read the sign? What's it say?"

Drayton squinted at a metal sign that was canted on top of a tall pole. "Katy Hill Road."

"Bingo." Theodosia slowed down and made a right turn.

"Now what?"

"Now we have to find Turnbull Road," she said. "And then 1120 Turnbull Road."

They drove along slowly, tires hissing against the blacktop.

"It's very agricultural out here," Drayton said. "Lots of corn."

"Here we go," Theodosia said. "Here's Turnbull." They hung another right and found themselves on a dirt road. They bumped along for a mile, then two miles, with not a single house in sight.

"This is the back of nowhere," Drayton said.

"Feels like it, anyway."

"Wait, there's something ahead."

"A mailbox," Theodosia said.

It was a dinged-up metal mailbox with peeling numbers. But they were the exact numbers they were looking for.

"Looks like somebody took a potshot at it," Drayton said. "Some good old boys out making mischief."

Theodosia turned down a narrow driveway shadowed by tall, dark pine trees, listening to gravel crunch beneath her tires.

"Sure is dark out here," Drayton said.

"And lonely," Theodosia said.

"No lights on anywhere. But I do see an outline of a house up ahead."

When they finally rolled to a stop, Theodosia said, "No car. I don't think Fox is here yet."

"Or maybe he's come and gone."

"Unlikely," Theodosia said. "In my experience, TV shoots always run late."

"If and when he shows up, he's not going to be happy."

"Too bad. Those are the breaks."

Drayton looked around. "So we just cool our heels and wait for him?"

Theodosia reached over and grabbed a flashlight from the

glove box. "Well, we could get out and take a look around. See what's so special about this place that puts it on a location shoot list."

"That's a thing? A location shoot list?"

"It is."

They climbed out of the Jeep and stood under a sweep of live oak.

"Are you sure we should be doing this?" Drayton asked.

"What's wrong, are you getting cold feet?"

"Truth be told, I am. A little."

"When Bettina first approached us, you were all gung ho about jumping in to investigate."

"That's me, an expert panel of one," Drayton said.

"C'mon," Theodosia said. "Let's at least take a look at this house."

They moved from a pocket of darkness into an open area with faint splashes of moonlight. The air felt clean and cool; the woods surrounding the house were lush, green, and alive with crickets and tree frogs singing their songs. Off in the distance came the low hoot of an owl.

"I'll be switched," Drayton exclaimed as they walked up to the old house. "Will you look at this!"

Theodosia clicked on her flashlight. "What?"

"It's a genuine dogtrot house." Drayton sounded almost giddy.

They stood and gazed at the old place. It was a one-story wooden building with a low roof, the exterior turned silver-gray from the elements, a fieldstone chimney anchoring one end. But that wasn't what made it so unique.

"I've heard of dogtrot houses before, but I've never actually seen one," Theodosia said. "The architecture is . . . unusual."

"I'll say," Drayton said. "It's built as a typical single-story home, but with a large open breezeway running smack-dab through the middle. You see, there are two completely separate living spaces on either side. But everything's contained under one roof."

"Unorthodox but kind of cool."

"Exactly the point," Drayton said. "They were engineered to take advantage of cross breezes and optimize airflow. Some historians say dogtrot houses originated in the Appalachians; others believe they were developed by farmers in our very own Carolina low country."

"I wonder how this house figures into Fox's shoot?"

"Maybe he's doing a historical documentary. Maybe he got a grant or something."

"Could be," Theodosia said as they stepped up onto the front porch and walked through the open breezeway. She stopped and peered in a window smudged with dirt and cobwebs. The room was empty with a scuffed wood floor and stone fireplace against the far wall. Dust lay everywhere. "Nobody home," she said.

"This place probably hasn't been inhabited for a number of years," Drayton said. "I'd guess the surrounding fields are leased out to a neighboring grower." He reached for a doorknob, rattled it, and said, "Locked. Too bad, I'd love to go inside this old place and look around."

"Maybe when Fox gets here," Theodosia said. "Maybe he'll have a key. I mean, if he's shooting a commercial or documentary here, he might need to get inside."

"This is fascinating," Drayton said. "Let's poke around some more."

"Sure."

They walked all the way through the open breezeway and stepped down into a backyard filled with knee-high weeds and an occasional thicket of buckthorn.

"There are two more buildings back here," Drayton said.

"One looks like a small barn," Theodosia said. "The other . . ."

"Looks almost like a miniature log cabin. Though the boards don't seem to be chinked with cement or clay."

"Corncrib," Theodosia said. Her aunt Libby's plantation, Cane Ridge, had one exactly like it. "Those gaps between boards are there on purpose. To allow air circulation so the corn can dry out."

"Air circulation, huh. Similar to the main house." Fascinated, Drayton led the way through the weeds. When they got close to the corncrib, the land turned to a mix of stubbly dry grass and hardpan. "You think there's any corn inside?"

"Doesn't look that way. But open the door and see for yourself."

Drayton reached a hand out, then hesitated and pulled back. "Somehow it doesn't feel right. Like we're overstepping our bounds."

"Oh, for goodness' sake," Theodosia said. "Nobody lives here. So what's the big deal?" She touched a hand to an old-fashioned rusted metal handle and pushed down hard. There was a metallic snap and then the door slowly swung open.

"Phew." Drayton waved a hand in front of his face. "Stinky. Whatever corn was left in here must have mildewed. Not even field mice would want to nibble that."

Theodosia snapped on her flashlight and played the beam along the inside walls of the small corncrib. Dust motes swirled in the air as she explored. She saw gobs of tangled gray cobwebs, a hook with a leather strap hanging from it, and . . . wait a minute, what was that hung on the wall? Something bony and white, almost bleached-looking! Her heart thumped inside her chest until she figured out what it was. A mounted skull from some kind of animal. Maybe a sheep or a small steer?

"Huh, I think this place was used more recently for storage," she called to Drayton.

Theodosia aimed her flashlight lower and flicked it around quickly. She was ready to get out of there, about to snap it off, when she caught a wink of something shiny. Hesitating, she aimed the beam into a far corner. Blinking, puzzled at what she was looking at, she moved the beam in a small circle. Then, as if she'd inhaled too much dust, her breath caught in her throat and she let out a sharp cry.

"What?" Drayton said. He'd turned and was about to walk away.

"Look," Theodosia said in a guttural tone. "Just . . . come take a look."

"I don't understand . . ."

Theodosia aimed her flashlight at what appeared to be a pile of rags. Then the yellow beam settled on the glistening thing that had first caught her attention.

It was a human eye. Wide open, but glazed and unseeing.

24

Drayton let out a yelp and jumped back. His jaw muscles tightened, and strange noises came from the back of his throat. Finally, he croaked out, "Is that what I think it is?"

"What do you think it is?" Theodosia asked. "What did *you* see?"

"An eyeball. Belonging to a dead body?"

"Yeah."

"Yeah?"

"And I do believe the dead body belongs to Eddie Fox."

Drayton threw out his arms as if to steady himself. "Whoa. Are you sure? Is this really happening?"

Theodosia nodded slowly, reluctantly. "I think it already happened." Suddenly, she didn't feel all that steady herself. Her head pounded like an anvil was inside it, and she felt sick to her stomach. What she'd hoped would be a simple Q and A session with Eddie Fox had suddenly turned tragic.

"But what . . . ?" Drayton was still fumbling for words.

Theodosia's flashlight carefully explored some more.

"It looks to me as if Fox was shot and then stuffed in this corncrib."

"Who would *do* that?"

"I don't know. Had to be someone who either lured him out here on false pretenses, or someone who knew he was heading here for a location scout."

"Who would know that?" Drayton asked.

"Probably everybody at the fashion show. He was off the chain when I tried to talk to him, babbling about how he was double-booked."

Drayton touched a hand to his chest. "And you're sure he's been shot?"

"Pretty sure." Theodosia re-aimed her flashlight at Fox's crumpled body. "From what I can see, he was nailed center of mass. Directly through the heart. Are you okay?"

"Not really." Drayton ran a visibly shaking hand through his hair. "I feel . . . creaky."

"Take a couple of deep breaths, okay?" There was a low rumble of thunder off in the distance, and Theodosia peered up at a sky lightly salted with stars. Low, gray clouds were starting to drift in. *Maybe a line of showers on the horizon? No, guess not.* She was just feeling . . . jumpy.

Drayton gulped air and swallowed hard, working to compose himself. Finally, he said, "Do you think Fox was killed by the same person who shot Nadine?"

Theodosia gave a disheartened shrug. "It's possible."

He straightened up and looked around. "Does this mean that Fox *didn't* kill Nadine?"

"Fox still could have shot her," Theodosia said. "But now we know . . ." She inclined her head in the direction of the corncrib. "We know there's another killer out there somewhere."

"You think maybe it's Fox's partner in the dope deal?"

"No idea," Theodosia said. Then she reconsidered her words. "I suppose it *could* be. No, it probably was."

"What are we going to do now?"

As if on cue, the wail of a siren rose and fell in the crisp night air. Then it was joined by two more sirens, a virtual cacophony of noise, followed by distant strobes of red and blue lights that glimmered through the scrim of trees.

"Sweet dogs," Drayton cried. "It looks as if the police are on their way and about to storm this place!"

"They can't be coming here!" Theodosia cried. "I haven't made a call yet, and I doubt we tripped any alarms."

"Must be Sheriff Burney," Drayton said. "This is his jurisdiction."

Theodosia gazed over at the driveway where lights bobbed and blinked liked crazy, motors roared, and cars slewed toward them. The lead car cut hard to the left, swerved past her Jeep, and then plowed through the weeds, headed in their direction.

"I'm still puzzled. There aren't any neighbors around for miles," Theodosia said.

"Well *something* tipped them off!" Drayton looked at his watch, as if that would somehow explain things, then threw up his hands and said, "That's it, we're going to be arrested for the murder of Eddie Fox. We're going to jail, the police will take those awful mug shots, and we'll have to wear orange jumpsuits."

"I doubt that's going to happen." Theodosia had to almost shout to be heard above the sirens.

"No? You'd better pray that Haley can scrounge up bail money for us," Drayton said as the lead car rocked to a stop ten feet from them.

But it wasn't Sheriff Burney who jumped out. It was . . .

"What are you two doing here?" Riley shouted. His face morphed from a hard mask to one of utter surprise.

Drayton raised his hands. "Don't shoot. It wasn't us that killed Eddie Fox."

"What!" Riley screamed.

"Eddie Fox. We found his body," Theodosia yelled at him. "Stumbled across it by accident."

"Hold up, guys," Riley said to the four uniformed officers that had followed him in. They stopped in their tracks and lowered their guns. Then Riley peered at Theodosia. "First I need you to answer my question. What the Sam Hill are you *doing* here?"

"Um, we were looking for Eddie Fox?" Theodosia said.

Drayton cleared his throat and pointed at the corncrib.

Riley strode forward and peered into the corncrib. He focused his larger, more powerful flashlight on the crumpled body and said, "Congratulations. I'd say you found him."

But the surprises didn't end there.

Two minutes later, while Theodosia was offering a hasty explanation to Riley, Sheriff Burney came roaring in.

In his khaki uniform, a pearl-handled revolver hung on his hand-tooled leather belt, and standing six feet two, the sheriff was a formidable presence as he rushed toward them.

"What in dang tarnation is going on here?" Sheriff Burney demanded.

Theodosia held up both hands in a gesture of surrender. "Not my doing," she said.

"Then why are you here?" Sheriff Burney demanded. He looked around, perplexed. "What's going on?"

"There's been a homicide," Riley said.

Sheriff Burney took a step back. "What?"

"Drayton and I drove out here because we wanted to talk to Eddie Fox," Theodosia said. "Kind of intercept him."

"Because he was doing a location scout here," Drayton added.

"And we found him shot," Theodosia said. "Dead."

"In there," Drayton said, pointing.

"They're here because they've been investigating," Riley said. He didn't cut a forbidding figure like Sheriff Burney, but he was radiating disappointment mixed with a serious amount of anger.

"We can't help that we *found* Fox," Drayton said, trying to smooth things over. "We wandered around the place and—boom—there he was. Dead as a doornail."

Sheriff Burney ducked into the corncrib to see for himself. He came out looking somber. "Dead just like that?" he asked.

"Yes, just like that," Drayton shot back.

Burney pulled off his Smokey Bear hat and scratched his head. "Well, shoot."

"Please don't," Drayton murmured.

Theodosia turned to confront Riley.

"How did you know to come out here?" she asked.

"We got a phone call," Riley said.

"So did my office," Sheriff Burney muttered.

Theodosia stared at them. It was starting to become clear to her that this whole thing had been a well-calculated setup.

"So you both received anonymous calls, right?" she said. "And they had to do with . . . let me take a wild guess . . . with drugs?"

Riley stared at her. "How'd you know that?"

Sheriff Burney just grunted.

"Because you were set up," Theodosia said. "Tricked." She turned to Sheriff Burney. "You both were."

"I'm not quite following your line of thought," Sheriff Burney said.

"Detective Riley got an anonymous call concerning a drug deal he's working on," Theodosia said. "It sent him rushing out here where he was supposed to find Eddie Fox's dead body and assume that Eddie was shot because he was a loose end in the drug deal that killed Nadine. His death might even suggest that his coconspirator had grabbed the drugs from Eddie and blew out of town. Which would mean the case is now pretty much a dead end. Sheriff Burney, you got the exact same call because the killer hoped you'd find Eddie Fox and make the assumption that *he* was the one who shot Nadine. And that Fox's partner was long gone."

Sheriff Burney scratched his nose with his thumb. He looked like he wasn't quite buying what she was selling.

"Drayton and I, on the other hand, came here on a fairly innocent errand. And we ended up discovering Eddie Fox's body on our own." Theodosia stared at Riley, hoping to dispel some of his anger. "I'm not sure that was part of the plan. Maybe it was, but my guess is we simply blundered in."

"A mistake," Sheriff Burney said. "And a setup." He gave a curt nod. "Damn."

Theodosia sighed. "And now the gang's all here."

"What happens now?" Drayton asked.

"We work it like we'd work any other case," Riley said. "We call in a Crime Scene team and check the body and surrounding area for possible forensic evidence."

"Oh," Theodosia said. "Forensics. There's something I should tell you."

"Yes?" Riley said, drawing out the word.

So Theodosia told Riley and Sheriff Burney about the two figures she'd encountered last night. And how, in defending her, Earl Grey had lunged after one of them and grabbed him by the leg.

"You think one of your so-called shadowy figures might have been Eddie Fox?" Riley asked.

"I don't know," Theodosia said. "Like I said, it was dark and they were both dressed in black. But if you look at Fox's leg, there could be marks. That would be positive confirmation, right?"

"You shouldn't have been out running," Sheriff Burney said in an almost scolding tone.

Theodosia shrugged. "It's what I do to stay in shape."

"Seems to me you spend more time tangled up in police business," Sheriff Burney said.

"You see?" Riley chided. "I'm not the only one who feels that way."

Drayton interceded gently. "What else can be done here? I mean in the way of collecting evidence?"

That helped divert some of Riley's anger. "We could start looking around for shell casings, fibers, tire marks in the driveway," he said.

One of the officers shined his flashlight beam at the ground. "Got some tire marks right here, Detective."

"There you go," Drayton said.

The same officer aimed his flashlight at the tires on Theodosia's Jeep. "Different from these," he said. "Wider."

They all shuffled across the grass and looked at the tire tracks. Careful not to step in them.

"Wide tires, like some kind of sports car," Riley said.

Theodosia and Drayton exchanged glances. They'd be at the Concours d'Carolina tomorrow. Lots of sports cars there.

Theodosia was about to mention it to Riley, then didn't. He'd lecture her even more aggressively and warn her to stay away. Just when things were getting interesting.

Some thirty minutes later the Crime Scene van showed up. Once the techs were suited up in their jumpsuits, Riley sent them in to photograph and begin processing Fox's body.

"We're specifically looking for bite marks on his legs. *Dog* bites," he said, casting a glance at Theodosia.

They didn't hear anything for a few minutes, then one of the techs called out, "No bites that we can see."

"No bites," Riley said as he approached Theodosia and Drayton. "He's clean."

"Clean but dead," Drayton said.

Riley put his hands on his hips. "Now I'd appreciate it if you both went home."

Theodosia made a face. "We'd like to stick around . . ."

"Not happening," Riley said.

"Come on," Drayton said to Theodosia. "It's late. We've got a big day tomorrow, and these folks have a long night ahead of them."

"Okay," Theodosia finally said. "Okay."

Drayton walked to the Jeep and climbed in. Theodosia lingered and let Riley walk over with her. As she was about to open the driver's side door, he put both arms around her and pulled her close.

"I worry about you," he said.

"Thanks, but you really don't have to."

"If I'd known you were driving out here tonight . . ."

"I know, you'd have handcuffed me and thrown away the key."

"No, I would have handcuffed you and dragged you to my place." He wiggled his eyebrows at her. "Taken advantage."

"You can do that anytime," she said.

"Just not tonight," Riley said. "I meant what I said. Go home. Drive carefully. Don't do anything crazy." He gave her a quick kiss. "Okay?"

"Okay."

Theodosia and Drayton were both quiet as they retraced their route. Drove down Turnbull, turned back onto Katy Hill Road, and then onto the Maybank Highway.

Finally, Drayton said, "Talk about Mr. Toad's wild ride."

"A definite shocker," Theodosia said.

"Why didn't you tell me what happened last night? That you were accosted by two strangers."

"After that awful e-mail warning, I didn't want to cause any more worry."

"But you do. Constantly."

They drove in silence for a while, then Theodosia said, "As strange as it sounds, it feels like we're a few steps closer to homing in on Nadine's killer."

"Because now we can rule out Fox?"

"Fox could still be Nadine's killer. But Fox has a partner that, I'm fairly sure, murdered him."

"So you think more craziness is coming down the pike?"

"A lot more. In fact, I think the murderer has been playing us all like a fiddle."

"I hadn't thought of it that way," Drayton said. He was fussing with something in his lap, shifting it from his right hand to his left.

"What's that you've got?"

"Hmm?" Drayton looked down at his hands. "Just something I picked up back there. A feather. I think it must be from an owl."

"Maybe an owl feather means good luck," Theodosia said.

Drayton shook his head. "Somehow, I don't think so."

25

Friday morning at the Indigo Tea Shop and Theodosia and Drayton were still puzzling over last night's murder.

"When you look at it in the cold, clear light of day, the killer pulled a fairly slick move," Drayton said.

"You mean drawing everyone out to the dogtrot house so we'd find Fox's body?"

"So *somebody* would find his body, yes."

Haley, who'd just emerged from the kitchen with a platter heaped full of cherry almond scones, jumped when she heard Drayton utter the word *body*.

"Wait. What?" Haley's shoulders jerked upward, and her eyes suddenly grew as large as the saucers Theodosia had been placing on tables. "Did you say *body*? As in dead body? Did somebody else get *killed*?"

"We were just about to tell you," Drayton said. He looked calm and collected in his summer-weight blue wool jacket and striped bow tie. As if discussing a recent murder were an everyday thing.

"What happened?" Haley shrilled. "Who got killed?" Her face had turned bright pink under her crisp white chef's hat, and she shifted uncomfortably from one Croc-shod foot to the other.

"It was Eddie Fox, the film production guy," Theodosia said. "We drove out to a house he was supposedly scouting for a location shoot and stumbled upon his body."

"In a corncrib," Drayton said helpfully, though it didn't really help matters at all.

"You mean like at a farm out in the boonies? Why'd you go there? Did you suspect him?" Haley asked.

"We wanted to ask Fox a few questions," Theodosia said. "About whether he used drones or not. And yes, he figured prominently on our suspect list."

"But obviously not anymore," Haley said. "Since he's croaked."

"Passed on," Drayton said. He picked up a tin of Namring Garden Darjeeling and studied the label.

Theodosia raised an index finger. "Unless Eddie Fox was one of the people directly involved in Nadine's murder."

Drayton set the tea tin back down. "Right," he said slowly. "Two people, just like we talked about before. The buyer and the seller. One of them could have been Fox."

"But was he the buyer or the seller?" Theodosia said.

"So you still think *two* people were involved in Nadine's murder?" Haley asked, practically fizzing with excitement. "A killer tag team? And now one of them murdered their own partner?"

"Could be," Drayton said.

"It does point in that general direction," Theodosia said.

"That's just *great*," Haley said. "Now you're only on the lookout for *one* killer."

"We promise we won't involve you," Drayton said.

"You already have," Haley said. "Besides, what if some crazed assassin comes storming in here waving a gun?" She shoved the platter of scones into Theodosia's hands. "What am I supposed to do, nail him with my salad shooter?"

"Ha ha," Drayton said. "Haley's going to nail the dude."

Haley looked startled. "Dude," she said to Drayton. "You said *dude.*"

He peered at her. "And that's a good thing?"

"It means you're loosening up," Haley said.

"That's right," Theodosia said. "If Drayton were any looser, he'd be positively unraveled."

"You guys," Haley said as she scurried back to the kitchen.

Theodosia placed the scones in the glass pie saver, then finished arranging the tables. Drayton busied himself behind the counter, setting out teapots like a small ceramic armada.

When Drayton looked up, Theodosia said, "I'm going to call Eddie Fox's studio. See if I can find out anything more."

"If anybody's even there," Drayton said.

Theodosia slipped into her office and made the call. It was answered all right, with a sniffle and a desultory, "Morning. Studio."

"Josie?" Theodosia said.

Another sniffle. "Yeah?"

"This is Theodosia Browning. We spoke last night. You were the one who told me where to find Eddie?"

"Eddie," Josie said, hiccupping loudly. "That poor guy. In my wildest dreams I never could have imagined he'd get murdered." Another sniffle. "I understand you were the one who found him."

"You talked to the police?"

"First thing, yeah. Everyone here . . . we're all heartsick about Eddie. He was an okay guy. A little into himself, but still okay."

"I know this has been a terrible shock, but I need to ask you something."

"What?" Josie blubbered.

"Did anybody else call the studio last night? I mean somebody looking for Fox?"

"I don't . . . I can't remember."

"Think hard, it's important."

"Yeah?"

"It could be," Theodosia said.

"A few calls came in, I guess. But they were mostly concerning the bank shoot. But I guess . . . yeah, somebody might have called."

"Was it a man or woman who called asking about Eddie?"

"I dunno."

"Did you tell them Eddie would be scouting a location at the dogtrot house?"

"I don't know anything about a dog. But maybe . . . yeah. They, um, might have called right before you did."

"*Before* I called." Theodosia's heart quickened a beat. Somebody had been looking for Eddie, planning to . . .

"I guess I *did* tell them." Josie's voice rose. "But I had to, it's my job!"

Back in the tea room, Theodosia leaned across the counter and replayed her conversation for Drayton.

"The killer was hunting him," Drayton said. "Maybe attempting to tie up loose ends?"

"It sure looks that way."

"We must have just missed him. The killer, I mean." Drayton gave a little shiver. He picked up a teapot and poured amber liquid into a teacup. "Here." He pushed it across the counter to Theodosia. "Take a sip."

"What is it?"

"Something strangely apropos. A strong black tea called Death by Tea."

"Death by Tea," Theodosia murmured. "You're right, it is rather fitting."

*   *   *

Soft morning light filtered through the windows, lending a warm glow to the Indigo Tea Room. Life went on as Theodosia welcomed guests, took orders, and poured tea into pristine china teacups. When the tea room was half-filled and she had a minute to spare, she grabbed her cell phone and called Marvin Chauvet. She wondered if their catering gig was still on.

"Oh my goodness," Marvin Chauvet wailed in answer to her question. "We're as shocked about Eddie Fox as you are!"

Are you really? Theodosia wondered.

"We were depending on him," Chauvet said. "Now I guess we'll have to edit all that raw footage ourselves. Or hire somebody . . . I don't know."

"It's certainly a bizarre twist of events," Theodosia continued. "Anyway, I wanted to make sure your hospitality tent at the Concours d'Carolina was still happening."

"Absolutely it is," Chauvet said. "Why wouldn't it be? You'll have the food ready, right?"

"Yes, so one o'clock, then," she said, not wanting to start an argument. "We'll be there."

Drayton looked up from measuring orchid plum tea into a pale green teapot. "I take it their hospitality tent is still on?"

"In the immortal words of Marvin Chauvet, 'Why wouldn't it be?'"

At ten thirty, Haley came out of the kitchen and said, "I just want to give you guys a heads-up. I've got a pan of French Quarter beignets in the oven along with two loaves of banana bread."

"Sounds yummy," Theodosia said.

"And you know I'm doing a slightly scaled-back luncheon today?"

"I assumed so, since you're also working on the appetizers for this afternoon."

"I'm going with lobster bisque soup, shrimp salad with tarragon, and two kinds of tea sandwiches."

"What kind?" Drayton asked.

"Cream cheese with roasted red peppers on rye and cashew chicken on homemade nut bread," Haley said. "Do you know what time Miss Dimple is coming in to help?"

Theodosia checked her watch. "Another hour or so."

"Okey dokey." Haley spun on her heels and ran lightly back to the kitchen.

Drayton looked up from his tea brewing. "She seems to be over her vexation."

"Looks like."

"Do you think she'll have the appetizers ready in time?" he asked. "We should leave by twelve thirty at the very latest."

"I ask you, when has Haley ever let us down?" Theodosia said.

"I'd have to say never."

"Then they'll be ready."

Miss Dimple arrived precisely on time and proceeded to bustle about the tea room, pouring tea, taking orders, refreshing glasses with ice water. She'd been helping out so much lately that she'd developed a real comfort level. Which was just fine with Theodosia since she considered everyone who worked there to be family. Even though some of her customers viewed her as the posh and elegant tea lady of Church Street, she was really a mother hen at heart.

Just as Theodosia delivered a pot of cardamom tea to table four, the front door whapped open and a red-faced Delaine stepped in. Theodosia hurried over to greet Delaine just as she burst into tears.

"Delaine!" Theodosia cried. "What?"

Delaine stood there trembling as tears streaked her face. Even though she was stylishly dressed in black slacks, a designer jean jacket, and a treasure trove of clanking gold jewelry, she looked for all the world to be in the middle of an emotional crisis. Actually, a whirlwind.

"What's wrong?" Theodosia asked again. When she'd left Cotton Duck late yesterday afternoon, Delaine had been in fine form. Laughing and joking with the fashion show guests, basking in the glow of a successful show, even writing up orders. Now she seemed completely unhinged.

"I'm . . . I'm sorry," Delaine stammered out.

"About what?"

"Everything!" she cried. "I just heard about Eddie Fox's murder—which is just plain *awful*. But mostly because I've been so callous about Nadine, about her . . ." A shudder ran through her entire body. "Her *murder*."

"You've endured a terrible shock," Theodosia said in what she hoped was a calm, comforting voice. Was it possible that Delaine was experiencing a delayed reaction?

It was indeed.

"I've been wandering around in a daze these last few days, sickened by my sister's murder yet unable to come to terms with it," Delaine said. "At the same time, I've been slightly intoxicated by my involvement in Lemon Squeeze Couture." She grabbed Theodosia's arm and squeezed hard. "But what I haven't done is take precious time to focus on the sad *reality* of Nadine's death. To actually *mourn* her passing."

Theodosia led Delaine to the small table by the window and got her seated.

Like the caring soul he was, Drayton hurried over with a pot of tea for Delaine. "Chamomile," he said. "To help settle your nerves." And then, seeing the abundance of tears that still flowed down her cheeks, he slipped her a clean hanky.

Delaine held it to her nose. "Thank you," she blubbered.

Theodosia sat down across from Delaine and poured her a cup of tea, pushed it across the table to her.

"I've acted like an idiot," Delaine said. "Put money and prestige ahead of family and friends." She blew her nose delicately and gazed at Theodosia with a mournful expression. "Can you ever forgive me?"

"The real question is, can you forgive yourself?" Theodosia said.

Delaine cocked her head to one side. "What do you mean?"

"Honey, you're not the terrible person you think you are. You've just endured a horrendous shock. And face it, you're a little high-strung to begin with."

Delaine nodded in agreement. "I am. I'll be the first one to admit that."

"What's most important is that you take care of yourself and look after Bettina as well. She's your immediate family, and she's still young and impressionable."

Delaine took a tentative sip of tea and said, "Bettina and I had a heart-to-heart talk this morning. I mean, we really went *deep*."

"And?"

"The amazing thing is that Bettina forgives me." Delaine took another sip of tea, then blotted her lips. "She said she completely understood why I'd reacted the way I did and how I'd probably reached my absolute tipping point. That I hadn't been myself all week."

"There you go," Theodosia said.

"Can you believe how *mature* she is?" Delaine dug in her bag for a mirrored compact. "For goodness' sake, I don't think *I'm* that mature."

Theodosia wisely remained silent.

26

With some gentle urging from Theodosia, Delaine stayed for lunch. Settled in with a pot of tea, a luncheon plate, and a few questions about Eddie Fox.

"I can't believe you and Drayton found him," Delaine said as she nibbled the top off a carrot muffin.

"Neither can we," Theodosia said.

"He must have been one of the drug dealers . . . from the Orchard House Inn, I mean."

"We're leaning that way as well."

"Are you still . . . investigating?"

"As a matter of fact, I'm hoping to quiz Harv and Marv when we get to the Concours d'Carolina." Theodosia checked her watch. "Drayton and I will be leaving in about five minutes. Haley's packing the last of the appetizers now."

Delaine gave a wistful look. "I was planning to go. But now, with everything so upended . . ."

"You shouldn't," Theodosia hastened to say. "Stay here, finish your lunch, then go home and take it easy. Put your tootsies up and cuddle with your cat. You've not only had a tragic loss, you've been working at a feverish pace all week long. So chances are any reserves you might have had are completely drained."

"I do feel a little peaked."

Theodosia patted Delaine's shoulder as she stood up. "Of course you do. But I promise, you *will* be fine."

"Ready?" Drayton asked as Theodosia approached the counter.

"Yup," Theodosia said. "Let's do it." She turned and waved at Miss Dimple. "Miss Dimple?" she mouthed. "It's all yours."

They hauled wicker baskets, picnic hampers, and coolers out to Theodosia's Jeep and packed everything in tight.

"Oops, there's one more," Theodosia said as she passed Drayton the final hamper.

Drayton shoved a cooler aside, frowned, mumbled something to himself, and proceeded to wedge in the hamper, but just barely.

"This reminds me of a tricky Chinese puzzle," he said.

They both held their breath as he closed the back hatch.

Driving through the stone gates of the Juniper Bay Country Club, Theodosia felt like a country cousin in her basic, somewhat ordinary Jeep. Because all around her were shiny, ultra-luxe exotic cars. She spotted a Porsche, Ferrari, Mercedes Benz, and Tesla. And those were just the cars driven by guests!

A man in a reflective yellow vest waved as he stepped out of a gatehouse.

Theodosia rolled down her window.

"Afternoon, ma'am," he said. "Welcome to the Concours d'Carolina. Do you have your tickets handy?"

"We're the caterers for the Lemon Squeeze Couture hospitality tent," she said.

"Oh sure, you're on the list," the gate guy said. He held a hand up to his forehead and squinted. "Follow the road to your left, drive right on past the clubhouse, and you'll spot the yellow tent."

"Okay, thanks."

"So this is what the Concours d'Carolina is all about," Drayton said as they bumped along, passing dozens of cars carefully parked on the manicured lawn, some even residing on their own room-sized carpets, like mini principalities. "Classic cars, high-test cars, collector cars. Quite a sight."

"I'm getting sticker shock just looking at these gorgeous autos," Theodosia said. The entire lawn surrounding the country club was filled with cars, strolling guests, colorful tents, and fluttering banners. There had to be almost ten acres' worth of activities.

"Such gorgeous weather, too. Blue sky, lovely breeze."

"And everyone's dressed to the nines," Theodosia said. She'd spotted lots of linen jackets, spring dresses, and hats. Panama hats on the men and large-brimmed straw hats on the women. *Almost like the Kentucky Derby*, she thought.

"Okay, there's the clubhouse," Drayton said as they drove past an enormous plantation-style building. It was painted yellow with white shutters, had a wide front porch and an enormous patio filled with tables that sported yellow and white umbrellas where guests sat sipping drinks.

"And there's a line of tents up ahead," Theodosia said. "I'm guessing we can just pull in back and unload."

"Works for me," Drayton said.

They found their tent among other sponsors' tents—Coronet Classic Cars, Mower's Fine Jewelry, Trembleau Wines, White Swan Vodka, Velacci Tires, and Touchstone Media.

Marvin Chauvet came out to greet them. He was wearing navy blue slacks with a matching golf shirt. A yellow cashmere sweater was slung around his shoulders and knotted in front.

"You found us," he said. "Good. We've got two tables set up inside right alongside our bar." He rattled the ice in his glass of amber liquid. "Which, I can happily attest, is fully operational."

Theodosia walked in and looked around. For a hospitality tent, it looked pretty spiffy. There was a plush blue-and-cinnamon-colored Oriental carpet on the floor, a dozen leather club chairs scattered around, and a makeshift bar with a young ponytailed bartender busily whipping something up in a silver shaker. The front of the tent was open with a swag of filmy curtains on each side.

Theodosia and Drayton quickly set up their tea and appetizers as Harv and Marv milled about, mumbling to each other as they puzzled over Fox's death.

Harvey Bateman, dressed in his trademark drab, snatched a steak bite off a silver tray and stared pointedly at Theodosia. "And you were there," he said. "Again." His mouth pulled into a nasty smile. "Maybe *you're* the one the police should be investigating."

"Nice try," Theodosia said. "But I don't go around murdering people."

Bateman let loose a hearty cackle, as if his words had been meant as a joke. "Neither do I."

That remains to be seen, Theodosia thought.

Since the appetizers were pretty much self-serve, Theodosia and Drayton decided to duck outside for a little exploring. They admired a bright red Maserati and a wicked black Dodge Viper. They also looked longingly at a classic Porsche and a vintage Alfa Romeo.

"Look at this beauty." Drayton indicated an artsy-looking, lime-green fastback car. "A 1970 Citroën 2CV. Besides champagne, this auto is one of the best things the French ever invented. Look at the custom upholstery."

Theodosia looked inside. "Pale green leather. Wow."

"You hardly ever see this particular model anymore, and this one's in tip-top shape."

"Does it make you want to drive?"

"Gift me with one of these sweet rides and I'd certainly consider it."

All the hoopla surrounding the cars made Theodosia think back to the tire tracks from last night—and the fact that Riley thought they might have been made by some kind of sports car with wide wheels.

Could the tracks have been made by one of the cars here? One on display or a car driven here by one of the attendees? Interesting idea. Did Harv and Marv own exotic cars? She'd have to keep her eyes and ears open.

Back at the hospitality tent, things had picked up considerably. So Theodosia grabbed a pair of silver tongs and began serving appetizers while Drayton poured tea for a few people who requested it. The guests for the most part were well-heeled and well-mannered. And Theodosia was happy she'd casually set a stack of her business cards in a small silver bowl. They were quietly and appreciatively being snatched up, which was always good for business.

At two o'clock the models burst into the tent. Six young women all impeccably coiffed and made-up, dressed head to toe in Lemon Squeeze Couture. Marvin Chauvet gathered them in a circle and instructed them to wander around the grounds for fifteen minutes, then head back to the tent, the idea being that interested parties might follow them in.

Theodosia didn't know how well that ploy would work but figured it was worth a shot. After all, there were a lot of movers and shakers in attendance today. Probably even some people in the retail industry.

There was also one nervous designer.

When Mark Devlin walked up to the appetizer table, he looked twitchy and ill at ease.

"Mr. Devlin," Theodosia said. "May I pour you a cup of tea? Or fix you an appetizer plate? The steak bites and shrimp gratiné are particularly good."

"Thank you, no, I believe I'll belly up to the bar for a cocktail instead," he said.

"Are you okay?" There was something off about him today. His clothing was impeccable—a pink linen shirt, cream-colored slacks, two-tone loafers—but his attitude seemed somewhat dulled.

Devlin gazed at her with a downturned mouth. "I just heard the news about Eddie Fox."

"Awful," Theodosia said, watching him closely. She wondered if he knew that she and Drayton had been the ones who'd found Fox's body.

But no, Devlin didn't seem to be aware of that fact. At least he wasn't mentioning it. He walked over to the bar, got a gin and tonic, and wandered back to the appetizer table.

"Are you sure you don't want something to eat?" Theodosia asked.

Devlin placed a hand on his stomach.

"No thanks, I'm not feeling one-hundred-percent today." He hesitated, then added, "I'm not ill or anything. I just have a bad feeling."

"About?"

"Everything. Nadine's murder, Fox's murder. It feels like a weird string of events that are all related."

"That's because they probably are," Theodosia said. She looked around the tent for Drayton, finally noticed him outside, talking to someone who was standing next to a shiny silver Volvo.

"I also had a long interview with the police this morning," Devlin said.

"I'd guess that's fairly standard since you were acquainted with both victims. No doubt the police are casting a relatively wide net."

Devlin sighed. "I suppose." He glanced around, then lowered his voice. "The other thing is, lately it feels as if someone's been following me."

"Why would you think that?" Theodosia asked.

He swirled his drink. "I don't know."

But Theodosia knew there had to be a reason. "Is it possible . . . that somebody thinks you know something?"

"That sounds dull and complicated, but yes. I suppose that could be it."

"Do you?" Theodosia asked. "Know something, I mean."

"Not really." Devlin put his glass to his lips and sipped gingerly. "Well, I have my suspicions of course."

"Did you mention them to the police this morning?"

Devlin shook his head. "Like I said, they're only suspicions. Just . . . vague feelings. You know . . . about what's happened."

"About who's responsible?"

"Maybe."

"Care to share?" Theodosia asked.

Devlin was about to say something when a smiling Meriam Chauvet came flying in and suddenly interrupted them.

"Mr. Devlin," she cried in a burst of enthusiasm. "Good afternoon. And Miss Browning, too. Isn't this a lovely event?"

"Nice to see you again," Devlin said as he hastily slipped away.

Meriam, who was dressed in a gorgeous raspberry-colored jacket and slacks, focused her upbeat mood squarely on Theodosia. "I can't tell you what a wonderful time I had at your tea shop yesterday. Everything was so elegant and graceful."

"Thank you."

"So I was thrilled when I heard you were catering Marvin's hospitality tent." She looked around. "Such as it is."

"I take it you've not been involved with the Lemon Squeeze Couture business?"

Meriam chuckled. "No, that's Marvin's bailiwick. I've got enough to keep me busy what with the retail store."

There was a volley of squeals and laughter as the models suddenly came rushing into the tent, trailed by Julie Eiden, the intern.

Theodosia decided to take full advantage of this serendipitous moment. She grabbed Julie and quickly introduced her to Meriam.

"So *you're* the intern," Meriam said. "Theodosia seems to think quite highly of you."

Julie's face reddened. "She's very kind."

"She also tells me that post-internship you're looking for a job in retail," Meriam said. "Maybe something to do with fashion merchandising?"

"The internship's been wonderful and given me tons of experience," Julie said. "But it's getting to the point where I need an actual job to pay the rent."

Julie and Meriam continued to talk as Theodosia suddenly got busy with some guests. When she finally turned her attention back to the two women, she was surprised to hear Meriam say, "I almost never do this, but I'm going to offer you a job on the spot."

"Really?" Julie squealed. "You mean an actual paying job?"

"The only catch is you have to start first thing Monday," Meriam said.

"Wow, thank you," Julie said. "I accept, oh, do I ever! Did you hear that, Theodosia? I'm hired. Just like that!"

"It's wonderful," Theodosia said. She felt like the two women had good chemistry together, that Julie would be an excellent fit for Meriam's shop.

"What's going on here?" Marvin Chauvet asked as he elbowed his way into their little circle.

"I have a new employee," Meriam said.

He looked back and forth between the two women. "Huh?" He wasn't sure what had just happened.

But Meriam was smiling like the cat who swallowed the canary. "I just hired Julie."

That rocked Marvin Chauvet back on his heels. "You. Did. Not." He looked at Julie with a pained expression. "But you're *our* intern!"

"Unpaid intern," Julie said. "And I do thank you for three months' worth of experience, but now I'm ready to strike out on my own."

"Strike out," Marvin grumbled as he turned and wandered off. "On your own. At my wife's company. Huh."

Five minutes later, a grumpy Harvey Bateman approached Theodosia.

"Did I hear right?" he asked. "Did Meriam Chauvet just poach our intern?"

"You heard right," Theodosia said. She wasn't about to tell him that she was the one responsible for the referral.

He grabbed a shrimp and popped it in his mouth. "That Meriam is some shark. As for the intern, some people just don't have any sense of loyalty."

"It's been my experience that a regular paycheck generally trumps an unpaid position."

Bateman scowled and shook an index finger at her. "You've got a smart mouth, you know that?"

"Thank you," Theodosia said. "It's not the first time I've been told that."

"And it probably won't be the last," Bateman muttered as he walked away.

Drayton edged in behind the table. "What were you and Bateman talking about? He looked upset."

"I introduced Julie to Meriam Chauvet, and she hired her on the spot."

"Intern Julie?"

"Yup."

"Goodness, that must have frosted Bateman's cupcake."

Theodosia smiled. "Marvin Chauvet took it even worse."

27

The rest of the afternoon proved fairly uneventful for Theodosia and Drayton. As shadows lengthened and the sun became a fuzzy orange blur on the horizon, they began to pack up their trays, serving utensils, and leftovers (of which there were very little).

Drayton hoisted a hamper, let out a faux groan, and said, "I'll start carrying these larger pieces out to your Jeep. If I shove them all the way in, we won't get stuck playing a game of Jenga again."

"I'm going to wrap up these shrimp and stick them in a cooler. Actually, I'll put all the leftovers in together. There aren't that many."

"None at all?" a voice asked.

Theodosia looked up to find Simon Nardwell staring at her.

"I'm afraid I arrived late," Nardwell explained. "And it appears I missed out on the refreshments." He gave a rueful smile.

"I can certainly fix you a plate," Theodosia said. She didn't really want to, but she didn't want to be rude, either.

Nardwell help up a hand. "No, thanks, I'll grab something

on my way home. After I take a quick spin around the grounds, that is."

"So you have an interest in classic cars as well as antique weapons?" Theodosia said.

Nardwell's eyes suddenly lit up. "Oh my, yes. In fact, I just saw the most beautiful Aston Martin DB5. As well as a Morgan and an Austin-Healey Sprite."

"You favor British cars."

"The older ones, anyway. The true classics. They're a feast for the eyes because of the handwork, the careful craftsmanship. You don't see that kind of attention to detail anymore." He stopped, gave an uncertain smile, and said, "Good evening, then." And left the tent.

It was almost dark by the time Theodosia and Drayton got everything packed up and loaded into the Jeep.

"What a day," Drayton said as they drove past the clubhouse where lights blazed and the festivities continued. The cocktail party had just started, to be followed by a fancy dinner and a trophy presentation for Collector of the Year.

"Tired?" Theodosia asked.

"Foot tired, anyway. But it was an interesting gig, wouldn't you say?"

"The cars were great, the people . . . meh."

"So you really tangled with Harvey Bateman?"

"Hard not to. He's one of those passive-aggressive guys," Theodosia said as she drove carefully past a line of parked cars. "Acts all friendly and laid-back, then—wham—he lunges for the jugular."

"I'll be glad when . . . whoa!" Drayton yelped as a red sports car suddenly blasted past them.

The car had come out of nowhere—engine roaring, horn

honking as it shot by them on the right-hand side of the road. Theodosia reacted just in time to touch her brakes and carefully swerve out of its way, barely missing a parked Bentley. Dust, motor oil, and grit were kicked back at her in the sports car's wake.

"Look at that little go-devil!" Drayton said. "Passed us doing sixty miles an hour and must have hit eighty by the time he reached the front gate."

"Redlining it all the way," Theodosia said. She approached the front gate, turned onto the highway, and floored it.

Who was that? she wondered. *Who was the jerk who almost caused me to have an accident?*

Up ahead, as the road spun out, they could see the little red car roaring along. It was coming up fast behind another vehicle, what looked like an SUV. The red car's brake lights flared, then it pulled directly behind the SUV, riding hard on its rear bumper, and staying there.

"What's that red car up to?" Drayton wondered. "Like it's almost harassing that SUV."

"Mark Devlin drives an SUV," Theodosia said.

"What?"

"I saw it parked outside of Lois's bookstore a couple of days ago. And Devlin was at the car show today. So . . ."

"You think that could be him up ahead?" Drayton asked.

"Could be."

"Why would someone be chasing him?"

"You're not going to believe this, but earlier today Devlin told me he thought someone was following him," Theodosia said.

"Following him why?" Drayton said.

"He was kind of foggy on that point. But I've been thinking—what if Devlin figured out who killed Nadine? And Eddie Fox?"

"Is that what he told you?"

"Not in so many words," Theodosia said. "But he said he had his suspicions. And he seemed nervous and agitated."

"If that's him up ahead he should be plenty agitated now," Drayton said as they watched the scenario between the two vehicles play out.

"That red car definitely seems like it wants to run the SUV off the road," Theodosia said. Feeling another blip of nervousness, she stepped on the gas.

"Quite a size differential though," Drayton said.

"But the sports car guy's a more skillful driver."

"Careful," Drayton said as they accelerated after the two cars. "The road's so dark and twisty out here."

When they rounded a turn and the road became more of a straightaway, they could see the red car and the SUV still involved in a dangerous game of cat and mouse. Every time the SUV braked, the red car was doggedly on its tail or running up on its side, pushing and taunting.

"Maybe it's just motor heads playing tag," Drayton said. "Especially that sports car."

Sports car.

Once again, Theodosia thought about the tire treads from last night.

Could that red car up ahead be the same car?

"I don't think they're playing tag," Theodosia said.

Drayton leaned forward in his seat. "Following him, then? Chasing him?"

Mark Devlin's words echoed in Theodosia's brain: *Someone's been following me.* Was that Devlin in the SUV? Was the red sports car the person who'd been following him? The same car that was endangering him right now?

All this roared through Theodosia's mind as, up ahead, the driver of the SUV drifted to the edge of the road and suddenly lost it. He swerved to the far left side of the road, then crossed back and hit the right berm, fishtailing all the way. There was a split second when the car seemed like it might regain control, then it tilted crazily and did a complete one-hundred-eighty-degree spin in the middle of the highway. There were two, three revolutions, then it began to slow. There was a sickening weeble-wobble, as if the vehicle were deciding what to do next, then it tilted and bumped down hard onto its right side.

The red sports car never hesitated, never stopped. In fact, its taillights were long gone by the time Theodosia and Drayton arrived at the scene of the accident.

Drayton immediately sprang from the Jeep. Theodosia was a split second behind him.

"You think he's alive?" Drayton cried as he sprinted to the SUV.

The man in the SUV wasn't just alive, he was conscious. And, amazingly, turned out to be exactly who Theodosia thought it might be—Mark Devlin.

"I need help," Devlin groaned when he saw them. "Somebody ran me off the road." His windshield was a network of cracks, and his side windows were completely smashed. Devlin was helplessly strapped into his seat, and the airbag had gone off, smooshing him like an exploded giant marshmallow.

"Theodosia's calling for help right now," Drayton said. "Just . . . try to remain calm."

Devlin groaned again and said, "I think my right arm is broken."

An ambulance and two highway patrol cars arrived a few minutes later. Thank goodness they were able to pry open the driver's side door and gently lift Devlin out onto a gurney.

"How bad?" Theodosia asked one of the EMTs once they'd slid the gurney, blankets fluttering in the wind, into the back of the ambulance.

"He's banged up, got quite a few cuts and bruises, but seems to be tracking fairly well. Maybe a mild concussion as well as a possible broken arm." The EMT looked back over his shoulder. "Judging by the condition of his SUV, this guy got lucky."

"You two are the ones who witnessed the accident?" one of the highway patrolmen asked Theodosia and Drayton. He aimed a flashlight at their faces.

"We saw it and called it in," Theodosia said.

He aimed the flashlight away. "I've got some questions for you."

They stood alongside the trooper's car while he placed his notebook on his front fender and scribbled notes. They answered questions and gave their version of the crash.

Finally, when they were finished, Theodosia called Riley.

"We just saw a little red sports car cause an accident and run Mark Devlin off the road."

"Who's Mark Devlin?" Riley asked.

"The designer who did most of the sketches for the Lemon Squeeze Couture line."

"Okay. Now the name rings a bell. So he had an accident?"

"More like Devlin was run off the road," Theodosia said. "On the way back from the Juniper Bay Country Club. You realize that he's basically the third person in the Lemon Squeeze Couture gang to be attacked?" She was upset and let some of her anger seep through in her voice.

"Tell me exactly what happened," Riley said. He sounded interested now.

"I was driving behind the two cars, coming home from the Concours d'Carolina, when we saw a red sports car force Devlin's car off the road."

"And then?"

"And then it rolled over into the ditch."

"Are you okay?"

"I'm fine." Theodosia glanced over at Drayton. "Drayton and

I are both fine. But Mark Devlin isn't. It looked like attempted murder to me."

Instead of responding to that, Riley said, "You called an ambulance, correct?"

"Already did that. They're here and about to take Devlin to the hospital. The highway patrol is on the scene as well."

"Ah," Riley said. "Good."

Theodosia took a gulp of air. "Last night at the dogtrot house, you thought the tire tracks might have been made by a sports car."

"And you think this might have been the same sports car?"

"Because of the Lemon Squeeze connection, yes, I do. It's certainly possible. So what I'm thinking is . . ."

"Yes?"

"Is there any way you can run that car down? I mean go through the South Carolina Department of Motor Vehicles' records?"

"And look for red sports cars? Do you know how long that would take? How many red sports cars there probably are? It's your basic needle in a haystack proposition."

"What if I gave you specific names? And you checked to see if they had a sports car registered to them?"

"Theo, last night when I said sports car, I could have been completely off base. There are all sorts of SUVs that run on wide tires as well. And trucks. A zillion trucks."

"Okay, I get that. Can I still give you a list of names?"

"You can, but not this minute. E-mail or text them to me later tonight when you get home." He paused. "You are going home, aren't you?"

"Sure thing," Theodosia said.

"No, you *have* to go home. Please do this for me. Tell you what, go home now and I'll take you to dinner tomorrow night, okay? Over a glass of wine and a juicy fillet I'll let you talk about this to your heart's content. Ask as many questions as you want, too. Deal?"

"Deal." Theodosia hung up and turned to Drayton. "We've got two dead people and a third one seriously injured. All of them involved with Lemon Squeeze Couture. What does that tell you?"

"That the fashion business is dangerous?" Drayton said.

"Or someone *involved* in it is dangerous."

Drayton touched a finger to his lower lip. "But who?"

"Not sure. But it feels like every time we settle on a suspect in Nadine's murder they end up dead or injured."

"Excuse me. Folks?"

They both looked up as another highway patrolman approached them. He was middle-aged with a slightly hangdog face. His shoulders slumped and he looked tired, as if he'd been working since early this morning and now his shift had been extended.

"I know you folks are the ones that called this in, but you're going to have to step back now," the trooper said. "We need to search the area for anything that might shine a light on what happened here."

"But we already told you what happened," Drayton said.

The highway patrolman spread his arms wide. "Please? I'm only following protocol."

"Okay," Theodosia said as she and Drayton retreated to a patch of tall grass. "We should probably take off anyway. I can't imagine . . ."

"What?" Drayton murmured.

"I said . . ."

"No, I wasn't talking to you. My toe just hit something." Drayton bent down, felt around in the grass for a couple of seconds, and came up with a brown leather wallet.

Theodosia knew what it was immediately. "Holy cats, Drayton," she whispered. "I'll bet that belongs to Devlin. It probably flew out of his car on impact. Open it up and check it quick. Is it his?"

Drayton flipped open the wallet and gave a quick nod. Then he held it up to signal one of the officers.

"No!" Theodosia grabbed his arm and pulled it back down. "Shh, don't say a word. Let's look through it."

Drayton frowned. "Do you think that's ethical?"

"Of course not," Theodosia said. "But we're going to do it anyway."

"I don't like this one bit," Drayton said as they drove through Charleston. "The idea of checking out Devlin's apartment makes me queasy."

"Then roll down your window and breathe some fresh air," Theodosia said. "I told you before, it's an exploratory mission."

They were rolling down Fishburne Street, heading for Huger Street.

"What's the address again?" Theodosia asked.

Drayton consulted Devlin's driver's license for a second time. "561 Huger, number 212."

"So an apartment building."

"That'd be my guess," Drayton said.

They turned on Ashley Avenue, passed Wingnut Ice Cream and Gordy's Deli, and finally hit Huger Street.

"It's gotta be along here somewhere," Theodosia said.

"I see 422, 426, must be the next block."

Theodosia drove slowly, scanning for house numbers. "I think that's it up ahead." She stopped in front of a dark brick building. "Yup, this is it, Devlin's apartment."

It was a three-story building with a yellow awning and two large palmetto trees out front.

Theodosia studied the place carefully, wondering what she'd find if she went inside Devlin's apartment. Drugs? A gun? Some sort of answer to this mess?

"Too bad we don't have a key," Theodosia said. She'd been planning to slide a credit card into the lock.

"We do have a key," Drayton said.

Theodosia spun in her seat and stared at him. "What did you say?"

"At least I *think* we do. There's a brass key tucked inside a hidden compartment here in Devlin's wallet."

"Dig it out, let's see if it works."

"I still don't think that's a very good idea," Drayton said.

"Of course it's not a good idea," Theodosia said. "But we're going to do it anyway." She climbed out of her Jeep, and Drayton followed her up the walk. Overhead, a streetlamp flickered once, twice, then fizzled out. Theodosia hoped it wasn't an omen.

Drayton furrowed his brow. "Going inside Devlin's apartment is breaking and entering."

"It's more like pushing the envelope. Daring to go where angels fear to tread."

"You make it sound like a Hardy Boys adventure."

"Because it kind of is," Theodosia said. "Besides, if we have a key it's technically not breaking and entering."

"Tell that to the police officers when they haul us in, book us, and take unflattering mug shots," Drayton said as they got to the front door.

"You really have a thing about getting arrested, don't you?"

"Because it frightens me."

Theodosia put her hand on the doorknob for the outside door and tugged. Nothing doing; the door to the lobby was locked tight.

"Let's try that key," she said.

They monkeyed with the key, but it didn't work.

"There you go," Drayton said. "Wrong key. We're stymied already because it's a security building."

"No problem." Theodosia punched six buttons to the right of the door and shouted, "Pizza delivery!" The loud BRIIING of a buzzer sounded almost immediately.

"Trickery," Drayton muttered as they opened the door and scrambled inside.

"Investigating," Theodosia said as they walked into a lobby with awful red flocked wallpaper and a gold chandelier that could have been a reclaimed Sputnik satellite. They climbed the stairs to the second floor.

"Which apartment is his?" she asked.

"Number 212."

"Here it is. Okay, now we need to try that key," Theodosia said.

Reluctantly, Drayton handed over the key to Theodosia.

"I hope it doesn't work," he said.

Theodosia stuck the key in the lock. It worked just fine.

28

"This scares the bejeebers out of me," Drayton said as Theodosia pushed open the door and switched on the light.

"Then you should go back and wait in the car," Theodosia said. "If you're that worried, I'm certainly not going to force you to do this."

"Truth be told, I'm worried sick."

"Then go. Really." Theodosia was sincere; she didn't want Drayton to be any more upset than he already was.

Drayton made a half turn, reversed himself, and took a tentative step back toward Devlin's apartment. "Well, maybe I can manage my nerves for a little while longer."

"Uh-huh."

Inside, Mark Devlin's apartment was spare, modern, and well organized. A gray modular sofa curved around a smoked glass coffee table. There were end tables with contemporary silver pharmacy lamps. And two large bookshelves filled with oversized art, design, and fashion books.

Instead of a dining table, Fox had a large white enamel Parsons table that held a portable drawing board and an iMac computer. A lime-green task chair was pulled up to the table; two white file cabinets sat next to it.

"His arrangement is actually quite functional and smart," Drayton said.

"Not what you were expecting?" Theodosia said.

"And look at these." Drayton picked up a clutch of drawings off the desk and showed them to Theodosia. They were all sketches of clothing, some of them rendered in Magic Marker, others computer printouts. "The man is not without talent."

"Looks like Devlin's both old school and new school," Theodosia said. "Some of his sketches were done freehand; others were done on a computer."

Computer, she wondered. *Could Devlin have sent me that weird computer animation with all the arrows?*

Drayton picked up another stack of sketches. "He's good."

"I'd say he's very good," Theodosia said. She poked around on Devlin's desk, then pulled open several file drawers, looking for a video camera. If Devlin had one, it might help explain the strange video. But all her searching and rummaging around failed to produce a camera.

"Do you think Devlin's been angling to take Nadine's place all along?" Drayton asked. "To take over as creative director?"

"From what I've heard, Devlin pretty much *was* the creative director. According to Delaine, Nadine had no design skills at all. Couldn't produce a single sketch."

"But could Devlin have murdered Nadine?" Drayton asked. "To get her out of the way?"

"Maybe. But that doesn't explain Eddie Fox's murder."

"Could be they're not related."

"Two people involved in almost the same business? I don't know. Seems a little strange."

"I see your point." Drayton looked around the apartment. "Do you think Mr. Devlin owns a gun?"

"There's only one way to find out," Theodosia said.

Drayton winced. "I was afraid you were going to say that."

They searched the entire apartment. Looked through Devlin's nightstand and closet. Knelt down and peered under the bed only to find a lone sock and a few dust bunnies. Did a cursory check of his bathroom and diligently went through all the kitchen cabinets. In the end, there was no gun. Unless Devlin kept it stashed in his car or at a friend's house.

Drayton dusted his hands together. "We'd better get out of here before Devlin comes home and finds us."

"Not much chance of that," Theodosia said. "He looked awfully banged up when the EMTs loaded him into the ambulance. I'm guessing he'll spend the next couple of days in a hospital bed."

"Probably a good place for him."

"Yeah," Theodosia said. "Considering everything that's happened, he might be a lot safer in the hospital than out here in the real world."

They stepped outside Devlin's apartment and locked the door. Drayton seemed to breathe a sigh of relief as they headed for the stairs.

"That was . . . ," he began just as a young woman came bopping out of her apartment across the hall. She was dressed in blue jeans and a bright yellow hoodie. Theodosia pegged her as a college student.

"Hello there," the young woman said. She seemed a little startled to see unfamiliar faces in the hallway.

"Good evening," Theodosia said back.

The woman stared at Drayton. "Are you, um, looking for someone in particular?" There was wariness in her voice now.

"We were. But, unfortunately, he wasn't home," Drayton said.

"Then how did you get in?" the young woman demanded. "This is supposed to be a security building."

"We're part of the Neighborhood Watch Team," Theodosia said. "Just checking on one of our volunteers."

"Oh," the woman said. "Okay."

"If you'd care to volunteer . . . ," Theodosia said.

The young woman turned and ran down the stairs ahead of them. Couldn't get away fast enough. "Nope, sorry," she called back. "I've got enough on my plate as it is."

"Fibber," Drayton said under his breath.

"One thing I've learned," Theodosia said. "You don't solve a murder by being polite."

By the time they got to the Indigo Tea Shop to unload the Jeep, they both felt tired and beat.

"This could wait until tomorrow, you know," Theodosia said. She could see the weariness on Drayton's face.

Drayton sighed. "Yes, but we're going to be frantically busy tomorrow. Plus, Haley's going to need these coolers. Better to do it now."

As they prepared to trundle their load inside, a sleepy Haley met them at the back door. Teacake was draped around her neck.

"What happened?" Haley asked.

Drayton straightened up. "What makes you think something happened?"

"Because you're back so late." Haley studied Drayton. "And you're looking kind of twitchy."

"We witnessed an accident," Theodosia said. She decided to play it straight with Haley, not sugar coat anything. "We saw someone run Mark Devlin off the road."

Haley rubbed the corner of one eye. "Isn't he the design guy?"

"The fashion designer, yes," Drayton said.

"Run off the road, like somebody tried to *kill* him?" Haley asked.

"Luckily, it didn't come to that," Drayton said.

"First Nadine, then that film guy, now the designer," Haley said. "Does that seem like a pattern to you?"

"I'm afraid it does," Theodosia said. "Which is why we're still trying to figure this whole thing out."

Haley stood there for a moment, then turned to go back upstairs. "Okay," she called over her shoulder. "Just please be careful."

Theodosia and Drayton unloaded all the hampers and boxes, then Theodosia drove Drayton home.

"Don't forget Haley's words," Drayton said as he bid Theodosia good night.

"She said to be careful," Theodosia said. "And I will be."

"You'd *better* be. Whoever this killer is, they're sure not fooling around."

Theodosia followed Drayton's advice. She went home, changed clothes, grabbed Earl Grey, and took him for a nice, safe walk around the block. There'd be no running down Stoll's Alley or padding through Longitude Lane tonight, she decided. They were going to do the smart thing—that is, remain on guard and stick close to home.

They were coming down the narrow alley that served Theodosia's cottage as well as the far larger Granville Mansion next door, when Theodosia saw a vehicle parked some thirty feet ahead. Her hand tightened on Earl Grey's leash, and her heart skipped a beat.

Now what?

Then Theodosia saw what it was—a delivery van from Wittaker's Wine & Spirits—and relaxed her guard.

"What's going on?" she asked.

The delivery guy, a young man in his early twenties, was so

startled when she spoke to him that he whirled around fast and said, "Huh?" He hadn't heard her coming.

Earl Grey strained at his leash, trying to give the guy a tentative sniff.

"Does he bite?" the delivery guy stammered out.

"Not usually," Theodosia said.

"Oh, well . . ."

"Looks like somebody's getting ready to have a party," Theodosia said. There were two cases of wine, pretty good wine at that, sitting in the driveway.

"I dunno what's going on," the guy said. "I just make deliveries."

"You know there's no one living here right now, don't you? The owner's still in London."

"That so?" said the delivery guy. "But they gave me a key."

"Who gave you a key?"

"The guy I work for." He indicated the Wittaker's logo and writing on the side of the van. "The liquor store owner."

"I wonder who gave him the key?" Theodosia said.

The deliveryman shook his head. "Dunno. I just work there."

Later that night, Theodosia sent Riley a text of all the names she could think of—people who might drive a red sports car and could be connected to Nadine's murder as well as Eddie Fox's murder last night.

She made sure to include Marvin Chauvet, Harvey Bateman, Simon Nardwell, Mark Devlin (although it felt like he was out of it), and a few others. As a final postscript, she added Julie Eiden's name to the list.

Then she typed, *I also have something to show you.*

Theodosia was about to attach a photo she'd taken of the gimbal spring, then decided not to.

Taking a deep breath, she pushed SEND.

29

It was early. Not yet eight o'clock on Saturday morning, but Theodosia, Drayton, and Haley were already hard at work. This was the day of the big Tea Trolley Tour, and they had to prep, make, and transport an entire luncheon to the Featherbed House B and B.

"Have you decided on a particular tea yet?" Theodosia asked Drayton. He was standing behind the counter, appraising a row of tea tins that were lined up in front of him.

"It's a matter of matching the right tea to our menu," Drayton said.

"Of course it is. It's what you do. What you're *best* at."

"But today I'm relegating myself to serving only one tea," he said. "So it's considerably more complicated."

Theodosia glanced over at him. "I can see that."

"A black tea is always a perennial favorite," Drayton said.

"So choose a Ceylonese black tea or a Lapsang souchong."

Drayton cocked an eye at a silver tea tin. "But Plum Deluxe's Crème Brûlée Earl Grey could be an unexpected surprise."

"You would know better than anyone."

A sudden knock rattled the front door.

Exasperated, Drayton threw up his hands. "We're not open," he called out loudly. Then shot a glance at Theodosia. "Please tell me you put a note on the door?"

"Yup. It says we're closed for a private party."

KNOCK, KNOCK, KNOCK.

"Some very persistent fool seems to be ignoring your message," Drayton said.

"I'm sure they'll get the idea. Eventually."

There was another knock and then a voice shouted, "Open up, it's me."

"Who's me?" Drayton muttered.

"Shoot, it's Riley," Theodosia said.

She scurried to the front door, turned the latch, and opened it.

"What are you doing here?" she asked.

Riley stood there blinking in the pale morning sunlight. He looked natty in his navy sport coat, blue shirt, and khaki slacks, but his eyes looked tired. "You sent me a major communiqué last night, remember? Along with a tantalizing promise that you had something for me?" He stepped inside. "I'm here for show-and-tell."

"Oh, that."

"Oh, that? Come on, Theo, it's early and I haven't had my five cups of coffee yet."

"There's tea here," Drayton called to him.

"Well, that would be nice," Riley said. "Considering."

Theodosia stepped to the counter, poured out a cup of Chinese black tea for Riley, then carried it to a table. "Come," she said. "Sit."

Riley sat. "Are there scones, too? Or are you hoarding them for your fancy luncheon?"

So Theodosia ran into the kitchen, grabbed two cream scones and a small pot of raspberry jam, and brought everything back out to Riley.

"Here," she said. "Two stolen scones in exchange for what you found out about red sports cars."

Riley slathered jam on a scone, took a bite, and chewed appreciatively. He swallowed and said, "There are lots more red sports cars than you have scones, I'll tell you that."

"How many more?"

"Thousands."

"Really?" This was bad news. Riley had been right after all. It was a needle in a haystack proposition.

"Now what's this mysterious *thing* you wanted to show me?" Riley asked.

Theodosia explained about finding the gimbal spring, then handed it over to him.

Riley stared at it, resting in the palm of his hand.

"You could have given this to me two days ago," he said. "It might have saved Fox's life."

Theodosia shook her head. "Doubtful. Whoever shot Eddie Fox had nothing to do with a drone. This is probably a false clue. A negative. Whoever killed Fox, they were there waiting for him at the dogtrot house. Literally hunkered down and ready to shoot."

"Yeah, maybe." Riley took another bite of scone.

"So where are you on this Eddie Fox thing?" Theodosia asked. "Have you talked to ballistics? Was it the same caliber gun as used on Nadine?"

"Afraid so."

"Well, that's something to work off, right?"

"Possibly. We're also waiting for results from the medical examiner and the Crime Scene techs. So we're really just getting started."

"I'm sorry to hear that. How's your other investigation, the drug deal, panning out?"

"I think we might have completely messed up," Riley said. "Or received bad intel. I've talked to every lowlife dealer and jackhole from here to Savannah, and there's not a whiff of a deal going down anywhere. And no sign of tough guys from Miami."

"Maybe that's a good thing?"

"Might be," Riley said.

Riley sat there working on his second scone while Theodosia finished using Bubble Wrap to pack up some of her better tea-cups and saucers. She was worried that Angie might run short and wanted the tables to look perfect. Drayton, on the other hand, was still mumbling about tea choices.

"Okay," Riley said, wiping his hands on a napkin. "I'll see you tonight." He leaned over and gave Theodosia a kiss on the nose. "We've got an eight o'clock reservation at the Charleston Grill. So plan to dress fancy."

"I will and I can't wait," Theodosia said. She'd already decided to wear a short black leather jacket over a black ballet skirt. Kind of Goth but cute Goth, if there was such a thing.

"We need to go over our menu one more time," Drayton said once Riley had left.

"Haley!" Theodosia called. "Drayton wants to do a menu check."

Haley came running out looking a little frazzled. Her long blond hair was pinned up, and she wore a red bandanna over it. With her white chef's jacket, she looked, Theodosia decided, like a biker chick who baked.

"Make it snappy, okay?" Haley said. "I've got four pans of scones that need to come out of the oven in, like, four minutes."

"Right," Drayton said. "So we're starting with gingerbread scones and Devonshire cream, yes?"

Haley bobbed her head. "And our second course is a roasted beet and pear salad on Bibb lettuce."

"Be still my heart," Theodosia said. It was one of her favorites.

"Then we'll serve our crab salad tea sandwiches," Haley said.

"And for the entrée?" Drayton asked. "Wait, *is* there an entrée?"

"Asparagus and ham tartines," Haley said. "But a petite version because we don't want our guests to get *too* stuffed. They've still got to jump on the trolley for their dessert course at the Lady Goodwood Inn."

"Does all this help you with your tea choice, Drayton?" Theodosia asked.

"Absolutely, it does. I'm going to go with the Crème Brûlée Earl Grey as well as my proprietary house blend of Cherry Frost tea."

"So two teas," Haley said. "Neat."

"You know me, always live dangerously," Drayton said.

"Okay, Haley," Theodosia said. "As soon as your food's ready, we'll pack everything up, load it into my Jeep, and you can drive over to the Featherbed House. With Drayton riding shotgun, of course."

"Are you gonna take the trolley over to the Dove Cote Inn?" Haley asked. "For the first leg of the Tea Trolley Tour?"

Theodosia shook her head. "Delaine's picking me up. We're going to do the Dove Cote cream tea together. Then, when she bugs out for Cotton Duck, I'll ride the Tea Trolley to the Featherbed House."

"So we'll see you there," Drayton said.

"With bells on," Theodosia said.

Just as she'd promised, Delaine pulled up in front of the Indigo Tea Shop at nine forty-five sharp. She tooted her horn a couple of times, and Theodosia went running out.

"You look like a fashionista," Theodosia said as she climbed into the front seat of Delaine's BMW. Delaine was wearing a pale pink skirt suit and black patent leather stilettos. Definitely sexy, but they had to be difficult to drive in.

"I *feel* like a fashionista," Delaine said as she pulled into traffic on Church Street, cutting off a white panel truck. "Actually, I'm super energized now that Bettina and I have had our heart-to-heart talk. I just know things are going to change for the better. I'm going to try to be a more open and giving person."

"Good for you," Theodosia said, meaning it.

"And you, in your fitted houndstooth jacket and black slacks. Well played."

"Thank you."

Delaine wove her way over to Lamboll Street and, despite Theodosia's protestations, parked in an EMPLOYEES ONLY parking spot in the small lot behind the Dove Cote Inn. Then they walked around to the front of the fanciful-looking Victorian inn and hoofed it up a winding cobblestone walk to the main entrance.

In earlier days, the Dove Cote Inn had served as a family residence. Now, with relatively new owners, the charming inn offered twelve luxurious suites (some with hot tubs) along with a large dining room addition that had been dubbed the Essex Room.

Inside, the Dove Cote's lobby smelled of lemon-scented candles while a fire crackled merrily in the brick fireplace. There were cozy armchairs and sofas in cream-colored leather with plump pink velvet pillows, and the Chinese carpet underfoot was an elegant shade of persimmon.

Isabelle Franklin, the inn's manager, stood in the lobby greeting guests and shepherding them back to the dining room.

"Theodosia," Isabelle said when she caught sight of them. "And Delaine, too. Welcome. I'm delighted you could make it." Isabelle was a small woman in her mid-thirties with shoulder-length blond hair. Today she wore a white ruffled blouse with a cameo pinned at the neck and a long black skirt.

"You look so *serious*," Delaine said as she enveloped Isabelle in a hug. "Darlin', we need to *talk*."

"I think 'need to talk' is Delaine parlance for choosing a new wardrobe," Isabelle laughed. "Am I right?"

Delaine wrinkled her nose. "Well . . ."

"I'm just trying to embody our Dove Cote brand," Isabelle said. "You know, historic and Victorian?"

"Then I'd say you're right on the money," Theodosia said as Isabelle led them down a short wood-paneled hallway hung with small oil paintings, and into the Essex Room.

It was, in a nutshell, the perfect spring venue. The inn's owners had started with a lovely, fairly spacious dining room, then taken it one step further and put on a large glass addition that included a curved glass roof. The finished product was light and airy—a room that not only looked out over a flourishing garden, but almost brought the garden inside.

"Gorgeous," Delaine said.

"And practically filled to capacity," Theodosia said, looking at the lively throng of guests already seated at the half dozen or so round tables.

"Now you know what you have to look forward to," Isabelle said to Theodosia. "For your luncheon tea."

"We'll be ready," Theodosia said. *At least I hope we will.*

"And I have to thank you for all your good suggestions," Isabelle said, grasping Theodosia's hand. "My kitchen people are terrific, but they've never done an actual morning cream tea before. Thank goodness Drayton gave us tea pointers and Haley shared her recipe for buttermilk scones."

"Goodness," Delaine said. "I hope the scones are low-carb."

They weren't, but nobody minded.

"What kind of tea is this again?" Delaine asked. They were sitting at a table with ten other guests where a lively conversation about tea and Southern tea traditions was ongoing.

"Spiced plum," Theodosia told her. "Basically a black Chinese tea with the essence of cinnamon and plums."

"Very nice. And this scone is positively luscious," Delaine said.

Theodosia couldn't agree more, because this was one of Haley's pride and joy recipes. Warm buttermilk scones, sliced in half and stuffed with fresh freestone peaches that had been judiciously sugared. Then the whole thing was topped with a generous dollop of fresh Devonshire cream. The kind whipped up with mascarpone.

"And isn't this dining room just adorable and done to the nines?" Delaine asked.

Theodosia had to agree. On the far wall was another impressive fireplace with a large Baroque mirror over it. An elegant brass clock and pair of lounging ceramic leopards rested on the mantel. Green topiary trees hung with pink and yellow silk flowers sat on two cocktail tables that flanked the fireplace. Perfection.

Theodosia alternately ate, chatted, and worried about the second leg of the Tea Trolley Tour that she'd soon be hosting at the Featherbed House. Had they planned too many courses? Was the event overloaded by having not one but two fashion shows? Would the weather hold and did Angie have the patio set to go? Most importantly, would Drayton and Haley be ready with the food and tea?

All those questions whirled through Theodosia's brain as she said goodbye to everyone and jumped on the first of two open-air trolleys that would ferry the Tea Trolley Tour guests to the Featherbed House.

Of course, the trolleys took their own sweet time getting there. They meandered through the Historic District as the driver pointed out such points of interest as White Point Garden, the Battery, the Gibbes Museum of Art, the Governor Aiken Gates, and the Charleston Library Society—all neighborhood haunts to Theodosia. So when they finally arrived at the Featherbed House some forty-five minutes later, she was in quite a dither.

30

When the Tea Trolley Tour pulled up in front of the Featherbed House B and B, Theodosia immediately hopped off and ran inside to check on Drayton and Haley.

She found them in the large restaurant-style kitchen, with Angie's two assistants, everyone looking relatively calm and collected.

"Is everything okay?" Theodosia asked, her words bubbling out in a rush. "Is the food set to go?"

"Sure is," Haley said as she carefully cut the crusts off a stack of sandwiches, then deftly quartered them. "Why wouldn't it be?"

"I was just . . . worried," Theodosia said, thinking to herself, *I gotta tone down this anxiety. I'm sure everything will go off without a hitch.*

"Don't be nervous," Haley said. "I got this. We got this."

"My one concern is that the guests won't be hungry," Drayton said.

"They'll be hungry," Haley said.

"But the Dove Cote's cream tea?" Drayton glanced at Theodosia. "You don't think the scone and peaches were too filling?"

"I'd say it was more like a taste of things to come," Theodosia said.

"Like an appetizer," Drayton said, looking pleased.

"Right." Theodosia was trying to breathe deeply, forcing herself to relax. Tea was brewing, beets were being grilled, salad plates were stacked, the asparagus and ham tartines were in the oven.

"See?" Haley said. "Our luncheon's going to be the star of the show. Of the entire day."

Drayton gave a quick nod. "We can only hope."

Theodosia wandered out of the kitchen and back through the lobby to check with Angie. But of course Angie was busy on the patio, basically directing traffic and seating guests. With the sun shining down, the patio looked adorable. Almost two dozen tables with Cinzano umbrellas, large earthenware pots spilling over with pink bougainvillea, and a small burbling pond next to a greenhouse where a row of purple orchids peeked through open windows.

Theodosia came up behind Angie. "Need any help?"

Angie turned around quickly. When she saw it was Theodosia, she visibly relaxed. "We're moving along fairly well," she said, then smiled at a group of four women and said, "That's right, you can have this table right here."

Then her focus was back on Theodosia.

"If you could do a quick check on the fashion people, that'd be great," Angie said. "I gave them two rooms in the annex to use for staging and as dressing rooms. And then . . ." She motioned to another group of women and said, "Over here, ladies, your table's right here."

"And then?" Theodosia said.

"Maybe get Anja and Katie, my two kitchen helpers, to start serving tea."

"Done," Theodosia said.

She walked to the edge of the patio, ducked around a woven wood fence that was covered with curls of green ivy, and peered into one of the annex rooms. Echo Grace was in there along with a half dozen models. The models were already dressed, and Echo was making wardrobe adjustments—more jewelry here, a casually draped scarf there. Echo was big on layering, just like Delaine.

In fact, a Delaine-styled outfit wasn't complete until there was a scarf, beads, bracelets, and a bag. Sometimes Delaine even styled her clients with two bags, one a large tote and the other a kind of smaller cross-body bag.

Echo looked up from where she was pinning glittery bee pins on a green velvet jacket. "Hey there," she said.

"Just checking in," Theodosia said. "You need anything?"

"Drayton brought us some tea a while back. Something called Cherry Frost, so we're good. Getting jazzed up, ready to roll. Just need to accessorize with a few of Kiki Everhart's bags and leather cuffs."

"Okay, see you later."

Theodosia popped her head into the second room and saw that Everhart had laid out all her bags and cuffs on the two beds. And did they ever look gorgeous. Angie had been right when she said Everhart was a true *artiste*.

So, okay. Theodosia threaded her way back across the patio, nodding at some of the guests, stopping to talk to a few others. Bill Glass was there, snapping photos, grinning from ear to ear. When he saw Theodosia, he gave a mock salute.

Giving him a casual wave, Theodosia walked back inside the Featherbed House, closed the double doors behind her, and headed through the lobby into the kitchen.

And found that teapots were already filled and scones were stacked on large silver platters ready to be served.

"You're ready to go," Theodosia said, pleased.

"We're on it," Haley said as she added a couple more scones to the stack. "Anja and Katie are heading out now with the tea. Drayton and I will follow with scones and Devonshire cream." She glanced sideways at her. "Okay?"

"Perfect," Theodosia said. "Now what can I do to help?"

"You, my dear, can finish slicing these pears for the salad. When I come back in, I'll start plating."

"You see," Drayton said as he edged by her with a tray of scones. "We've got this."

Theodosia sliced pears, checked on the grilled beets and the baking tartines, and generally puttered around the kitchen until everyone came back. Then Haley, little martinet that she was, gently eased her out.

"Maybe you could check on how the first course is going," Haley said. "Give us the high sign when it's time to start clearing. After that we'll bring out the salads."

Back in the lobby, Theodosia ran into Angie.

"It's going great out there," Angie said, her face flushed with excitement. "People are loving it."

"When are you going to start the fashion show?" Theodosia asked.

"I thought we'd wait until the salad course. Okay with you?"

"Works for me," Theodosia said. She glanced out the double doors to the patio. And what she saw gave her a sudden start.

Harvey Bateman and Marvin Chauvet were sitting at one of the tables, chatting with a few of the guests.

"Bateman and Chauvet," Theodosia stuttered out to Angie. "What are those two guys doing here?" A sick feeling had begun to grow in the pit of her stomach.

"Actually, it's kind of exciting," Angie said. "For Kiki Everhart, anyway. It seems that Mr. Chauvet and Mr. Bateman heard all about her bags and leather cuffs and are quite interested in the entire line."

"Interested how? Investing in it or buying the line outright?"

"Well, I heard the words *seed money* thrown around so it struck me as more of a partnership deal." Angie frowned. She'd detected Theodosia's negative vibe. "Why? Is something wrong? Something I should know about?"

Theodosia waved a hand. "Not at all, everything's perfect. I'm just overreacting. Go back out there and have fun. Be the lively hotelier we know and love."

Angie laughed. "When you put it that way . . ." She held up a finger. "But first I do have to check something in the kitchen."

Theodosia stood there, not sure whether she should be angry or worried about Harv and Marv. Was it possible that one of them was a stone-cold killer? That one had pinned a threatening note to her door and then sent a harassing e-mail? The question was—which one?

Both of them?

She stared out at the patio again. Harv and Marv worried her. Just the fact that they were here today felt hinky. What was going on? Could they be fashion people *and* drug dealers? Had they been involved in the cocaine deal that had gotten Nadine killed?

Theodosia's mind was working overtime as she ruminated on the possibilities. Had one of them run Devlin's car off the road last night? When Devlin had mentioned his suspicions to her, had he been obliquely referring to Harv or Marv?

Suddenly, Theodosia had to know. In fact, she was kicking herself for not getting in touch with Devlin earlier.

Slipping into Angie's office, she dialed the number for the hospital. When she reached the central operator, she asked to be put through to Mark Devlin's room. There was a pause and then the operator said, "That would be room 516. I'll connect you now."

"Thank you."

There was a hollow click, then the phone started ringing on the other end. And rang and rang and rang.

Dang, he's not there.

Theodosia strode from one end of the lobby to the other, thinking about the two murders and the car crash last night. It all seemed to be connected. And yet . . . she couldn't quite make it all connect.

She stopped pacing, sat down hard in a wingback chair, and pressed her hands to her forehead. If she could just relax and clear her head, not let the monkey brain take over and pull her thoughts in a million different directions. Maybe then she could figure this out.

Lifting her head, she stared at a plush goose that sat on one of the chintz sofas.

With its white, feathery body, shiny oil spot eyes, and yellow webbed feet, it was adorable.

That's when something deep inside her brain went CLICK.

She exhaled slowly. *What just happened here?*

Theodosia had literally felt a palpable tick, a sensation that made her feel as if a missing piece of the puzzle had suddenly dropped into place. Only she wasn't exactly sure what puzzle piece that was. Or where it was taking her.

Then she gazed at the plush goose again and something about it joggled her memory. She thought about the feather Drayton had picked up Thursday night at the dogtrot house murder scene.

No, it can't be.

She shoved the thought away only to have it come rushing back at her.

A feather. Drayton had thought it was an owl's feather. Only Theodosia suddenly had a different idea. What if he'd actually found an ostrich feather? A fluffy, showy ostrich feather that had come off one of Echo Grace's gorgeous suede jackets!

She reached out, picked up the plush goose, and held it in her hands, thinking, *Echo? Really?*

There was a soft snick as the patio door opened and a breath of wind crept in.

Theodosia looked up as sun mingled with shadows and wondered if her eyes were playing tricks on her. Then she saw Echo Grace standing there, staring at her, a look of supreme curiosity on her face. Then Echo gazed at the stuffed goose Theodosia held in her hand, and her expression changed to one of wariness.

And was that a hint of resignation? At being found out?

Theodosia saw the change come over Echo's face, plain as day. She must be involved! Theodosia didn't know how or why, but she suddenly *knew* that Echo was . . .

"Echo," Theodosia stammered. "We need to . . ."

A curtain dropped over Echo's face, turning it dark and hard and filled with rage. She turned and started moving fast, flitted through the lobby as if she had a hundred demons nipping at her heels. Echo gave Theodosia one angry backward glance over her shoulder. And then, like a wraith in a moonlit cemetery, slipped quietly out of sight.

Theodosia's only thought was, *Where'd she go?*

31

Theodosia dropped the goose and jumped up from the chair just as her phone started to ring.

She pulled it from her pocket and said, "Hello?" as she strode forcefully down the hallway toward the kitchen.

"Theo, it's me," Riley said. "I ran those names like you asked."

"Riley," she said, fear and anxiety coloring her voice as she blasted through the kitchen door and rounded one of the stainless steel kitchen counters, banging her hip in the process. "Something happened. I think . . ."

"And I added a couple more names," Riley said, talking over her. "I might have found . . ."

Theodosia only half listened to him as she pushed past Haley, who was plating salads, and Drayton, who was adding little sprigs of parsley. They stared at her, looking surprised and a little worried.

"Did Echo come through here?" Theodosia asked. There was urgency in her voice.

"She ran through here like somebody was chasing her," Haley said. "I'm not sure where she was going."

Theodosia ran back out to the lobby, looked around, then charged out onto the patio.

No Echo in sight. Just people calmly eating scones.

"Theo, are you listening to me?" Riley said in her ear.

"Yes . . . I mean sort of," Theodosia replied. She actually wasn't listening to him. She had something more important on her mind.

Where did Echo run off to?

Back inside the Featherbed House, feeling frantic, Theodosia dashed down a short hallway and pushed open the door to the breakfast room. It was dark inside. With no lights on she could barely make out the table and chairs, another piece of bulky furniture.

Did Echo run in here?

"Theo?" Riley said again in her ear.

Theodosia ignored him. Because someone *was* standing in here. Over in the corner, kind of crouched and swaying.

Is that her? What's she doing?

Theodosia crept in silently. The only light in the room came from a faint glowing lamp built into a maple highboy that held Angie's small collection of copper luster dishes.

Theodosia blinked, trying to let her eyes get accustomed to the dark. And then, more than a little startled when she saw Angie standing there, said, "Angie? Is that you?"

Why, Theodosia wondered, was Angie hiding in the dark, quaking like a frightened kitten, when she was supposed to be playing hostess out on the patio?

Theodosia's eyes searched the dim room as Riley continued to rattle away in her ear.

Then she saw that Angie's shoulders were pinched forward, as if she were trying to pick up a heavy load. And that Angie's normally placid face wore a brittle, almost paralyzed expression.

The image was so strange and incongruous that Theodosia immediately blurted out, "Angie, what's . . . ?"

"What?" Riley said in her ear.

That's when Theodosia realized that Angie wasn't alone in here. Echo Grace was standing directly behind Angie, practically hidden in shadows. Except for the fact that Echo had one arm bent around Angie's neck with a knife pressed hard to her throat.

Time stood still for Theodosia. She was aware of a ticking clock, of a pinpoint of light reflecting off something, and of her own quiet breathing.

It took Theodosia a split second to process this horrible scene. And realize the terrible danger Angie was in. The knife Echo held was nasty, a long, thin knife that had no doubt come from Angie's own kitchen. A knife you'd use for something serious. Like deboning a chicken or filleting a fish.

Or slicing someone's throat.

"Theodosia?" came Riley's insistent voice. Loud enough now for everyone in the room to hear.

"End that call," Echo hissed at her.

"Sure," Theodosia said. "Just don't *hurt* her, okay?" She pressed a button and carefully placed her cell phone on a nearby shelf, hoping against hope that Riley would be able to hear what was going on. What *would be* going on if she could figure out what to do. How to defuse this terrible situation.

"Now get in here and shut that door," Echo ordered. Echo's face had turned dark and saturnine as she pressed the blade harder against Angie's neck.

"Why are you doing this?" Theodosia asked.

Echo spit her words at her. "You know why."

"You killed Nadine," Theodosia said as Angie squirmed in Echo's clutches and her face turned another shade of pale.

"What of it? She was in the way," Echo snarled. "Blundered in, stupid cow."

"Blundered into your drug deal?"

"You're so smart, why don't you tell me what happened," Echo said.

"Eddie Fox was your partner," Theodosia said, venturing a guess. "And you killed him, too."

"Eddie was a disaster. Sure, he had connections all over the place, good connections. But all he really wanted to do was put the stuff up his nose." Echo shook her head. "I have no tolerance for druggies."

"Just drug dealers," Theodosia said. She gazed at Angie, who was imploring her with her eyes, begging Theodosia to do something. And she wanted to, she really did. But what?

"Drugs were only a sideline, babe," Echo said in a haughty voice. "But now . . . well, you've made things difficult, haven't you. Complicated." Echo pushed her knife harder against Angie's throat, and a bead of blood appeared, shimmering like a tiny ruby.

"Don't you dare hurt her." Theodosia's voice was cold as ice with a hard expression to match.

"Or what?" Echo taunted.

There was a sudden bump at the door, then Drayton pushed his way into the breakfast room.

"Theo, are you in here? Haley needs . . ." He stopped. "Goodness me, why is it so dark in here? It's like the inside of a tomb."

Drayton stood there, curious, posture as erect as a ballet instructor, balancing a silver tray that held a steaming pot of tea.

"Wonderful," Echo sneered. "Your little toady has arrived."

Drayton did a sudden double take as Echo spoke from out of the darkness. "Excuse me?"

"Set your tray down," Echo ordered. "Then stand over there with the tea shop lady."

Drayton didn't budge an inch. Instead, he slowly took in the scene—the knife pressed hard against Angie's throat, Theodosia's grim expression, Echo's anger—and was so genuinely flustered that he simply stood there immobile, hands clutching his tray.

Echo gritted her teeth. "I said put it down!"

"Sorry, sorry," Theodosia said as she started toward Drayton, a half-apologetic, half-cowed look on her face. "Better let me help with that." She pulled the tray away from him, wrapped one hand around the teapot's sturdy handle, and set the tray down on the mahogany table.

A split second later, teapot gripped firmly in hand, Theodosia swung it with all her might at Echo's head. It was a swing like no other, a farm team batter stepping up to home plate and swinging against a veteran pitcher for the New York Yankees. Only Theodosia added a desperate, whispered plea. *Gotta do this right, gotta connect and back off this crazy lady!*

And back her off she did.

The teapot sounded like a gunshot as it struck hard against the side of Echo's head, sending shock waves through her entire body. The force of the blow cracked a tooth, split Echo's lower lip wide open, and knocked her completely off-balance. The scalding-hot tea was a lucky strike extra as it splashed everywhere, giving Angie a chance to escape her captor's clutches while it drenched Echo from head to toe.

Echo reacted as if she'd just received a ten-thousand-watt jolt of raw electricity. Screaming in pain, she frantically clawed at thin air as the hot tea, burning like Hades, sent her yowling and crashing to the floor.

As she fell, the knife skittered out of her hand.

No stranger to a life-and-death struggle, Theodosia quickly dropped to her hands and knees. And, in a puddle of hot tea and a melee of broken shards, scrambled madly for the knife.

Echo, also on the floor, flailed blindly, her cries turning to urgent, angry bleats as she tried desperately to reclaim the knife . . .

32

Theodosia got there first. She wrapped a hand around the handle, snatched up the boning knife, and scrambled to her feet. She was breathless and scared, still feeling shaky, but resolute that she'd been forced to act in Angie's defense.

Still not willing to accept defeat, Echo growled like a wild animal and spun herself around, hands pulled into claws. There was blood in her eye as she struggled to her knees, trying desperately to pull herself up and launch a murderous attack—this time aimed at Theodosia.

Seeing her adversary coiling like a venomous sidewinder, Theodosia responded with another split-second move. She whirled around, balanced carefully, and lifted her right leg. With precision aim, she cocked her knee and launched a murderous kick.

Oof.

Theodosia's leather loafer connected squarely with Echo's chin. The woman folded like a cheap card table and went down, sprawling flat on her face for a second time.

That's when the door suddenly crashed open with a resounding WHAP! and a perturbed Haley came flying in.

"What the hell-o!" Haley cried as she slid to a stop. Stunned, her mouth gaped open and her eyes grew large with shock as she saw the slightly wounded Angie and a crumpled Echo Grace. Finally, she managed to stammer out a breathy, "What happened here?"

"Echo tried to kill Angie," Theodosia managed to gasp. She was out of breath from fear, exertion, and the extra shot of adrenaline that coursed roughly through her veins. "With a knife."

"Kill her?" Haley wheeled around to face Echo, who was now crouched in a sad heap on the floor, moaning and holding her jaw. "You tried to *kill* Angie?"

"Echo's the one who murdered Nadine and Eddie Fox," Theodosia said. "Probably drove Mark Devlin off the highway, too."

"She did?" Haley cried. "Why?"

"Drug deal," Theodosia said.

"*She's* the one?" Haley focused blazing eyes on Echo and muttered, "You witch."

Echo pulled herself into a tight little ball of indignation and glared. "You crack muh toof!" she cried at Theodosia.

"Here's the thing," Theodosia said, her words short and clipped. "My manners fly out the window when someone threatens a friend of mine with bodily harm." She paused. "I find it . . . unforgivable."

"Theo, did you call the cops?" Haley cried. She was suddenly jumping up and down. "You gotta call the cops, like, ASAP. Tell 'em you solved two murders. Bing, bang, boom, just like that." Haley dusted her hands together, her mood suddenly bordering on ecstatic.

"We're calling, I'm calling," Theodosia said wearily. She wondered if Riley had caught any of this drama as she grabbed her phone off the shelf and put it to her ear. Nope, he'd hung up. She sighed and hit 911.

Drayton, in the meantime, had picked up the heavy metal tray and cocked it at a crazy angle, ready to whack Echo again should she attempt to get up. She did not.

"They're coming," Theodosia said, finally, after a short conversation with the 911 operator. "The police are on their way."

Angie touched a tentative hand to Theodosia's shoulder and said, "Theo, she was about to slit my throat. You . . . you saved my life." Then, tears streaming down her face, Angie began to shake uncontrollably.

Theodosia pulled Angie close to her and hugged her. "You're okay, you're okay," she murmured over and over until Angie finally managed to calm down.

"I know I am," Angie said, swallowing hard. "Now. But you saved me. Thank you, Theo. Thank you so much."

Theodosia pointed to Echo, who had crawled into a corner and was looking angry and sullen. "We should check her leg."

Haley peered at Echo. "Check her for what?"

"A dog bite. Earl Grey might have bit her."

Haley reached out, pushed up Echo's long skirt to her knees, and said, "Yup, looks like a dog bite to me. Earl Grey did that?"

"Yes, thank goodness," said Theodosia. "He went after her when she and Eddie tried to waylay me the other night. Lord knows what they had in mind."

"I'm sure it wasn't good," Drayton said.

Five minutes later, with a tidal wave of sirens approaching, Theodosia ran into the lobby to meet the police.

Riley and Tidwell both showed up. Along with a cavalcade of uniformed officers that seemed to bring the entire tea party to a crashing halt.

One of the guests, a red-haired woman in her seventies, rushed in to see what all the excitement was about. As she stood there gaping, several good-looking male officers streamed past her. She looked up with eager eyes and said, "Strippers? You hired male strippers? Who-hee!"

Theodosia actually laughed out loud. Then had to give the woman the bad news that these were genuine police officers, not the Chippendales in costume.

"Theo!" Riley called. "We need to talk."

Bill Glass suddenly came running in, cameras dangling around his neck, and shouted, "What did I miss? What did I miss?"

"Please go back outside," Tidwell urged. "We'll tell you all about it later."

Theodosia finally collapsed into an easy chair as she explained to Riley and Tidwell exactly what had gone down—the knife at Angie's throat, Drayton stumbling in, her taking a wild chance and smashing a teapot against Echo's jaw.

Once Riley and Tidwell had finished quizzing her at length, Theodosia took time to phone Cotton Duck and give Delaine and Bettina the good news.

"It's over," she said. "Echo Grace has been arrested for the murder of Nadine and her own coconspirator Eddie Fox. They'll probably press charges against Echo for causing Mark Devlin's car crash as well. Oh, and the drugs, too."

Delaine and Bettina were on the phone together, both of them shouting questions and squealing at Theodosia's answers.

"You did it!" Bettina cried. "You said you'd find Mom's killer and you did it!"

"I never doubted Theodosia for a minute!" Delaine shouted.

Then, because Angie was still awfully shaky, Theodosia went outside and carefully explained the strange circumstances to the guests who were still seated at tables on the patio, waiting for their tea sandwiches and entrées. She didn't give them the whole version, just a kind of CliffsNotes summary.

When Theodosia finished, she figured they'd be angry and upset at having their luncheon ruined. Instead, she received a hearty round of applause.

"Bravo!" one woman cheered and stood up, which prompted the rest of the guests to stand, too.

"Brave girl," another guest shouted.

"Thank you, thank you very much," Theodosia said, raising her arms and making a *please sit down* gesture in the air. "But I want to assure you that the luncheon *will* go on. In fact, we'll be serving tea sandwiches shortly, as well as our special asparagus and ham tartines. Along with plenty of Drayton's fresh-brewed tea."

Tidwell suddenly came sauntering out, looking pleased with himself.

Saved by the burly detective in the bad suit.

"And this, ladies," Theodosia said, "is Detective Burt Tidwell who heads the Robbery and Homicide Division of the Charleston Police Department."

As the applause started up again, Theodosia decided to be a little mischievous and take it one step further.

"In fact, I'm quite confident the good detective would be delighted to say a few words about his role in solving these two recent homicides."

"What?" Tidwell snarled. "Me?"

The applause grew louder as Theodosia flashed an encouraging smile at Tidwell.

Bill Glass leaned in with his camera and grinned like a malevolent jack-o'-lantern. "Go ahead, bucko," he whispered. "Give it to 'em straight." At which point Theodosia shoved Glass out of the way.

Nonplussed, Tidwell gazed around at his audience, trying to

decide exactly what to do as anxious eyes stared at him. Then he lifted his chin and drew himself up to his full height. "Perhaps I could deliver a quick rundown . . . from a law enforcement perspective, of course."

At that moment, Theodosia could have sworn she saw a rare smile flit across Tidwell's craggy face.

Or maybe not.

The Indigo Tea Shop

Killer Lemon Cream Scones

2 cups flour

⅓ cup sugar

1 Tbsp. baking powder

¼ tsp. salt

1 tsp. lemon peel, grated finely

1 cup heavy cream

3 Tbsp. water

PREHEAT oven to 375 degrees. In a medium bowl, combine flour, sugar, baking powder, salt, and lemon peel. Stir in cream and water using fork, then mix until dough forms a rough ball. Knead dough 4 or 5 times on a lightly floured surface. Place on greased cookie sheet and pat into an 8-inch round circle. Using a large knife, cut into dough halfway, making 8 wedges. Bake 20 to 25 minutes, until golden brown. Cool on wire rack and cut into wedges while still warm. Serve with lemon curd or Devonshire cream. Yields 8 scones.

Strawberries with Balsamic Vinegar

16 oz. fresh strawberries, hulled and halved
2 Tbsp. balsamic vinegar
¼ cup sugar

PLACE strawberries in a bowl. Drizzle balsamic vinegar over strawberries, then sprinkle with sugar. Stir gently to combine ingredients. Cover and let sit at room temperature for 1 to 2 hours. Serve. Yields 6 servings. (Note: These tasty strawberries are the perfect accompaniment to tea and scones.)

Roasted Red Pepper Hummus

1 can (15 oz.) garbanzo beans
2 cloves garlic, minced
⅓ cup tahini
⅓ cup lemon juice
½ cup roasted red peppers
¼ tsp. dried basil
Salt and pepper to taste

IN a food processor, combine garbanzo beans, garlic, tahini, and lemon juice. Process until the mixture is smooth and creamy. Add roasted red peppers and basil. Process again until peppers are finely chopped. Transfer hummus to small bowl, cover, and chill until ready to serve. Yields 2 cups. (Note: Excellent with pita bread or savory scones such as cheddar cheese scones.)

Haley's Lemon Bars

    1 cup butter, softened
    2 cups sugar, divided into ½ cup and 1½ cups
    2 ½ cups cups all-purpose flour, divided into 2 cups plus one
        extra ½ cup
    4 eggs
    2 lemons, juiced

PREHEAT oven to 350 degrees. In medium bowl, blend together butter, ½ cup sugar, and 2 cups flour. Press mixture into the bottom of an ungreased 9-by-13-inch baking pan.

BAKE for 15 to 18 minutes or until firm and golden. In another bowl, whisk together 1½ cups sugar and ½ cup flour. Whisk in the eggs and lemon juice, then pour over baked crust. Bake for an additional 20 minutes and remove from oven. Bars will firm up as they cool. Yields 12 good-sized bars.

Drayton's Favorite Lemon Curd

    ¾ cup fresh lemon juice
    1 Tbsp. grated lemon zest
    ¾ cup sugar
    3 eggs
    ½ stick unsalted butter, cubed

IN a 2-quart saucepan, combine lemon juice, lemon zest, sugar, eggs, and butter. Whisk and cook over medium-low heat until mixture thickens enough to hold marks from the whisk and the first bubble appears on the surface. (This will take about 6 minutes.) Pour into storage container, cover surface with plastic wrap, and refrigerate. Yields about 1²/₃ cups. (Note: Serve lemon curd as topping for your favorite scones.)

Honest-to-Goodness English Crumpets

1 pkg. active dry yeast
1 tsp. sugar
¼ cup warm water
1 egg
⅓ cup milk, room temperature
4 Tbsp. butter
1 cup all-purpose flour
½ tsp. salt
Baking rings or round cookie cutters

IN large bowl, combine dry yeast, sugar, and warm water. Let stand for 15 minutes, until bubbly. Blend in egg, milk, and 1 Tbsp. butter. Now add flour and salt and beat until smooth. Cover and let stand in a warm place until mixture doubles (about 45 minutes). Place remaining 3 Tbsp. of butter in griddle over low to medium heat. Add baking rings. Pour about 3 Tbsp. of batter into each ring. Cook about 7 minutes or until small holes appear and tops appear dry. Remove rings and flip crumpets over and brown lightly. Serve crumpets warm with butter or preserves. Yields 6 to 8 crumpets.

Yummy Butterscotch Brownies

    2 cups flour
    2 tsp. baking powder
    1½ tsp. salt
    1 pkg. (12 oz.) butterscotch morsels
    ½ cup (1 stick) butter
    1 cup brown sugar
    4 eggs
    1 tsp. vanilla extract
    1 cup chopped nuts (optional)

PREHEAT oven to 350 degrees. Combine flour, baking powder, and salt, then set flour mixture aside. Melt butterscotch morsels and place in large mixing bowl. Add butter and brown sugar and cream together. Let cool for 5 minutes. Now beat in eggs and vanilla. Blend in flour mixture and nuts (if desired) and spread evenly in a 13-by-9-inch pan. Bake for 30 minutes. Then let cool and serve. Yields about 12 brownies.

Muffuletta Olive Salad Sandwich

SALAD

    ½ cup chopped green stuffed olives
    ½ cup chopped black olives, pitted
    4 peperoncini, minced
    ½ cup roasted red peppers, diced
    1 cup extra-virgin olive oil
    3 Tbsp. fresh parsley

¼ tsp. basil

2 Tbsp. balsamic vinegar

SANDWICH

1 large round loaf of bread (Italian or sourdough)

⅓ lb. salami, thinly sliced

⅓ lb. prosciutto or capicola ham, thinly sliced

½ lb. provolone cheese, thinly sliced

½ cup Havarti cheese, thinly sliced

½ red onion, thinly sliced

COMBINE all salad ingredients and let stand so that flavors can meld. Slice the bread in half, removing the top portion like a cap. Scoop out some of the center loaf. Drizzle oil from the salad on both top and bottom halves. Now layer in the olive salad, cold cuts, cheeses, and onion slices—and layer again until all the ingredients are used. Place top on sandwich and slice into 6 wedges. Serve with soup or chips. Yields 6 sandwich wedges.

Chicken and Fruit Luncheon Salad

4 cups cooked diced chicken

2 cups chopped celery

1 cup chopped apples

1 cup pineapple chunks, drained

1 cup mayonnaise

½ tsp. salt

2 Tbsp. lemon juice

½ cup chopped toasted almonds

Lettuce for 6 lettuce cups

COMBINE all ingredients in a large bowl and toss until well combined. Place 6 lettuce cups on luncheon plates and scoop in salad. Yields 6 servings.

Baked Brown Sugar Salmon

2 Tbsp. lemon juice
⅓ cup brown sugar, packed
4 salmon fillets
2 Tbsp. butter, melted
4 slices of lemon, thin

PREHEAT oven to 375 degrees. Pour lemon juice into ungreased 8-by-11-inch baking dish. Sprinkle in brown sugar. Arrange salmon fillets in dish and drizzle with melted butter. Bake uncovered for 15 minutes. Turn fillets and top each piece with a lemon slice. Bake for an additional 12 to 15 minutes. Place fillets on plate and drizzle with juices from pan. Yields 4 servings.

Devonshire Cream with Mascarpone

½ cup heavy cream
2 Tbsp. powdered sugar
8 oz. mascarpone cheese
½ cup sour cream

PLACE all ingredients in a medium-sized bowl. Using a hand mixer, whip all ingredients together until fully combined. Store in refrigerator; let sit at room temperature for 30 minutes before serving. Yields 1½ cups.

Laura Childs

Silk Road Tea Party

Theodosia is always up for a themed tea party, and this Chinese tea is no exception. Smooth on a bright red tablecloth, then grab some Chinese cups and a few sets of chopsticks. Got a bamboo plant? Add it to the table with any Chinese ceramics you might have. Start with steamed pork buns then add in dim sum favorites like shrimp rolls or pork pot stickers. Noodles sautéed with chicken and vegetables are always satisfying. When it comes to Chinese teas, you can't go wrong with Lapsang souchong, red Fujian, or silver needle.

Irish Tea

For a wee taste of the old country, pull out your lace tablecloth, add your favorite pottery or Irish bone china, and put on some Celtic music. Begin your tea with Irish soda scones and marmalade. Then it's time to move on to potato-leek soup and an assortment of tea sandwiches. Think English cheddar with mustard and corned beef on hearty bread. For tea choices opt for Super Irish Breakfast black tea from Stash Tea or Lucky Irish Breakfast tea from the Republic of Tea. For dessert try your hand at baking chocolate and Irish cream cupcakes or even a Victorian sponge cake.

Herbal Tea Party

With so many excellent herbal teas available—Stash Tea's Ruby Orange Ginger Tea, Celestial Seasonings Bengal Spice—why not have an herbal tea party? Give your table an herb garden look with multiple pots of fresh herbs. You could even add a few white candles and some gardening books. Make your first course rosemary scones, then serve tea sandwiches such as cream cheese and watercress on sourdough bread or chicken salad with tarragon on fresh-baked herb bread. You could also serve an herb salad with tomato, parsley, and mint or opt for pasta with pesto sauce. Mint chocolate brownies or cinnamon ice cream would make a lovely dessert. And if you'd like to give favors to your guests, consider (what else!) seed packets of herbs.

Lemon Tea

You can host a lemon tea party much like Theodosia and Drayton did (but without the murder). Decorate your table with yellow place mats, any china that has a splash of yellow, and pots of yellow daffodils or jonquils. For the pièce de résistance, set out an enormous glass bowl filled with fresh lemons. With that lovely scent wafting through the air, start with lemon scones, then move on to eggs Benedict with hollandaise sauce. Instead of a traditional tea sandwich, try strawberry and goat cheese bruschetta, then serve lemon chicken for your entrée. Capital Teas has a Lemon Drop Tea, while Grace Tea Company offers a Lemon Verbena Sweet

Limonetto. If you opt to serve a black or white tea, don't forget to have plenty of thin-sliced lemons on the table. Lemon bars make the perfect dessert.

Charles Dickens Tea

You'll have a dickens of a good time when you invite all your friends in for a Charles Dickens Christmas Tea. The theme here is Olde English so think paisley, lace, and velvet when it comes to decor. Then pull out all your antique dishes and tea ware, add a few pewter candles, as well as a few copies of *A Christmas Carol*. Start with cream scones loaded up with Devonshire cream and lemon curd and a hearty English breakfast tea. Simpson & Vail offers a Charles Dickens' Black Tea Blend and the Republic of Tea has several *Downton Abbey* tea blends. For a second course, consider tea sandwiches with turkey and cranberry or salmon with cream cheese. Shrimp in aspic makes a fine entrée. For dessert, wow your guests with English sticky toffee pudding or a peach trifle.

Fairy Godmother Tea

This magical tea is perfect for moms and daughters or grand-mothers and granddaughters. It's also a grand excuse for the young-sters to dress as Cinderella in their finest princess dresses. Decorate your table in purple and pink then add a sprinkle of stars, crowns, and magic wands. If you can find some white pumpkins and a glass slipper, so much the better. Start with jeweled scones (cream scones with colorful candied fruit added), then segue to tea sand-wiches. Chicken salad, egg salad, or tuna salad are perfect. For an entrée, try a cheddar quiche. Dessert could be petits fours, fruit skewers with raspberry yogurt sauce, or cupcakes decorated with a princess theme. Serve juice for the young ladies, a lovely Assam tea for the moms or grandmothers.

Baby Reveal Tea Party

Forget the blue or pink balloons. Instead, surprise your guests with cream scones frosted with blue or pink frosting. Or you can serve pinwheel tea sandwiches—cream cheese blended with pimento for pink, cream cheese with blueberries for blue. For your next course consider white bean soup or a Waldorf salad. Grilled chicken breast with asparagus makes a delicious entrée, and you can source pink or blue macarons for dessert. Some tea favorites might include cardamom or Formosa oolong.

GET CREATIVE WITH SCONES

The Indigo Tea Shop gang isn't afraid to break the rules and get creative with scones, and neither should you. Here are a few "scone toppers" to get you started:

- **Jam and Devonshire Cream**—You can't go wrong with this classic version.

- **Cream Cheese and Maple Syrup**—Turn your scone into a nouveau version of French toast.

- **Banana Split**—Top a cream scone with banana slices and drizzle on some chocolate sauce.

- **Fig and Cheese**—Spread some fig jam on your split scone and top with blue cheese crumbles.

- **Honey and Ricotta Cheese**—Spread with softened ricotta cheese and add a few drops of honey.

- **Fresh Fruit**—Split your scone, add blueberries, strawberries, or sliced pears, and top with a dollop of Devonshire cream.

- **Smoked Salmon with Cream Cheese**—Turn a basic scone into an updated bagel.

- **Cheese and Chutney**—Spread on your favorite chutney and top with a slice of cheddar cheese.

- **Herbed Butter**—A butter seasoned with tarragon or your favorite herbs is delicious on scones.

- **Guacamole**—Don't be afraid to top your scone with guacamole and a bit of hot sauce.

- **Gruyère and Bacon**—Spread on some softened Gruyère cheese and add a slice of bacon.

- **Fried Egg with Hot Sauce**—This takes your scone into the realm of hearty breakfast sandwich.

TEA RESOURCES

TEA MAGAZINES AND PUBLICATIONS

TeaTime—A luscious magazine profiling tea and tea lore. Filled with glossy photos and wonderful recipes. (teatimemagazine.com)

Southern Lady—From the publishers of *TeaTime* with a focus on people and places in the South as well as wonderful teatime recipes. (south ernladymagazine.com)

Tea House Times—Go to www.theteahousetimes.com for subscription information and dozens of links to tea shops, purveyors of tea, gift shops, and tea events.

Victoria—Articles and pictorials on homes, home design, gardens, and tea. (victoriamag.com)

Fresh Cup Magazine—For tea and coffee professionals. (freshcup.com)

Tea & Coffee—Trade journal for the tea and coffee industry. (teaandcof fee.net)

Jane Pettigrew—This author has written seventeen books on the varied aspects of tea and its history and culture. (janepettigrew.com/books)

A Tea Reader—By Katrina Avila Munichiello, an anthology of tea stories and reflections.

AMERICAN TEA PLANTATIONS

Charleston Tea Plantation—The oldest and largest tea plantation in the United States. Order their fine black tea or schedule a visit at bigelow tea.com.

Table Rock Tea Company—This Pickens, South Carolina, plantation grows premium whole-leaf tea. (tablerocktea.com)

Great Mississippi Tea Company—Up-and-coming Mississippi tea farm. (greatmsteacompany.com)

Sakuma Brothers Farm—This tea garden just outside Burlington, Washington, has been growing white and green tea for over twenty years. (sakumabros.com)

Big Island Tea—Organic artisan tea from Hawaii. (bigislandtea.com)

Mauna Kea Tea—Organic green and oolong tea from Hawaii's Big Island. (maunakeatea.com)

Onomea Tea—Nine-acre tea estate near Hilo, Hawaii. (onotea.com)

Minto Island Growers—Handpicked, small-batch crafted teas grown in Oregon. (mintoislandtea.com)

Finger Lakes Tea Company—Tea producer located in Waterloo, New York. (fingerlakestea.com)

Camellia Forest Tea Gardens—This North Carolina company collects, grows, and sells tea plants. Also produce their own tea. (teaflowergardens.com)

TEA WEBSITES AND INTERESTING BLOGS

Destinationtea.com—State-by-state directory of afternoon tea venues.

Teamap.com—Directory of hundreds of tea shops in the United States and Canada.

Afternoontea.co.uk—Guide to tea rooms in the United Kingdom.

Cookingwithideas.typepad.com—Recipes and book reviews for the bibliochef.

Seedrack.com—Order *Camellia sinensis* seeds and grow your own tea!

Jennybakes.com—Fabulous recipes from a real make-it-from-scratch baker.

Cozyupwithkathy.blogspot.com—Cozy mystery reviews.

Thedailytea.com—Formerly *Tea Magazine*, this online publication is filled with tea news, recipes, inspiration, and tea travel.

Allteapots.com—Teapots from around the world.

Fireflyspirits.com—South Carolina purveyors of sweet tea vodka.

Relevanttealeaf.blogspot.com—All about tea.

Stephcupoftea.blogspot.com—Blog on tea, food, and inspiration.

Teawithfriends.blogspot.com—Lovely blog on tea, friendship, and tea accoutrements.

Bellaonline.com/site/tea—Features and forums on tea.

Napkinfoldingguide.com—Photo illustrations of twenty-seven different (and sometimes elaborate) napkin folds.

Worldteaexpo.com—This premier business-to-business trade show features more than three hundred tea suppliers, vendors, and tea innovators.

Fatcatscones.com—Frozen ready-to-bake scones.

Kingarthurflour.com—One of the best flours for baking. This is what many professional pastry chefs use.

Californiateahouse.com—Order Machu's Blend, a special herbal tea for dogs that promotes healthy skin, lowers stress, and aids digestion.

Vintageteaworks.com—This company offers six unique wine-flavored tea blends that celebrate wine and respect the tea.

Downtonabbeycooks.com—A *Downton Abbey* blog with news and recipes.

Auntannie.com—Crafting site that will teach you how to make your own petal envelopes, pillow boxes, gift bags, etc.

Victorianhousescones.com—Scone, biscuit, and cookie mixes for both retail and wholesale orders. Plus baking and scone-making tips.

Englishteastore.com—Buy a jar of English Double Devon Cream here as well as British foods and candies.

Stickyfingersbakeries.com—Scone mixes and English curds.

TeaSippersSociety.com—Join this international tea community of tea sippers, growers, and educators. A terrific newsletter!

Melhadtea.com—Adventures of a traveling tea sommelier.

Bullsbaysaltworks.com—Local South Carolina sea salt crafted by hand.

PURVEYORS OF FINE TEA

Plumdeluxe.com
Adagio.com
Elmwoodinn.com
Capitalteas.com
Newbyteas.com/us
Harney.com
Stashtea.com
Serendipitea.com
Marktwendell.com
Republicoftea.com
Teazaanti.com
Bigelowtea.com
Celestialseasonings.com
Goldenmoontea.com
Uptontea.com

Svtea.com (Simpson & Vail)

Gracetea.com

Davidstea.com

VISITING CHARLESTON

Charleston.com—Travel and hotel guide.

Charlestoncvb.com—The official Charleston convention and visitor bureau.

Charlestontour.wordpress.com—Private tours of homes and gardens, some including lunch or tea.

Charlestonplace.com—Charleston Place Hotel serves an excellent afternoon tea, Thursday through Saturday, from one to three.

Poogansporch.com—This restored Victorian house serves traditional low-country cuisine. Be sure to ask about Poogan!

Preservationsociety.org—Hosts Charleston's annual Fall Candlelight Tour.

Palmettocarriage.com—Horse-drawn carriage rides.

Charlestonharbortours.com—Boat tours and harbor cruises.

Ghostwalk.net—Stroll into Charleston's haunted history. Ask them about the "original" Theodosia!

Charlestontours.net—Ghost tours plus tours of plantations and historic homes.

Follybeach.com—Official guide to Folly Beach activities, hotels, rentals, restaurants, and events.

Gibbesmuseum.org—Art exhibits, programs, and events.

Boonehallplantation.com—Visit one of America's oldest working plantations.

Charlestonlibrarysociety.org—A rich collection of books, historic manuscripts, maps, and correspondence. Music and guest speaker events.

ACKNOWLEDGMENTS

An abundance of thank-yous to Sam, Tom, Elisha, Stephanie, Sareer, M.J., Bob, Jennie, Dan, and all the wonderful people at Berkley Prime Crime and Penguin Random House who handle editing, design (such fabulous covers!), publicity (amazing!), copywriting, social media, bookstore sales, gift sales, production, and shipping. Heartfelt thanks as well to all the tea lovers, tea shop owners, book clubs, bookshop folks, librarians, reviewers, magazine editors and writers, websites, broadcasters, and bloggers who have enjoyed the Tea Shop Mysteries and helped spread the word. You are all so kind to help make this possible!

And I am filled with gratitude for my special readers and tea lovers who've embraced Theodosia, Drayton, Haley, Earl Grey, and the rest of the tea shop gang as friends and family. Thank you so much, and I solemnly promise many more Tea Shop Mysteries to come!

KEEP READING FOR AN EXCERPT
FROM LAURA CHILDS'S NEXT
TEA SHOP MYSTERY . . .

Honey Drop Dead

It was politics as usual. Or unusual in this particular case. Because tea maven Theodosia Browning had never hosted a tea party before where a superambitious, over-caffeinated politician had suddenly leaped from his chair to deliver a boastful, impromptu speech.

Of course, it was election time in Charleston, South Carolina, and politicians were thick as flies in a hog barn. Which was why Osgood Claxton III was rambling on to an acutely bored audience about his prodigious accomplishments and why they should surely award him a seat in the state legislature. It was also why Theodosia hovered nervously at her tea table while her team readied scones and tea sandwiches.

"He's trying to hijack Holly's event," Theodosia murmured to Drayton Conneley, her tea sommelier and trusted friend. They were gazing out at the dozen or so tables that had been set up in Charleston's gorgeous new Petigru Park, getting ready to plop fresh-baked glory bee honey scones on all their guests' plates.

"This has the makings of a train wreck," Drayton agreed. He

touched a finger to his yellow bow tie as if to punctuate his sentence.

Theodosia turned sharp blue eyes on Holly Burns, the owner of the Imago Gallery, who was seated nearby. As Claxton droned on, Holly's face turned blotchy and her jaw went rigid. Clearly, she wasn't one bit happy.

Oh dear. This was, after all, Holly's outdoor tea party in honor of the relaunch of her Imago Gallery. Dozens of art lovers, patrons, and artists lounged at the elegantly appointed tables while, all around them, large colorful paintings were displayed on wooden easels. A brilliant yellow sun shone down and a cool breeze wafted in from Charleston Harbor to stir the park's newly planted native grasses. Hives from a community beekeeping project were stacked like bee condos a safe distance away.

"I'm going to go over there and try to disarm that walking, talking dictionary," Theodosia said to Drayton. A self-made tea entrepreneur who'd made it on her own terms, Theodosia was confident, nimble at handling tricky situations, and unimpressed by boastful politicians. Her ice chip blue eyes matched her tasteful sapphire earrings while masses of Titian-red hair swirled around her lovely oval face. Theodosia also possessed a gracious manner that was poised yet purposeful.

"Watch your step with that fellow," Drayton warned. "He's powerfully . . ."

"Connected. Yes, I know he is," Theodosia said as she grabbed a pink floral teapot filled with Darjeeling tea, fixed her mouth in a bright smile, and headed directly for the red-faced, overbearing politician.

Osgood Claxton III saw her coming and seemed to lose focus for a moment. He blinked, trying desperately to sputter out a few more words. But that tiny hesitation was all Theodosia needed.

"Mr. Claxton," Theodosia said with a warm lilt to her voice. "Bless your heart for expounding on your many qualifications.

Now that we're all familiar with such prodigious talents, you must surely take your seat so my staff and I can begin serving our delicious luncheon of honey scones and tea sandwiches."

Theodosia grabbed a quick breath, faced the forty or so guests, and continued, not allowing the startled Claxton a moment to jump back in. "As you all know, Holly Burns has recently upped the ante at her marvelous Imago Gallery." She smiled as Claxton reluctantly slumped in his seat. "Along with a new partner, and a higher profile in Charleston's thriving art scene, Holly now represents an amazing group of talented and well-known South Carolina artists."

There was a spatter of applause, and Holly half rose in her chair to wave and acknowledge her guests. She had long dark hair, was skinny as a wet cat, wore armfuls of clanking silver bracelets, and jittered with anxiety. With dozens of potential art buyers and a few wealthy collectors among her guests, today would prove to be a make-or-break day for her.

Theodosia continued. "And lucky for us, we have on display here"—she gestured at the paintings resting on their easels—"a number of intriguing and colorful paintings—works by Holly's new artists that are here for your appreciation and careful perusal." There was more applause, and then Theodosia added, "So please, sit back and enjoy this special Honeybee Tea as we fill your teacups with our house blend of honey child tea and serve our first course of fresh-baked glory bee scones. Following that, we'll present a tempting array of tea sandwiches that will include honey ham on rye, shrimp with tarragon on crostini, and chicken salad on brioche."

As Drayton poured tea, Theodosia and her young chef, Haley Parker, slipped from table to table, serving scones, dropping off bowls of Devonshire cream, and encouraging guests to also drizzle some of their specially sourced raw honey onto their scones.

When the guests were all sipping and munching (even Osgood

Claxton III seemed to be making short work of his scone), Theodosia wiped her hands on her apron and gazed about contentedly. This is what she did, after all—and she did it rather well. Yes, Monday through Friday you could find her at the Indigo Tea Shop, a devastatingly adorable tea shop on Church Street. But she also reveled in catering special event teas. And this Sunday's tea, her themed Honeybee Tea, seemed to be going off without a hitch. The weather was gorgeous, Petigru Park was clearly the perfect venue, and there were already small red stickers on several of the paintings—which meant they'd been earmarked as either on hold or sold. So a feather in Theodosia's cap as well as Holly's.

As a former marketing executive, Theodosia loved nothing better than to spin out new ideas. These included event teas, tea trolley tours, even catering gigs. She'd draw up a business plan, work out all the nits and nats, then bring the whole shootin' match to fruition. Right now she was making plans for a line of organic, tea-infused chocolates that would be sold at the Indigo Tea Shop. Two of the brand names she was considering were Church Street Chocolates and Cacao Tea.

"This is going well, yes?" Drayton said to her. He'd just made the rounds pouring tea and looked elegant in his cream-colored jacket and matching linen slacks. Sixty-something and always projecting the manner and bearing of a true Southern gent, Drayton was a tea sommelier and skilled orator, and served on several boards of directors.

"I just got a quick read from Holly and she's over the moon," Theodosia said. "She believes she's already made several sales to a few serious collectors, and that the Imago Gallery is finally on the right track to success."

"Holly was smart to hook up with that silent partner. Jeremy something . . ."

"Slade. Jeremy Slade."

Drayton nodded. "Right. The one who gave her the infusion of cash."

"She lucked out," Theodosia said. Then she gazed across the tables and said, "Oh, bother."

"What?" Drayton said.

"Bill Glass just showed up." Glass was the publisher of *Shooting Star*, a local tabloid that specialized in gossip, unfounded rumors, and glossy photos of the nouveau riche acting badly. Today, Glass was wandering among the tables, taking photos and doing a skillful bit of glad-handing. His razor sunglasses were pushed up on his forehead, and he wore a khaki photographer's vest, sloppy brown pants, and red high-top tennis shoes.

"He's not exactly the vision you want to see at a tea party, but he's harmless," Drayton said. "Besides, most people are thrilled to see their picture in his little rag of a magazine."

"Maybe," Theodosia said as Haley nudged her and said, "Time to put out the sandwich trays?" Haley was twenty-six, petite, and blond with stick-straight hair. But underneath her sweet appearance, she was a little martinet. And it was woe to the baker or fishmonger who tried to deliver day-old goods to Haley's kitchen.

"Let's do it," said Drayton. "While everything's so perfectly fresh."

"Right down to my edible flowers," Haley smiled.

Theodosia had just placed a three-tiered tray stacked with tea sandwiches on one of the tables when a woman glanced past her, pointed, and said, "Will you look at that. One of the beekeepers just showed up." She sounded amused.

Theodosia looked over at the colony of twelve white hives where a man (she thought it was a man) in protective gear was aiming a smoker at one of the hives.

"Going to harvest some honey," another guest said, excitement coloring her voice.

"Good thing he's wearing that bee getup, the protective jacket, pants, veil, and whatnot," a man said. "Dealing with beehives is quite an art."

Now more guests had turned in their chairs to watch.

"This really is quite charming," the man's companion said. "It must be part of the event."

"Has to be," another person at the table chimed in.

Theodosia knew this hadn't been planned. It was completely serendipitous that one of the beekeepers had shown up at this exact moment. All the same, she was pleased because it made for an exciting diversion. Especially since the event had been promoted as a Honeybee Tea and the invitations had even made mention of the park's community beekeeping project.

Unfortunately, two tables over, Claxton had jumped to his feet again. He was suddenly spearheading a round of applause for the beekeeper, whipping up the crowd's enthusiasm.

"Not him again," Drayton muttered as he came up behind Theodosia.

"The man's incorrigible," she said. "Looks as if he's trying to take credit for what's really a city-funded project."

They watched Claxton vigorously thrust both arms in the air in a V for Victory sign as the guests cheered.

"He thinks the applause is for him," Theodosia said.

Everyone watched as Claxton puffed up his chest, practically busting the buttons on his vest. Then he turned with a flourish and faced the beekeeper.

"Great job," Claxton called out to him. "Phenomenal project, these bees."

He took a few steps in the direction of the hives as the beekeeper moved forward to greet him.

"You see what your city officials can do when they put their mind to it?" Claxton said loudly. "Native grasses planted in this park, all these wonderful hives. Come on over here, Mr. Beekeeper. I want to shake your hand."

The beekeeper advanced on Claxton, his helmet obscuring his face, his smoker held at waist level. It looked a lot like a stainless steel watering can, Theodosia decided. Only with a shorter spout.

As Claxton reached a hand out, the beekeeper snapped his smoker up to eye level and a faint motorized hum suddenly sounded. Then the beekeeper aimed the smoker directly at Claxton's face and sent a milky white vapor spewing out at him.

"Wha . . . ?" came Claxton's startled, garbled response as he was suddenly engulfed in a thick white cloud. Terrified, Claxton began to stumble about aimlessly, his face turning red as he started to choke. It was a dry, raspy AR-AR-AR, as if he was unable to pull in a single sip of oxygen. Then, eyes rolling back in his head, knees beginning to buckle, Claxton batted his arms frantically as if to ward off the continuing billows of smoke.

Or was it smoke? Theodosia wondered a split second later. Because everyone in Claxton's vicinity was suddenly coughing and choking like crazy and rubbing their eyes.

No, it has to be some kind of toxic bomb.

The cloud drifted across the tea tables, threatening to engulf everyone. Dark shapes darted back and forth as they fought to escape. Visibility was almost down to zero.

Undaunted, Theodosia covered her mouth with her apron and ran smack-dab into the fray.

"Everybody! We have to get away from this right now!" she cried. Then she raised a hand in a wild gesture. "This way!"

Coughing and crying, shouting and screaming, many of the guests were openly weeping from the toxic fumes as they stumbled toward Theodosia and she tried to lead them away from the smoke.

Haley suddenly appeared next to Theodosia, eyes bleary and

red, tears streaming down her face. Her cell phone was clutched in her hand.

"Did you call 911?" Theodosia choked out as she led her flock to safety.

"Talking to them now," Haley cried. "They want to know what . . ."

"Toxic fumes, tell them some kind of toxic smoke bomb." In the melee, with people all around her, Theodosia lost sight of Haley for a few moments. Then she found her again. "Are they coming?" she asked.

"They're coming." Haley had to shout to be heard above the cries and screams.

"Tell them to send ambulances, EMTs, everything they've got." Theodosia looked around. "We probably have a couple dozen injured people here."

"The dispatcher wants to know who released the . . ."

"I think it was just the one guy," Theodosia shouted back. "A phony beekeeper who . . ."

BOOM!

That noise—an explosion, really—rattled Theodosia's teeth and rocked her back on her heels. But her brain instantaneously sorted out exactly what she'd heard.

A gunshot? Oh, my Lord, I think it was. I know it was.

Wiping her eyes, squinting into the filmy cloud that was slowly starting to dissipate, she saw the phony beekeeper standing there. He had a gun clutched in his right hand with Claxton's body sprawled at his feet.

The beekeeper's protective suit still obscured his identity, and he held the smoker in his other hand. But it was his attitude that chilled Theodosia to the bone. He seemed to gaze at Claxton's body in a gloating, self-satisfied manner. Taking pride in his kill as well as the terrible panic he'd brought about.

The phony beekeeper cocked his head, as if making some sort of critical decision. Then he spun on his heels and began to sprint awkwardly across the park. He obviously had one single, burning thought in mind—get away from this place fast!

At the same time, a nugget of white-hot rage exploded inside Theodosia's brain. She took in Claxton's prone body—the man had to be dead—as well as the tearful guests that milled about, still looking panicked. And she was gripped by one all-consuming thought—run the killer down!

Not having access to a weapon, not even thinking all that clearly, Theodosia grabbed the first thing she saw—a tall glass vase filled with bright yellow jonquils. Tucking the vase under one arm, Theodosia took off running.

"Stop!" Theodosia cried as she pounded across the vast expanse of green parkland, in hot pursuit of the phony beekeeper. She leaped across a bed of daylilies and dodged a small copse of dogwood. She saw that, up ahead, the phony beekeeper was running badly. He was hindered by his bulky suit and clanking smoker that banged against his legs. So, little by little, as Theodosia chased after him, she was beginning to close the gap.

He killed a man was the terrible thought that spiraled through Theodosia's brain and propelled her forward. *And spewed out some kind of toxic smoke that made people sick. Made my guests sick.*

She lowered her head, hunched her shoulders forward, and forced herself to lengthen her strides, to kick it into high gear. She was a longtime jogger with an abundance of stamina. So maybe she could catch him?

Maybe, but then what?

Her answer came in the form of a black-and-white dog, a kind of collie-Labrador mix, that suddenly sprinted out of a nearby wooded area. Legs churning, haunches bunched like a jackrabbit, the dog began chasing after the running man. The dog probably saw it as a game, but Theodosia was grateful for the help.

Catching up fast, almost running on the man's heels now, the dog let out a series of high-pitched barks. When the man didn't stop to play, the dog gathered itself into a coiled bunch and lunged forward, his teeth catching the legs of the man's flapping suit.

That's it, get him! Theodosia's heart was suddenly filled with hope.

But no. The dog's interference had slowed the man down some, but didn't stop him completely. Angered by the canine intrusion, the man spun around and lifted his pistol. Half running, half backpedaling now, the man aimed his weapon directly at the dog.

He's going to kill the dog! Theodosia loved dogs more than anything.

"Don't!" she shouted.

Startled to hear someone shout at him, the phony beekeeper's hand jerked sideways. He looked around hastily and saw Theodosia running full tilt in his direction.

Then the beekeeper readjusted his aim and pointed the gun at her!

Theodosia ducked her head and threw herself down on the grass just as he pulled the trigger. There was another loud BANG and a high-pitched ZING as something—presumably the bullet—flew past her head.

That's when Theodosia made a split-second decision. Scrambling to her feet, she assumed a power stance and cocked her right arm. Then she let fly, hurling the glass vase directly at the phony beekeeper with as much force as she could muster. The vase sailed through the air, flipping over and over, spewing water and flowers as it went. Theodosia watched, hypnotized, following the arc of the vase, feeling as if this whole thing were happening in slow motion. Then the scenario seemed to jump ahead into hyperspace and speed up, like super-cranked film footage, as the vase smashed hard against the side of the man's helmet. Instantly, shards of glass, water, and flowers exploded everywhere.

Caught completely off guard, momentarily stunned by the direct hit to his head, the assailant was knocked off-balance. He stumbled to his left, caught a foot on the turf, tripped, and started to go down. One of his knees hit the ground and his arms flew out to try and steady himself. As his arms flailed wildly, seeking to regain his balance, he also fumbled his gun.

Yes!

"Stop!" Theodosia shouted as the dog, undaunted, circled back around, barking loudly. Then, as the man searched frantically for his gun, the dog dashed back in and nipped his pants leg for a second time.

Hindered by his mask, unable to locate his gun, the phony beekeeper spat out a single harsh word. Then his leg flew up and he kicked the offending dog right in the head, sending the poor mutt spinning.

"The police are on their way!" Theodosia shouted as she reached down and snatched up a piece of broken glass. It was the bottom of the vase and it made a dandy weapon.

The phony beekeeper ignored her and lumbered up a small hill where a stand of palmettos waved in the breeze. Once he'd reached high ground, he spun around to face her.

Theodosia stopped in her tracks.

Now what?

Was she tough enough to rush in and attack this jackhole? Try to wrestle him to the ground until law enforcement could arrive? Probably not. She could hear the faint drone of sirens off in the distance—answering Haley's 911 call, thank heavens—but they wouldn't reach her, wouldn't *find* her, anytime soon.

Theodosia held up the hunk of glass and made a cutting gesture.

As if to retaliate, the phony beekeeper hoisted his smoker and pointed it at Theodosia. But when he flipped a lever with his finger, he was clean out of smoke.

Disappointed and frustrated, the phony beekeeper tossed the smoker on the ground where it clattered and rolled away. Then he lifted an arm and pointed directly at her. It was a silent, ominous gesture. A clear message that said he wouldn't soon forget this confrontation. Then the phony beekeeper turned and bounded across the grass into a copse of trees. Seconds later, he'd disappeared from sight. There was a loud revving sound and then . . . silence. A few birds, the wind through the trees.

Theodosia stood there, out of breath, scared, and frustrated. She was also shocked at herself for having sprinted after the man without benefit of weapon or serious plan.

She'd been motivated by . . . what? Just good old retaliation, she guessed. Hard-boiled anger had sunk its talons into her and almost gotten the better of her.

Not good. Not smart, Theodosia told herself.

As adrenaline continued to fizz through her body, Theodosia turned and slowly retraced her steps. On a path that was strewn with shattered glass and broken yellow jonquils.